She settled the laurels in my blonde curls and then stepped back to admire her work.

Her eyes flicked over my body just once, so quickly it's possible I was imagining it, but I flushed all the same.

For one white-hot instant, that dark instinct to overcome and overpower, to kiss and bruise, flared to life in my stomach. I imagined myself slotting my fingers into all that black hair and tugging until her mouth was hovering over mine. I imagined the soft, surprised sound she might make, the sweetness of her breath ghosting across my lips.

And then she was gone, disappeared into the crowd to treat another girl to her undivided attention. I swayed a little, because of either the punch or the brief but electric encounter.

Pressing the cool back of my hand to my flushed cheek, I squeezed my eyes shut and took a deep breath, quieting the beast circling restlessly inside me.

"Ah," Maisy said, sidling up beside me with a knowing smile. "I see you've met Carmilla."

Praise for S. T. Gibson

An Education in Malice

"*An Education in Malice* is an ode to girlhood: ribbons, blood, poetry, and rage. Gibson's fang-sharp prose and unflinching honesty create a delicate and fearless exploration of loneliness, love, and—as the bridge between those two absolutes—longing."

—Sydney J. Shields, author of
The Honey Witch

"From sinful all-night salons to hedonistic Halloween parties, Laura's world thrums with dark pleasures that will leave you wanting more."   —*Kirkus*

"An isolated women's college, a Gothic aesthetic that would make the Brontë sisters proud, an all-consuming passion between sapphic academic rivals...what's not to like here? Light a candle to maximize the moody vibes and dive in."   —*People*

A Dowry of Blood

"A dizzying nightmare of a romance that will leave you aching, angry, and ultimately hopeful."

—Hannah Whitten, *New York Times* bestselling
author of *For the Wolf*

By S. T. Gibson

A Dowry of Blood
An Education in Malice

AN EDUCATION IN MALICE

S. T. GIBSON

REDHOOK

Copyright © 2024 by Sarah Gibson
Interview copyright © 2024 by Hachette Book Group, Inc.
Excerpt from *A Dowry of Blood* copyright © 2021 by Sarah Gibson

Cover design and illustration by Tim Byrne
Author photograph by Elizabeth Unseth

Redhook Books/Orbit
Hachette Book Group
1290 Avenue of the Americas
New York, NY 10104
hachettebookgroup.com

First Paperback Edition: September 2024
Originally published in hardcover and ebook in Great Britain by Orbit and in the U.S. by Redhook in February 2024

Redhook is an imprint of Orbit, a division of Hachette Book Group.
The Redhook name and logo are registered trademarks of Hachette Book Group, Inc.

The publisher is not responsible for websites (or their content) that are not owned by the publisher.

The Hachette Speakers Bureau provides a wide range of authors for speaking events. To find out more, go to hachettespeakersbureau.com or email HachetteSpeakers@hbgusa.com.

Redhook books may be purchased in bulk for business, educational, or promotional use. For information, please contact your local bookseller or the Hachette Book Group Special Markets Department at special.markets@hbgusa.com.

Library of Congress Control Number: 2023944413

ISBNs: 9780316501866 (trade paperback), 9780316501972 (ebook)

Printed in the United States of America

CW

10 9 8 7 6 5 4 3 2 1

For those who didn't make it out of the ivory tower
unscathed: you have always been worthy.

Author's note

This work of fiction explores dark themes, so I've elected to provide the following content guidance. If you choose to proceed, please read with self-compassion.

An Education in Malice contains depictions of:

~ Uneven power dynamics
~ Inappropriate relationships between a professor and students
~ Toxic academic environments
~ Blood, gore, and murder
~ Consensual sexual content, including public sex
~ Kink, negotiated and spontaneous
~ Alcohol and drug use
~ Smoking

S. T. Gibson

It also contains brief references to:

~ Racist political policies
~ Homophobia
~ Religious discrimination against women

CHAPTER ONE

Laura

———◆◇◆———

September 7, 1968

assachusetts greeted me with a riot of autumn color. Gold, ochre, and russet were my welcoming committee as I stepped off the plane and loaded my two suitcases into the car that would take me deeper into the state, and on to the next four years of my life. Mississippi was a study in green, crawling with Spanish moss and bedecked with heavy-laden magnolia trees, but I never realized how many colors there were to be found in nature until that first fall in New England.

As beautiful as Massachusetts was, the memory of Mississippi sat inside me like a stone. I missed the electrical buzz of cicadas; the muggy twilight; the slow, easy greetings between strangers on the street. I missed sitting in the creaking rocking chair on the porch each morning, reading selections from the newspaper and sipping coffee. I missed the solitude of my attic room in our farmhouse, the way thunderstorms lashed against my windowpane in summer. I even missed my dull old teacher and her French and Latin drills, the silent camaraderie of the other girls grinding away at their translations in the schoolhouse.

Most of all I missed my father, his booming laugh, his quick wit, the hugs he gave that nearly squeezed the breath from my lungs.

My father had always nurtured my interest in writing, which burned brightly from a young age and sometimes bordered on the obsessive. I was perfectly happy to shut myself away in my room for hours at a time, reading W. H. Auden and Gertrude Stein and scribbling nonsense in my notebooks. I never thought my work was strong enough to share with anyone, but at my father's insistence I sometimes let him read little snippets. I had a great talent, he said, and that talent should be nurtured somewhere capable professors could coax it out of me.

Somewhere, my father had decided, like Saint Perpetua's.

Saint Perpetua was affectionately referred to as the forgotten youngest sibling of the Seven Sisters, and the school that bore her name, Saint Perpetua's Women's College, was tucked away in a remote corner of the state. Just far enough from Boston that weekend trips were impractical. The school was Episcopal in charter, which suited me just fine. My nervous temperament was soothed by the rote prayers of organized religion, even if I developed a reputation back home for questioning the priest at every turn. I had spent much of the year after graduating high school reading, writing, going to church, and taking long walks through the woods behind our house, but, as my father gently reminded me, my intellectual meandering couldn't last forever. Even if I followed my well-laid plans to become a small-town parish priest, I would need a degree. Moreover, I needed the structure of higher education to sharpen my mind, and I needed the companionship of other girls to prevent me from growing into eccentricity.

I had walked over every contingency, good and bad, in my head a thousand times before arriving at Saint Perpetua's. I imagined crushing failure and soaring success and everything in-between. But nothing could have prepared me for turning the tree-lined corner and entering the campus.

I saw the chapel first, rising proudly from the tallest hill to pierce the cloudy sky with its steeple. Then the academic buildings, all gray Gothic stone in the Princeton style, with their carved wooden doors open to the grassy quadrangle. The green was littered with girls, many dressed in Mary Janes and practical calf-skimming tweed skirts, but others sporting skinny ankle pants and berets, or tiny mini-dresses worn over jewel-tone tights. They were walking in tight formations of three or four, or laying on their stomachs eating brown-bag lunches while reading from textbooks, or giggling while spinning hula hoops around their waists. I had been educated at a tiny school and had never seen so many young people in one place, much less so many girls of my same age.

The car that picked me up from the airport circled the quad, then stopped in front of a stately four-story building with gargoyles leering from the parapets. Upon thanking and paying the driver, I found myself standing on the stoop of the dormitory with a suitcase in each hand, the cool September breeze rippling the tartan of my skirt. It was one of my favorite pieces of clothing, as it cinched at the waist and flattered my ample hips.

"Watch your head!" someone called from behind me. I swiveled around just in time to dodge a Frisbee, which pinged off the side of the dormitory. A pretty, sturdily built white girl in a varsity sweater jogged over, her brown curls bouncing merrily.

"Nice reflexes," she said with a broad smile. Gloss the color of cherry juice gleamed on her lips. Her skin was spattered generously with freckles. "Say, you aren't Laura Sheridan, are you?"

"That's me," I said, adjusting my grip on my suitcase so I could shake her hand. She had the enthusiastic grip of an athlete.

"Maisy Cohen. I was waiting for you to show up. I'm your senior sister."

Saint Perpetua's assigned all rising freshmen to a graduating senior, hoping to nurture a sense of mentorship. I had filled out some sort of questionnaire months ago that was supposed to match me with the perfect senior, and while I was leery at the prospect of forced friendship with anybody, Maisy's warmth put me at ease.

"It's a pleasure to meet you," I said, shifting from foot to foot. I wasn't great with first impressions, and I defaulted to an almost chilly courtesy in order to cover up the butterflies that hatched in my stomach at the prospect of meeting new people. Maisy didn't seem to mind.

"Well, let's get you moved in. Is that all you brought with you?"

I looked helplessly at my pair of suitcases.

"I suppose so."

"Fine by me," Maisy said, taking one of the stuffed suitcases as though it weighed nothing. "Less to lug around. Come on. You're in 412. Swell view, by the way. You really lucked out."

I followed her though the doors and up the stairs to the fourth floor. The halls were strewn with furniture and cardboard boxes, and there were girls drifting in and out of the rooms, calling down the hall to each other while propping open doors with heavy textbooks. Someone played Motown loudly from one room, and the scent of nag champa incense drifted out of another. Giving me a grin, Maisy shouldered open the door to my new home.

My father had secured me a private room, for which I was grateful. The single window looked out through the branches of an elm tree to the quad beyond, affording me a perfect view of the comings and goings of my classmates. Maisy plopped my suitcase down on the bare bed and took me in with an enterprising air, her hands on her hips.

"All the way from Mississippi, huh?"

"That's right."

"Well, Massachusetts welcomes you. I'm Boston born, myself. Have you got your classes all sorted out? If you haven't, I can help with that. I'm friendly with the registrar."

"That shouldn't be necessary," I said, grasping my hands together in front of me. I had no idea what to do with them. "I'm enrolled in all my prerequisites, and the poetry seminary for the writing program."

"Ah," Maisy said. "You're one of De Lafontaine's."

"I think that's the professor's name, yes," I said carefully, not catching her drift. This wasn't entirely unusual for me, as I often felt on the outside of conversations I was involved in.

"You haven't heard any rumors about her, have you?"

I shook my head dutifully. I did virtually no research into my declared major; I only knew that the writing program at Saint Perpetua's was well regarded, and that writing was the only thing I could imagine myself doing for four years.

"Good. She's demanding, but absolutely electric in the classroom. You'll see. You're coming to the bonfire tonight, aren't you?"

"I was thinking of an early night, actually."

"Oh, come on," Maisy said, clapping me on the shoulder like we were chums already. "You can't miss the bonfire! It's how we ring in every new school year. Absolutely everybody will be there, and they'll want to meet you. You know how it is: everyone's gotta scope everybody else out before classes start on Monday. Take it from me, cliques form fast."

This watering-hole ritual sounded absolutely harrowing to me, but I found myself nodding, mostly because Maisy didn't seem like the kind of person who took no for an answer.

"Perfect. I'll pick you up at your room at eight sharp and play escort, at least until you get your bearings. Don't worry," she said with a wink, "I won't throw you to the wolves right away."

"Thanks," I said, my voice thin.

Before I could protest further, a slender Black girl appeared in my doorway. She looked devastatingly chic in her cigarette pants and sailor shirt, and she wore her dark hair in a Brigitte Bardot bouffant.

"Maisy! I was scouring the quad for you. The rest of the team said you were in here with a frosh. Hey, new girl," she said in a not unfriendly way, then turned her attention back to Maisy. "Listen, word on the street is Siobhan's roommate somehow got her hands on the new Jimi Hendrix album – you know her dad's in the music industry – and if I don't listen to it right now I'm going to keel over."

"Elenore, Laura; Laura, Elenore," Maisy said by way of an introduction. "Elenore's in the writing cohort, you'll probably be seeing a lot of her."

"Maisy, this is life and death," Elenore said seriously. She had the slightly haughty air of someone who enjoyed experimental French cinema, which I found charming despite my better judgment. "You know how that girl gets; if too many people start buzzing around she won't share her goods. You coming or what?"

"I'll let you get situated," Maisy said, already drifting out of my room. "So nice to have you at Saint P's, Laura."

And with that, she was gone, the sound of her and Elenore chattering disappearing down the hallway. And I was left with my own nerves and the wisps of hope about what the night might hold.

—◆—

Bonfire Night was a Saint Perpetua's institution, one I had read about in the glossy college brochure my father proffered. It was part alma mater tradition, part social mixer. The senior girls were in charge of welcoming the new years with a roaring fire, crowns of laurels, and cups of bracing spiced punch. It was the place to make one's debut on the Saint Perpetua scene, to establish with clothes and hairstyle and turn-of-phrase what sort of clique one might fit into.

I agonized over my outfit for an hour as dark fell outside, cycling between half a dozen get-ups until I settled on a suede skirt and a cream-colored cashmere sweater with practical brown loafers. It was polished but invisible, and I hoped it would raise no eyebrows.

Maisy arrived at my room as promised at 8 p.m. sharp, with Elenore in tow. They were in high spirits, probably because of the flask of whiskey they were passing between them. I declined a drink but allowed them to link their arms through mine and walk me proudly, one on either side, to the bonfire.

The quad was swimming with girls when we arrived, and I was quickly swept up into the milieu. Maisy made a number of booming introductions to people whose names fell right out of my head, including half the rowing team. The fire had been stoked high and hot despite the tepid night, and I was soon sweating in my cashmere. I accepted a plastic cup of punch out of desperation more than anything, and put away enough deep swallows to file the harsh edges off the evening. I'm not sure how long I drifted around, as silent and unsmiling as a chaperone, but at some point, Maisy squeezed my elbow and disappeared to pass her flask around her team. Just about the time I was about to make an Irish exit, our senior hosts arrived.

A cheer went up from the rest of the girls, and I found myself clapping awkwardly, straining to see over the jostling shoulders of the partygoers. We had waited by the bonfire for an hour or so, and anticipation was coiled tight in the air. Through the sea of bodies, I caught a glimpse of white, and then another, and I carefully pressed my way to the front of the crowd.

Twenty-five girls in long white dresses strode solemnly towards the crowd, their arms strung with crowns of greenery and their feet bare. As they got closer I could see their dresses were really robes, belted in the front with a sash. They looked like vestal virgins processing towards the offertory flame. I harbored a suspicion that most collegiate traditions were bunk, an excuse to see and be seen, but in that moment I understood the strange power of ritual. I felt as though I was being transported back to a wilder era.

One of the girls raised her voice in Saint Perpetua's school song, and all the other partygoers quickly joined in. It was strangely dour, more hymn than pep rally cheer, and I didn't know the words, but it still gave me goosebumps.

The young women in white began to circulate, picking out the freshman girls and crowning them with laurels. We were a small incoming class of less than three hundred, but I was impressed that the seniors knew everyone else so well they were easily able to identify strange faces. I considered shrinking to the back of the crowd, never having been much for the spotlight, but before I could make my retreat, someone touched my wrist.

She wore her dark hair long and it fell over her shoulders in waves. Her lips spread into a smile as she silently took me in with warm caramel eyes, and I thought, for a shining moment, that she was seeing me as I was seeing her:

As absolutely perfect.

"What's your name?" the girl asked. Her voice was rich and low.

"Laura."

"Well, Laura," she said, lifting the crown high above my head, as though this was some sort of coronation, "Saint Perpetua's welcomes you."

She settled the laurels in my blonde curls and then stepped back to admire her work. Her eyes flicked over my body just once, so quickly it's possible I was imagining it, but I flushed all the same.

For one white-hot instant, that dark instinct to overcome and overpower, to kiss and bruise, flared to life in my stomach. I imagined myself slotting my fingers into all that black hair and tugging until her mouth was hovering over mine. I imagined the soft, surprised sound she might make, the sweetness of her breath ghosting across my lips.

And then she was gone, disappeared into the crowd to treat another girl to her undivided attention. I swayed a little, because of either the punch or the brief but electric encounter.

Pressing the cool back of my hand to my flushed cheek, I squeezed my eyes shut and took a deep breath, quieting the beast circling restlessly inside me.

"Ah," Maisy said, sidling up beside me with a knowing smile. "I see you've met Carmilla."

CHAPTER TWO

Laura

he first day of classes started at 8 a.m. on the dot, with a mandatory church history survey course taught by a professor who had probably been alive during the reign of Charlemagne. I'd always been precocious about religion, and already knew all about the desert fathers he was droning on about, so I tuned out most of what he had to say. Instead of taking notes, I sipped some hot tea with honey out of my thermos as I scribbled in my day planner. New starts made me exceptionally nervous, but my day planner helped. It laid out my whole life in neat little time blocks, with tasks listed off to the side, ready to be checked off. After church history came typing, also mandatory, then a break for lunch, then astronomy, which seemed like the least offensive science I could choose to satisfy the prerequisite.

Then, after nightfall, my academic life really began.

From seven to nine I had poetry composition with Ms. De Lafontaine, a course I was personally invited to after submitting a few writing samples along with my application essays. It was supposed to be off-limits to freshmen, but I pleaded my case, citing my gap year, my publication in a few small-time journals down South, my devotion to the written word, and the professor granted me an exception. I was so excited for the class I was barely able to eat any dinner.

Ms. De Lafontaine's classroom was a third-floor oratory in the main academic building, Seward Hall. I arrived ten minutes early, a habit brought on by my anxiety, and took in the chairs dragged into a tight circle in the middle of the room. There were only a dozen girls registered for the class, all upperclassmen who were writing in notebooks or reapplying lipstick in compact mirrors or otherwise ignoring me. Luckily, I recognized one of them.

"Hello," I said, setting my bag down next to Elenore. She looked up at me with eyes that had been carefully lined in black, and smiled warmly.

"Hey, new girl," she said, pulling out my chair for me. I sat down gingerly, holding my day planner in my lap. "That's a pretty dress."

I smoothed my corduroy pinafore and smiled back at her, grateful for the olive branch of trading compliments.

"Thank you. I love your eye makeup."

"Thanks yourself," she said, batting her heavily mascaraed lashes. She flipped the leather-bound notebook she was writing in closed, then leaned in close and conspiratorial. "How are you holding up after the bonfire? I had a splitting headache for the whole day afterwards. No more mixing brown liquor with punch, that's for sure."

"I felt fine. I'm not a big drinker."

"Lucky you. You know, not many first years can get an audience with De Lafontaine, much less a spot in her class. Who'd you kill to get in?"

"Nobody. I just sent her over some of my poetry, and she enrolled me."

"You must be something special, then. I applied three times before she let me in and not to toot my own horn, but I'm very good. If you ask me I think she just dislikes non-fiction writers. I'm going to work for the *New Yorker* someday, write investigative pieces that really matter and shine light on the way the world works, you know? But De Lafontaine requires that all students in the writing cohort study poetry; she says it's the foundation of language. She brings out the best in all of us, though. You'll have to give me your take on her after class." Elenore patted her bouffant hairdo. "Say, did you do the reading? I skimmed it."

"Reading?" I echoed, suddenly terrified. I hadn't seen anything about reading in the syllabus.

Elenore snickered, jostling her shoulder against mine.

"Just kidding. Man, you went white as a sheet. Loosen up a little, okay? De Lafontaine can smell fear."

"Where is she, anyway?" I asked, craning my neck to look around the shadowy oratory. The room was lit with standing lamps, not overhead lights, and the resulting glow was warm and dim.

"Oh, she's always a little late. Not to worry."

Before I had the chance to ask anything more, the door opened and a tall and brutally lovely white woman strode into the room. She wore breezy green satin trousers that matched the scarf tied around her bobbed brown curls, a billowing white blouse, and chunky heels that increased her already formidable height. She was probably in her mid-forties, and she had a stately Romanesque nose that grounded her otherwise delicate features.

"Hello, class," she said, in a throaty voice that dropped right into the pit of my stomach. She stood ramrod straight in the middle of the circled chairs and took us in one by one, ponderously smoking a lipstick-stained Virginia Slim. "You're a sorry-looking lot this morning. Too much revelry at the bonfire on Saturday?"

"Yes, Ms. De Lafontaine," one of the senior girls said, laughter in her voice.

"I hope you celebrated so ferociously you called down the old gods, my bacchantes," the professor said with a mischievous smile. My heart skipped a beat when her green eyes fell on me, pinning me in place. "And it looks like we have some new additions to our little *cultus*. Wonderful."

I swallowed hard and nodded.

One by one, she counted us off on her tapered fingers.

"But there's only eleven of you. Where's Carmilla?"

"Probably keeping the party going," Elenore muttered, too low for the professor to hear.

"I won't start without her," Ms. De Lafontaine went on, tapping her foot.

As if on cue, the girl from the bonfire burst into the room. I had pressed Maisy for details about her that first night, but all my senior sister had to say about Carmilla was that she was "a genius" and "quite the bitch". Naturally, I had spent the next two days looking for her face on the quad or in the lunch line, spurred forward by my pet fixation.

I wasn't obsessed, I assured myself. I was only curious.

Carmilla was dressed strangely, in short ruffled bloomers over dark tights, and a men's vest worn buttoned over a white shirt with puffed sleeves. She looked like she was getting ready to go on stage as Romeo; all she was missing was the short sword and maybe a hat to cover up her long hair. She wore her bangs short, in curly wisps that reminded me of something out of Jane Austen.

"There's our prodigal daughter," Ms. De Lafontaine said.

"Hiya, Ms. D," Carmilla responded, and waltzed right up to her, an unlit cigarette between her fingers. "Can I bum a light?"

I watched, gobsmacked, as Ms. De Lafontaine bent down to let Carmilla light her cigarette off her own smoldering one.

"So happy you decided to grace us with your presence," De Lafontaine said drolly, but there was a fond smile tugging at her lips. She reached out and straightened Carmilla's collar, very much like a mother would.

"I never skip a seminar; you know that," Carmilla responded, dropping into the only seat left open in the room. It happened to be directly across the circle from me. I did my best to keep my eyes on the day planner in my lap.

"Now we can begin," De Lafontaine said, tapping her cigarette delicately into a crystal ashtray set out near the chalkboard. "Shall we start with a recitation? Carmilla, you were late, so you can pay the piper."

Carmilla didn't seem bothered in the least. She stood with a sort of sweeping gesture, then pressed her hand over her chest and began to speak.

Nature, with all her airs and graces, attends on her
    favorites,
painting cheeks with a rosy bloom,
filling lungs with the sweet breath of life.
Youth, in all her splendor, gleams on the skin of girls
who process, heedless of death,
towards beauty's consummation.

She finished with a smirk, and Ms. De Lafontaine brought her hands together in a clap.

"Inspired as always," she said.

"I penned it just this morning," Carmilla said proudly.

"Does anyone else want to share what they've been working on?"

There was abashed murmuring in the room, but no one volunteered. Carmilla was a hard act to follow.

Then, to my absolute shock, the professor turned her attention to me.

"Laura," she said, my name practically a purr. "You were so keen on enrolling. Why don't you show the class something you've been working on?"

I flipped open my journal, thumbing through the pages for something short, something brilliant, something that would convince the class that I deserved to be there. With trembling fingers, I settled on one of the pieces I had submitted as part of my application.

I read it aloud in as strong a voice as I could manage, unable to make eye contact with the professor.

Love turns some people into birds or beggars,
but you make me into architecture,
into a sanctuary of soft and holy spaces
shaped to catch the sound of your voice.
These eyes: rose windows bathing you in light.
These arms: alcoves open in shadowed embrace.
This heart: a confessional dark enough for your sins.
This mouth: a bell driving away demons
and calling you home.

For an awful, brittle moment, there was silence. I just kept staring at my journal, willing the moment to pass. Eventually, I lifted my gaze and found that De Lafontaine was looking at me intently, her arms crossed over her chest. There was a strange fire in her eyes.

"Glorious," she said finally, and I found that I could breathe again. "Absolutely glorious. The tender spareness of language, the rich sensuality of religious metaphor. Your style is unapologetically modern yet accessible. Well done, Laura."

She clapped, and all the girls in the room followed suit. I found myself swimming in the sound of applause, and my cheeks reddened immediately. Elenore gave me a friendly nudge with her foot, reminding me to lift my chin and not avert my gaze from the praise. I was rewarded with the professor's proud, feline smile. Only Carmilla frowned, clapping with a briskness that bordered on violence.

"Well," De Lafontaine said, casting her eyes around the circle again, "it seems that a little new blood in the water is going to be good for everyone. Now. Down to business. Let's talk Voltaire."

The next hour slipped past as though in a dream. De Lafontaine was rhapsodic. When she spoke, the whole room held their breath. She had committed vast swaths of Voltaire, as well as plenty of other poets, to memory. She knew the Classicists, she knew the Beats, and she knew everyone in-between. It seemed almost impossible that one woman's mind could contain so much beauty.

She favored live readings of the assigned texts, and would ambush girls by requesting them to compose verse on the spot, so one had to remain forever on your toes. The class was participatory, visceral, and I felt almost physically exerted when it was over.

As I gathered up my things, my hand cramping from all the notes I had taken, I felt a presence behind me.

I turned to see Carmilla, lovely and dark, surveying me with a haughty air.

"You're very good," she said without bothering with an introduction. "Where are you from?"

"Mississippi," I responded, a little taken aback by her closeness. Her mouth was the color of a rosebud, and it was flushed as though she had been biting her lips. "Nowhere you would have heard of."

"Interesting," she sniffed.

"Where are you from?" I asked, because it seemed like the polite thing to do.

"Austria," she replied, as though the answer bored her. I was immediately enchanted, having never been out of the States myself. When I opened my mouth to ask for more information, she cut me off. "Have you ever been in love?"

I blinked a few times, dazed. To tell the truth, I hadn't. There had been plenty of schoolgirl crushes on my class-mates, and a few doomed infatuations with women old enough to be my mother, but none of them had ever been reciprocated. Not that I had given the other parties much of a chance. I kept my feelings so hidden that they were almost invisible to myself, much less to other people. So no, I had never experienced that all-encompassing sensation of falling into something bigger than myself, that exquisite pain all the poets wrote about.

But now, gazing up at Carmilla with her perfectly arched brows drawn together, I wondered if this wasn't the start of something distinctly love-shaped. And why else would she be asking me, if she didn't feel the same way?

"No," I answered honestly. "But I'd like to be, one day."

She smiled in a way that showed all her teeth. It was, I realized a moment too late, not a friendly smile.

"I could tell. There's a certain quality to your work that just doesn't feel authentic. If you want my advice, I suggest you write from life instead."

Immediately, my blood ran cold. We weren't alone in the room. There were still girls milling around, and Elenore was standing only a few feet away, brows up to her hairline in shock. Carmilla made a pleased little sound that told me she had been angling to hurt me, and was happy that she had.

I immediately regretted the weekend I had spent searching for her in crowds, asking around about her. Foolishly, I had projected all my pent-up desires onto a pretty face, oblivious to the snake underneath. I thought I had made a friend, perhaps kindled the spark of something more, but now I saw that all I had made was an enemy.

"Is that what you do?" I asked flatly.

"Certainly. All my poems come from life. They're the real deal."

"And mine aren't?" I asked, heating a little. I was horribly defensive of my writing. "You've barely seen any of my work, how could you possibly know?"

"I've got an eye for these kinds of things," she said, as though she were appraising a piece of jewelry, not talking about another human being.

"Jealousy gives you wrinkles, Carmilla," Elenore said, coming to my defense. She touched me on the wrist, probably hoping to lead me away from an altercation, but I was transfixed by Carmilla's cruelty.

Carmilla laughed, a musical sound that had no right to be so beautiful.

"I'm not jealous of a *freshman*. I'm just giving her some advice. If she doesn't want to take it, that's not my problem."

She pulled her hair up with a pale blue ribbon, almost exactly the color of the veins showing through the delicate skin of her wrist. I lost myself for a moment in the vision of tying her hands together with that same ribbon, of forcing them down into a coverlet. Inexplicably, the hatred blooming between us sharpened my attraction even more.

"Thanks for the advice, but I think I'm doing fine on my own. De Lafontaine certainly seems to think so," I said, twisting the knife.

Something shuttered behind Carmilla's eyes and I saw that I had hit a nerve. Mean-spirited triumph coursed through me.

Fine. If it was an enemy she wanted, it was an enemy she would get.

"Let's go, Laura," Elenore said, tipping her chin up imperiously at Carmilla.

I followed her out of the room without another word. I couldn't resist a glance over my shoulder as I went and I found Carmilla Karnstein watching me, her eyes burning.

CHAPTER THREE

Carmilla

kicked open the back door to Seward Hall, slouched against the moonlit exterior wall with an unlit clove cigarette between my lips, and seethed.

Never in all my days and nights had I been shown up by someone in class like that, much less by a cow-eyed country hick with a taste for sparse poetry. Who the hell did this Laura girl think she was, crashing a senior seminar she had no right to be in and throwing herself at De Lafontaine? I decided right away that I hated her, hated her stupid bouncy curls and her soft-edged Southern drawl and that little red notebook she kept scribbling in like a pastor's pet during a sermon. She had no sense of her place, of the delicate hierarchy that Saint Perpetua's was built on. My mother would have undoubtedly called her an unrepentant social climber, if my mother had stuck around long enough to actually see me matriculate into college.

When I had encountered her at the bonfire I had thought Laura pretty if in a plain sort of way, inoffensive, but now she chafed against me like poison ivy on my skin.

Shaking my head furiously, I retrieved the prized golden lighter that De Lafontaine had given me as a twenty-first birthday present and lit up. I drew the smoke deeply into my lungs, muttering a few lines of *Paradise Lost* to calm myself down. Poetry was the only antidote to my temper.

> "Me miserable! which way shall I fly
> Infinite wrath, and infinite despair?
> Which way I fly is Hell; myself am Hell;
> And, in the lowest deep, a lower deep
> Still threatening to devour me opens wide,
> To which the Hell I suffer seems a Heaven."

A few moments later, the back door swung open, and De Lafontaine stepped out, as poised as ever. She was so tall she had to duck to avoid the oak branches hanging overhead, the ones that sequestered the back lawn of Seward Hall from prying eyes. That was why we often met here: the privacy, and the ease of access.

"Quite a little temper tantrum you threw in there," she observed, taking me in with her keen eyes. I could never lie to her when she looked at me like that.

"I don't like show-offs," I said, shrugging as though I wasn't deeply bothered by what had just happened in the classroom.

De Lafontaine plucked the cigarette from my fingers and took a drag, her lipstick and mine mingling on the filter. Then she passed it back to me, shaking her head.

"Just admit you hate sharing the spotlight."

"I just don't know why I have to share it with some new girl," I muttered. Every time we met, I told myself I was going to carry myself with maturity and worldliness, to prove to my professor that I was indeed as wise beyond my years as she told me I was, but every time I just ended up feeling like a silly little girl who couldn't control her emotions.

"You've got no one to challenge you. You're resting on your laurels. If Laura can keep pace with you, then I for one welcome a little competition."

"Competition." I spat the word out like a curse. "You just think she's clever, that's all. Clever and charming."

"Don't be jealous," De Lafontaine said, her voice soft as silk but unyielding as iron. I knew that tone, the one that told me there would be consequences if I continued walking down whatever path I was on. Another day, when I was feeling surer of myself, I might have risked her wrath. But that day, I relented.

"Sorry, Ms. D," I said, kicking at a clod of dirt with my foot. De Lafontaine touched the toe of her loafer to my Mary Jane, stilling the idle action.

"Why did you ask to meet with me?" she said, to the point as ever.

My throat got a little dry. What could I say that didn't make me sound desperate? I knew the terms of our arrangement: she led, and I followed. She called, and I answered. Never the other way around. Any attempt to exert authority in this situation was probably doomed, but I still had to try.

"You haven't invited me over for weeks," I said, trying to keep my tone light. "I was worried you were sick or something."

De Lafontaine gave me a small smile that didn't touch her eyes, like she was indulging a toddler.

"It's been the summer vacation, Carmilla. Why would I invite you over when our lessons aren't in session?"

I opened my mouth and then closed it again.

"What have you been up to, then?"

"Research. That's all."

"If you would take me on as a formal assistant, if you would tell me *anything* at all about your research, I could help you. I don't mind the extra work, honest."

"That won't be necessary."

"It's just . . . Listen, if there's someone else, I would rather just know. You can tell me. I won't get angry."

"Careful what you say in public," she said, glancing over her shoulder. Her mood was quickly edging towards irritable. "Someone might hear."

"If you're worried about getting caught, maybe you should invite me over. In private."

I was being overly bold, I knew, but I was getting desperate. Without the frequent clandestine meetings I had grown accustomed to, I felt antsy and ready to burst, like an overly ripe peach. I worried I had been forgotten. I worried that I had been replaced.

Worst of all, I worried that De Lafontaine was getting bored.

"Carmilla." De Lafontaine sighed, making my name sound like an admonishment. I scowled at the ground, refusing to meet her eyes. This was the part when she told me I was being clingy, where she suggested that we take a break, explore other options. This was the part where I broke. Hot, angry tears pricked at my eyes.

Then, to my surprise, De Lafontaine reached out and smoothed her hand down my hair.

"I take too much from you," she murmured.

I snapped my gaze up and looked into her lovely face, the skin like marble, the mouth like a knife wound.

"You don't take anything I'm not willing to give. I'm not afraid of you. I want to keep going."

De Lafontaine breathed in deeply through her nose, something giving way behind her eyes.

"You're too good to me," she said, lifting my hand up and ghosting her lips across the tender skin on the underside of my wrist. I shuddered as my pulse quickened, beating against her teeth as they scraped across my flesh. I knew what came next, but every time was still a little terrifying.

"Some day . . ." De Lafontaine said, voice hoarse with

want. This is how I liked her best, in her fleeting moments of vulnerability. "You'll get tired of all this. You'll realize what I really am, and you'll go off to have your own adventures. You'll forget all about me."

"I could never forget you," I said firmly. "And I'm not going anywhere."

De Lafontaine's piercing eyes met mine, stealing the breath from my lungs, and then, without remorse or hesitation, she bit down.

CHAPTER FOUR

Laura

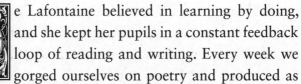

De Lafontaine believed in learning by doing, and she kept her pupils in a constant feedback loop of reading and writing. Every week we gorged ourselves on poetry and produced as much as we could in response, experimenting with form, verse, meter, and style. The reading was nearly impossible to keep up with, and you could always spot one of De Lafontaine's girls because they were constantly leafing through poetry books during meals or under their desks in unrelated classes. We all wanted so desperately to please her, to prove that we belonged in her class, so none of us complained about the workload. De Lafontaine had no patience for those who fell behind, and her syllabus clearly outlined an expulsion policy for anyone who failed to turn their work in on time.

I was in and out of the library every week just to keep

S. T. Gibson

up with the number of books she assigned. My father
provided me with a little spending money in the mail
each month, but it wasn't enough to cover all the classics
and contemporaries De Lafontaine demanded we read,
so I became very friendly with the girls who worked at
the circulation desk. I also became intimately acquainted
with the labyrinthine stacks.

I would wander my favorite sections for hours on end,
trailing my fingers along the spines of theology and
philosophy. The Episcopal Church had passed a movement
to ordain women just the year before, and I was excited
by the new opportunity it offered to studious minds like
mine. In some ways, I was well suited to the priesthood.
I was a talented writer, I knew the holy texts almost as
well as I knew my Shakespeare, I was a good listener, I
was patient, and I didn't spill other people's secrets. In
other ways, I was a terrible candidate for the priesthood.
I was terrified of public speaking, argumentative with
male authority figures, and of course, I had my vices,
which I had no intention of giving up.

Sometimes, when the library was particularly quiet, I
would indulge in one of my favorite sins and acquaint
myself with Saint Perpetua's small but engrossing collection of vintage erotica. I was almost positive it was there
for enterprising students doing research into sexology, or
psychology, or women's liberation, and was certainly not
there for recreational reading, but I had developed a taste
for erotic literature early in my teens, when a well-meaning

distant relation had gifted me a copy of *Delta of Venus*, thinking it to be one of Anaïs Nin's autobiographical works.

So, as a little treat after picking up that week's Hesiod and Aeschylus from the classics section, I rewarded myself by flipping through a pamphlet of Victorian pornography. The inked illustrations of ferocious women in corsets and garters whipping prone men made me smile because of their fanciful nature, but they also stoked that dark fire forever smoldering in my chest. Erotica was one of the only places I could find frank discussions of my own proclivities, rendered in fantastical prose that both titillated the body and delighted the mind. Reading those books felt like slipping on a beribboned mask and surrendering myself to the whirl of a hedonistic masquerade, plunging into a world where I was at once at home and a stranger in a strange land.

"*There* you are," somebody said behind me.

I nearly jumped out of my skin, snapping the pamphlet closed and shoving it between the classical poetry balanced in my arms. Carmilla stood glowering at the end of the aisle, her arms crossed across her chest. She was actually tapping her foot, which was something I thought people only did in stage plays.

"The girls at circulation said you checked out the last copy of Aeschylus in the entire library. I could hardly believe my bad luck. I thought I might find you in the classics section. What are you doing sulking back here?"

"N-nothing," I stammered. I wanted to dissolve into the stacks.

Carmilla took a few thudding steps towards me, dragging her feet like a put-out child. She was wearing a maroon sweater over a sliver of mini-skirt that showed plenty of thigh, and I tried not to stare at her pink knees.

"Give it over," she said, holding out her hand expectantly.

"What? No, I'm not giving you my book; I just checked it out. Didn't you just say it was the last copy in the library? Buy your own."

I felt certain that Carmilla, who summered in the Alps and seemingly never wore the same outfit twice, could afford a schoolbook or two. She blew air through her lips in an unladylike way, and the resulting breeze ruffled her bangs.

"Listen, I waited too long. There's no time to have a new copy shipped in. I'll buy it off you if you want, I don't care; I just need that book."

I bristled at her assumption that she could toss a couple dollars my way and buy my acquiescence.

"This is my copy," I said, enunciating clearly because I wanted to get my refusal through her head, but also perhaps because I wanted to draw out this conversation, to savor her closeness just a few moments more. "I found it and I need it, so I'm not going to give it to you. You'll just have to borrow another copy from one of your friends in the seminar. You do have friends, don't you?"

She wrinkled her nose in irritation.

"At least let me *look* at the assigned poems, then. It will only take five minutes. Surely you've got that to spare. I seriously doubt your social calendar is full."

Without so much as asking permission, she plucked the book from the middle of my stack, disrupting the delicate balance I had created. I nearly dropped my Hesiod, and in the process, the salacious Victorian pamphlet fluttered to the floor. I scrambled to pick it up, but Carmilla beat me to it, snatching up the tract in her hand.

"What's this?" she wondered, then, horrifyingly, started to read the title out loud. "*Lady Danube's Guide to the Ecstasies and Agonies*—"

Panicking entirely, I dropped my books to the floor and clapped my hand over her mouth.

I had never touched her before then, and now suddenly she was captured in my arms, her lips pressed against my palm, her hip bone digging into my thigh. Carmilla's eyes burned as she stared at me with outrage, but she didn't try to wrench away. All at once I was enveloped in the heat of her body, the delicate scent of soap and rosewater still clinging to her skin.

For an instant, my head swam with pleasure, and then I came to my senses and released her.

"Sorry, sorry," I babbled, stooping to gather up my assigned reading. My face burned like a furnace. "I don't know why I did that. Just please . . . be discreet."

Carmilla delicately wiped a smudge of lipstick from

the corner of her mouth with her pinky, then arched an imperious eyebrow at me. A delighted smirk crept across her face.

"The good little church girl's got a taste for dirty books, has she? Oh, that's rich."

"Wait, how do you know I go to church?" I had certainly never seen Carmilla at the university chapel services, nor at confession or vesper prayers.

She shot me a strange look over the edge of the pamphlet, her eyes half-hidden by sooty lashes.

"Maybe I asked around about you. What's it to you?"

"It's plenty to me, if you're going to start malicious gossip."

"I've got far better things to do in my life than sit around and think about you," she said crisply.

"Please give it back," I said, thrusting out my hand for the pamphlet. Carmilla just leaned against the bookshelf, then thumbed open the tract and began reading leisurely.

"No, I don't think I will. These illustrations certainly are imaginative, aren't they?"

"Carmilla," I said, practically begging.

"Quite the smorgasbord of sex acts here. Fellatio, bondage, dominance and submission . . . This is real *Story of* O stuff. Do you have a taste for the rougher aspects of love? Bold, carrying this kind of literature around in the daylight. Perhaps you're a bit of an exhibitionist?"

I couldn't bear to look her in the face. I closed my eyes,

drawing in a deep breath through my nose, and contemplated throwing myself out the nearest window. This was worse than humiliating. When I opened my eyes, I found, to my horror, that I was blinking back tears.

"Oh, come on," Carmilla said, her voice a little gentler, though only barely. "That's nothing to be ashamed of; it's not even a novelty anymore in this day and age. You need to lighten up; you're wound too tight. Are you a virgin? I'll bet ten dollars you are."

"Take the Aeschylus. I don't care anymore. Just stop making fun of me."

"Come on," she sighed, "if I was making fun of you, you would know it. I should be thanking you. I didn't even know Saint Perpetua's *had* books like this. This is a treasure trove! Come here, you're making a scene in the middle of the stacks. You don't want a librarian to come and check up on us, do you?"

I had to admit that I did not. In fact, that was the only possible worse outcome than the one I was currently living in.

Sullenly, I gave in to Carmilla's beckoning and drew closer to her. She was still flipping through the pamphlet, eating up the illustrations with wide, eager eyes. I marveled at how unashamed she was. I wondered what it must be like to walk through life with her self-assured air. She was like a modern-day princess, with a face sculpted by generations of thoroughbred intermarriage and a mouth shaped for giving orders.

I was desperate to know what she looked like on her knees.

"This one is quite acrobatic," she said, flipping the pamphlet upside down to get a better look at a picture of a woman suspended from the ceiling by an intricate latticework of rope.

"It doesn't look very comfortable," I admitted, my voice barely above a whisper in the silent library.

Carmilla flipped the page, revealing two women in lacy negligees and Madame Pompadour wigs tangled together on a bed.

"Now that, however, looks quite comfortable."

Any blood left in my body that wasn't inflaming my cheeks rushed between my legs, and I squirmed. It wasn't a sensation I was used to experiencing except in my most private moments in my own bed, and I wasn't used to it being prompted by another flesh-and-blood person. Certainly not a beautiful, mean-spirited girl that I had to look at in class for hours at a time.

Something about the delirium of arousal spurred me to action, and I reached behind Carmilla to pluck a book off the shelves. It was one of my favorites, though I had never gathered enough courage to walk it downstairs and check it out in clear view of God and the circulation girls.

"Try this," I said, pulling the pamphlet out of her hands and pressing the slim clothbound volume into them instead.

She turned the book over, flipping open the cover to read the dedication.

"*To women who crave the sweet juice of familiar fruit.*"

"It's a book of poems in translation," I said. "Though I doubt they're the kind of poems that De Lafontaine would ever assign. Light bedtime reading, if you have the time for it."

"I'll make the time," Carmilla murmured, leafing through the little book. She glanced up at me and I was struck once again by the shifting quality of her eyes, sometimes golden, sometimes deepest brown. Now they were dark and round, her pupils wide.

I wanted nothing more than to be the voyeuristic ghost in the room when she read those poems in her bed at night.

I opened my mouth to say something brave, something bold, something that one of the heroines in my erotic novels would say, but words failed me. They so often did, when I wasn't writing and rewriting them until I achieved the perfect effect. Instead, I nodded to the Aeschylus in her hands.

"You can have it," I said. "I'll look on with Elenore."

Carmilla looked to the book and then at my face, then back again. Then she snapped the book of Sapphic poetry shut and tilted her chin up, as though she were about to pass a monarchical decree.

"No, I think I'll buy my copy. I found what I was looking for today. See you in class, Sheridan."

And with that, she turned on her heel and left me alone and reeling in the shadowed stacks of the university library.

CHAPTER FIVE

Carmilla

y schedule was as sparse as any precocious senior's who had already completed all their graduation requirements; the poetry seminar with De Lafontaine was the centerpiece, accentuated by two credits of chorale, three credits of a lecture series De Lafontaine was giving on the Beats, and four credits of independent study with De Lafontaine, which generally entailed me reading in her office, submitting my poems for private critique, or baring my neck for her appetite in her apartment. I didn't need any other teacher, not when the light of her brilliance shone bright enough to illuminate my whole life.

I was twenty years and nine days old when I met Professor De Lafontaine for the first time. Newly released from an arduous winter semester at a Swiss finishing school and fresh off the plane to the States, I was still wearing the red beret and coordinating uniform of my previous school. I had unenrolled myself from the finishing school the moment my twentieth birthday granted me the right to access my trust fund, then hastily packed up my favorite books of poetry and hightailed it to America.

I knocked on De Lafontaine's office door before letting anyone on the school's welcoming committee know that the girl who had paid her semester's tuition in full, with Swiss francs no less, had arrived. There was no point in getting settled in until I had introduced myself to the one person on campus who really mattered. She had opened the frosted-glass door, every inch the creature out of myth in her platform shoes and a stiffly starched blouse, and looked down at me with a mixture of weariness and curiosity. She was just as beautiful as the drawing of her in the *Paris Review* had suggested, if a little older, with elegant crow's feet blossoming at the corners of her eyes.

"I'm afraid office hours are over," she had said. "Can I help you?"

"Carmilla Karnstein," I had said, because I had scripted our entire exchange out in my head for months and I wasn't about to divert from my lines. "Your most ardent admirer. I've traveled all the way from Europe to study under you. I trust you received my letters?"

"Oh yes," she said, arching a dark brow. "The Austrian girl. I'm afraid I don't accept new students mid-year, Ms. Karnstein, and even if I did there's simply not enough room in the class—"

This was not how this exchange was supposed to go. Refusing to give in to panic, I set my round suitcase down in front of her door, tugged my gloves off with my teeth, and planted my feet the way my acting instructor had always told me to. Without asking permission, I launched into my newest poem, a modified cinquain about the crushing melancholy I had experienced in Switzerland. My father, tiring of my disastrous dalliances with local boys and girls and my propensity for blowing off my tutors to go horseback riding or running up bills on his credit in the city bars, had shipped me off at his earliest convenience. I had found Switzerland unspeakably dreary, and had done my best to flunk all my classes before being informed by the headmistress that failing to apply myself would only saddle me with kitchen duties and a tighter curfew, not send me back to Austria as I hoped.

I had committed the entire poem to memory, and I performed it without hardly taking a breath.

De Lafontaine stared at me for a long while after I had finished, tapping her fingers against the doorframe. Then she leaned in a little closer, lowering her voice so we wouldn't be overheard by any of the professors in the neighboring offices. My heart skipped a beat. I had always so loved being loomed over, especially by beautiful people. I was, at my core, a brat who adored the guidance of a firm hand. Maybe it was because my parents had been so absent when I was growing up, or maybe it was simply a delicious aberration in my soul, but as she looked down at me, I couldn't help but feel small and trapped and thrilled.

"Did you really mean what you wrote? In those letters?" she asked.

"You read them?" I breathed, rapt by her simple presence. I had written her four, and she had never responded.

"Of course I read them. You spoke so eloquently of my poetry; it's like you knew it better than I did."

There was a strange, vulnerable gleam in her eye, one I would spend countless days chasing after.

"I meant every word."

De Lafontaine smiled at me then. Her teeth, I noticed, were rather pointed.

"Then come in, Carmilla," she said, stepping aside to welcome me into her office. "Tell me, what have you been reading lately?"

Everything she asked of me afterwards, all the little agonies and offerings she required to keep me in her good graces, was given without hesitation or regret.

If we transgressed boundaries or dove into the dark waters of something taboo together, I never noticed, as lost as I was to her. For the entirety of the spring semester of my junior year, I was her morning glory, her silver spoon, her prize mare. I devoted myself entirely to a life of letters under her tutelage, wringing every last drop of emotion I had into my poems. And oh, how she praised me. Whether she was lauding me in front of a classroom or whispering encouragement to me in private, I was always her little star. Our spirits were kindred, she would tell me, linked by art and blood in a chain no man's disapproval or god's judgment could break.

And then the Sheridan girl arrived. In one fell swoop, my station as the favorite became precarious. In class, I maintained a cool demeanor, but in private, I fumed over her very existence. I lay in bed at night, my face hot with rage, imagining smashing her fingers in the door of De Lafontaine's office or tripping her up on her way to class. Besting her wasn't enough; I wanted her out of the picture entirely. School had only been in session a month, and already she had ingratiated herself with De Lafontaine. Laura had no idea what she was doing, what she was dealing with. If she knew the truth about De Lafontaine she would run screaming. Only I was brave enough to face down all that darkness and open my arms to it. That's why I had been chosen: my bravery and talent, both undeniable to someone like De Lafontaine, who truly appreciated such things.

De Lafontaine, who had been so cold to me lately, and who refused to share the details of her mysterious research with me no matter how much I asked.

One crisp night, I threw back the covers from my bed, slipped my feet into my oxfords, and wiggled a coat over my pajamas. I was training myself to keep to De Lafontaine's schedule, just in case she called for me, and had become semi-nocturnal already. Stifling a yawn, I plucked up my miniature flashlight and discreetly made my way through the hall, down the stairs, and out into the quiet of two a.m. There was dew on the grass, along with the first of the leaves that would fall and blanket the quad by the time October was out, and I squelched through them as I made my way briskly to the library. In my pocket, a surreptitious slip of paper burned. I had plucked it from between the pages of De Lafontaine's planner when she wasn't looking during one of our last meetings.

If De Lafontaine wasn't willing to share her secrets with me, I would simply have to uncover them myself.

I had learned from an older girl who used to slip into the library after hours for quickies in the stacks with her beau that the lock on the side door was broken, and could easily be jimmied open with a hairpin. I crouched in the dark, flashlight balanced between my teeth, and worked the lock until it gave way.

The library was eerie at night, the maroon carpet spreading out before me like Homer's wine-dark sea, the shelves casting weird shadows across my hands and face. Swallowing my trepidation, I made a beeline for the circulation desk, and began to flip through the seemingly endless card catalog, comparing call numbers on the cards with the neatly handwritten numbers on the slip of paper

I had swiped from De Lafontaine. There were eight titles in total, and I collected the cards and made my way towards the appropriate section of the library to pull the books.

I gathered them up in a precarious stack in my arms and then settled into a chair at a table in the main reading room, careful not to let my light shine out the window. With a scholar's fervent focus, I began to review the titles.

A Concise Survey of Women's Colleges in the United States.

The Young Woman's Guide to Higher Education, Edition 3.

A History of Saint Perpetua's Women's College, 1841–Present.

There were pamphlets too, collections of notable lectures from Saint Perpetua's faculty, and a book of blueprints featuring the original designs for the school, masterminded by a mysterious architect who had died before the university opened its doors.

De Lafontaine, it appeared, was preoccupied with Saint Perpetua's college, particularly its origins.

I flipped open the history of the college to a dog-eared page, and my breath caught in my throat when I noticed tiny notes scribbled in the margins. I would recognize the handwriting anywhere: it was De Lafontaine's neat, looping script. She annotated all her books, and I had often lovingly run my fingers along the notes she left in volumes of poetry that she lent me from her private collection.

Next to one underlined paragraph, she had written, simply: *the answer lies beneath.*

Suddenly, the front door to the library swung open with a clang and the invading beam of a flashlight swept through the room.

I gasped, ducking down from my seat and clambering underneath the table. I had enough foresight to grab the history book as I went and stuff it into my bag. Doing my best to keep my breathing quiet, I sat hunched in the shadows as a security guard made a routine perusal of the premises. Thankfully, he didn't seem to notice me.

I waited until he had rounded a corner, then snatched up my bag and made a mad dash for the exit. I pushed my way out through the front door, then sprinted across the quad until my lungs burned. With every step, I expected to hear a rough male voice calling out to me, telling me to stop, to drop the bag, but I somehow made it back to my dorm without being detected. I locked my door behind me and collapsed onto my bed, sweating and panting.

After taking a few moments to catch my breath, I fished the stolen library book out of my bag and began reading by the light of the lamp propped up next to my bed on a stack of novels. I tore a fresh piece of paper from the nearest notebook and started feverishly writing, transferring De Lafontaine's notes to my own. I didn't stop until the harsh light of morning pricked my eyes through the window, dragging me back into reality.

I would get to the bottom of whatever De Lafontaine was researching. And once I presented my findings to her, she would have no choice but to welcome me back into her confidence.

She had to.

I didn't know what would become of me if she didn't.

CHAPTER SIX

Laura

armilla's poems were all about Youth, or Eternity, or any of those other ineffable ideals that seemed only appropriate to render in capital letters. De Lafontaine was absolutely rhapsodic about Carmilla's work, and the two women shared a strange rapport that was difficult to pin down. Carmilla trailed after the professor as eager as a pup, and De Lafontaine doled out praise at random intervals, like little training treats. They weren't friends – De Lafontaine was impassable as a Calvinist God and refused to give students the illusion that she was their contemporary – but I would sometimes see the two of them smoking under the awning of the academic building before class, talking with their heads close together. De Lafontaine would occasionally arrive a half-hour late to seminar or cut out early, complaining of headaches, though girls whispered about seeing her walking the quad at night alone. Carmilla, while she never lowered herself to participating in gossip about our teacher, would sometimes smile in a way that suggested she knew more about De Lafontaine's late-night activities than anyone else.

I wondered at their strange intimacy, the way Carmilla had been so clearly chosen out of our cohort as the favorite. I wondered what made her so special, and if De Lafontaine might get bored of her allegories and similes after a while.

I wondered if Carmilla's position could be usurped.

I threw myself into my studies. I had always been academically minded, but the competitive atmosphere of De Lafontaine's classes sharpened my predilection into an obsession. Maisy and Elenore, who I suspected had conspired between themselves to adopt me, were always trying to convince me to go out with them, on the hikes that Maisy so adored or to the jazz clubs where Elenore liked to go hang out with her boyfriend. I had no interest in men or the great outdoors, especially not when De Lafontaine kept grading my poetry with notes like "push yourself past what is comfortable" or "you can produce better work than this". I wondered if Carmilla received similar notes on her work, or if De Lafontaine was as effusive about the other girl's work in private as she was in front of the class.

Carmilla, for her part, seemed bound and determined to vex me at every turn. She smirked at me whenever I got up in front of the room to read my latest work, or scribbled in her notebook loudly while ignoring me entirely. I rarely saw her outside of the classroom, since she lived in an upperclassman dorm and spent her free time doing God knows what with that little clique of hers, but on the rare occasion our paths crossed she averted her eyes. I wasn't sure what I had done to earn her ire. I'd always thought of myself as an unassuming, bland sort of person, not worth remarking on, much less taking offense from. But then again, my writing was the most interesting thing about me, and it was my writing that riled Carmilla.

Can I confess that I loved it?

I loved getting under her skin. I loved knowing that, if I tried hard enough, my words could pierce the armor of her popularity and her persona and disturb something inside her. I could see that I had an effect on her, even if she tried to hide it. It was evident in the furrowing of her brows and the tightening of her mouth every time I stood up in class to read.

If I couldn't touch her, I would settle for making her squirm.

I devoured De Lafontaine's reading list, and I used the inspiration of literature to fuel my own poetry. I wrote about everything, about the scintillating scarlet of the leaves outside, of my aching longing for Mississippi, but most of all I wrote about *her*. I was never so brazen as to call her by name, of course; I called her Persephone, or Puck, or any of those other literary figures that she seemed to conjure up with her costumes and posturing. I wrote about her tangle of black hair, her lithe tanned arms, her delicate bird-boned ankles. I worked myself into a fever over her, hunched over my typewriter in my dorm room while my tea went cold on my bedside table. Sometimes my poems venerated her like a saint, other times they cast her as the Devil herself, but Carmilla always played a starring role.

I was never going to possess her, of course. I would never get to taste her skin or hear the sweetness of a moan from her lips. But if I couldn't have the real Carmilla, I would settle for an illusion of my own design.

If it was writing from life she wanted, it was writing from life she was going to get.

I was, I knew full well, a creature composed of strange desires. They'd always been with me, these hungers. As a child I played villain in every game of "capture the princess", tying my pretty playmates up with jump ropes and spiriting them away to my faux castle on the playground. I wrestled my friends to the ground in bursts of emotion, or punctuated kisses on the cheek with a sharp nip. It didn't help that I had absolutely no interest in pursuing companionship with boys in the same way I did with girls, no matter how many limpid first dates I went on. Love and pain grew in a thorny grove inside me, impossible to disentangle from one another. And as I grew older, I withdrew into myself, becoming less brazen in my friendships. I learned to keep my hands to myself, to sit on them until they went numb or to dig my fingers into my palms until they bled. I learned how to guard my heart against the sweeping, heady sensation of a crush. I learned how to survive in the cutthroat world of girlhood, where all strangeness was unrooted as ruthlessly as weeds from a garden.

I domesticated my own wildness, starved the odd appetites inside me. I remade myself into Laura the saint, Laura who never causes any trouble, Laura who is reliable and dependable, if a little boring.

Now I might have been a virgin, but I was no innocent. I'd read de Sade. I knew there were words for my proclivities, and no shortage of people in the world who shared them. I didn't feel any shame for liking what I liked, especially since I had no intention of exerting my diabolical will over any but the most willing of subjects. I kept my tastes quiet, kept them private, feeding them only rarely and when I was sure I wouldn't get caught. I often felt like a wolf wearing the skin of a girl, balancing on two legs and hoping no one would notice.

But this girl, this Carmilla . . . she undid all my domestication. One smile from her and I wanted to loose my hair and chase her barefoot through the woods, I wanted to knock her to the ground and pin her like a butterfly, I wanted to dig my teeth into her plush lower lip, I wanted, *I wanted*.

One rainy Tuesday evening, De Lafontaine stopped me outside her classroom. I was halfway across the quad already and she jogged to catch up to me, calling my name. She was holding a black umbrella, which she chivalrously extended over my head as she drew close to me.

"Laura, a word?" she asked.

"Of course, Professor," I said, slowing my pace so we could walk side by side on the path and share the protection of the umbrella.

"You've been making excellent progress in your studies," she said, strolling with one hand tucked into the pocket of her oversized tweed slacks. They matched a vest she wore buttoned over her crisp white shirt, and the pairing gave her a debonair, androgynous air. "I want you to know that I notice how hard you're working to better yourself, and I've noted marked improvement."

"Thank you," I said, warming a little under the praise. I wasn't used to anyone but my father esteeming my work so much.

"I hoped you might be available this Friday night?" she asked, and she almost sounded nervous. As though a single bone in my body had the power to reject her. "I host a breakout seminar of poetry students at my apartment, very discreet, very selective. We meet weekly to take the course of study deeper, and to critique each other's work. Iron sharpens iron, isn't that the saying?"

"I think it is," I said, a little stunned. Was I hearing her right? Had I really made such a positive impression?

"Grand," De Lafontaine said, squeezing my shoulder with a grip that was unexpectedly strong. She grinned at me, flashing white teeth. "Nine p.m. then, my place?"

She produced a pen from her pocket and paused to take my hand in hers. My heart, treacherous as always and weak in the presence of beautiful women, stuttered. She uncapped the pen and scribbled her address on my palm, dotting the Is with little flourishes that felt like pinpricks.

"I'll look forward to it. How many other people are in this seminar?" I asked, curiosity getting the better of me.

De Lafontaine pressed a finger to her crimson lips, pondering or miming the act.

"Counting you? Two total."

CHAPTER SEVEN

Laura

hat Friday I stood with sweating palms outside De Lafontaine's home. She lived on the third floor of an old brick apartment complex perched on the edge of campus, catering mostly to faculty with a few older residents who had been grandfathered in from the previous landlord. Ivy, already fading in the chill of early autumn nights, crawled up the side of the building.

I swallowed hard, steeling my nerves. I wasn't great at first (or second, or third) impressions, but I was determined to make this a good one.

There's always something staggeringly intimate about seeing someone's living space for the first time, and I wasn't sure I was prepared to see my professor in such a new light. But then again, I had been invited. I had been *chosen*. Plucked out of the milieu of eager girls and dusted off and given a special privilege.

Maybe I did deserve to be here, after all.

With that thought emboldening me, I rang the doorbell for De Lafontaine's apartment. Moments later, the woman herself appeared in the doorway. She was graceful as a swan in wide-legged linen pants, a low-cut wrap blouse, and a jeweled barette pinned in her short hair.

The artist at home, at rest. The god made vulnerable by a freshly washed face and stocking feet.

"Laura," she said, so warmly I flushed miserably. She slid one arm around my shoulder and drew me into the cool dim of her apartment building. "So happy to have you. You're just in time. I haven't poured the drinks yet."

I followed her silently up the winding staircase to the third floor, where she popped open her door with her shoulder. Inside, the room smelled richly of rumpled linen and jasmine and the faint undercurrent of something green and peaty that I suspected was illegal.

There was a low orange velvet couch in one corner of the small living space, and a trio of overstuffed throw pillows tossed on to the floor around a coffee table. Precariously crammed bookshelves stood in the corners of the room, boasting poetry, prose and non-fiction. As I rounded the corner, I caught a glimpse of a small galley kitchen jutting off the side of the main room, with delicate china cups hanging from iron hooks above the sink. Much of the rest of the floor space in the front room was taken up by a shockingly crimson armchair.

And there sat Carmilla, curled up with an open copy of John Donne's poems in her hands. When she looked up at me, there was an arresting softness to her features, the vulnerability of surprise. Then her gaze shuttered and the hatred returned to her eyes.

"Well," she said, snapping her book shut with more force than was strictly necessary. Her thin eyebrows shot up towards her hairline as she looked towards De Lafontaine for an explanation.

"Laura will be joining us this evening," the professor said in that kind but firm tone that she used in the classroom, the one that brooked no argument.

"That's fine," Carmilla said airily, swinging her legs over the armrest of the chair and planting them firmly on the floor. "Drinks for three, then?"

"You do drink, don't you?" De Lafontaine said, in a quiet aside to me laced with a smirk. There was no denying her.

"Of course," I blustered.

"Good, good," she said, clapping me on the shoulder and guiding me towards the couch. The touch was as intoxicating as whatever Carmilla was brewing up in the kitchen. De Lafontaine didn't strike me as effusive with her affection, but here she was, touching me at every turn. I didn't know what to make of it, but I knew I didn't want her to stop.

I took a seat on the edge of the sofa as Carmilla puttered

and clattered in the kitchen. De Lafontaine sat beside me, one ankle crossed over her knee like a proper gentleman, and smiled at me widely.

"How are you finding Donne?" she asked. "Carmilla and I were just discussing his work."

"I find his religious devotion touching," I began, warming up to sharing the entirety of my thoughts on the man. Generally, I liked Donne, although I sometimes felt like he could get lost in metaphor.

From the kitchen, Carmilla audibly scoffed.

"Yes, Carmilla?" De Lafontaine said drolly.

"It's just . . ." Carmilla said, appearing from the kitchen carrying some sort of contraption in two arms. It was mostly glass and metal, and featured two dainty spigots protruding from a vessel containing cold water. "Donne's religious devotion is a smokescreen for his carnal desires. '*Batter my heart, three-personed God*'? You've read it, I assume."

"Of course," I said, prickling at her insinuation that I had been skimping on my reading.

Carmilla smirked right at me as she plopped down on one of the cushions arrayed around the coffee table. It was at that very moment De Lafontaine decided to disappear into the kitchen, leaving me alone with my rival.

"It's about sex, Laura."

I wasn't sure I had ever heard her say my name, and to hear her say it in the same sentence as the word *sex* was shamefully electrifying.

"In what way?" I shot back.

"*Take me to you, imprison me, for I, except you enthrall me, never shall be free, nor ever chaste, except you ravish me,*" she quoted, with a little flourish of her fingers. "All that talk of taking and ravishment and you don't think he has the beast with two backs in mind?"

"Carmilla, don't be crude," our professor called from the kitchen, but there was laughter in her voice. She reappeared moments later carrying three tiny glasses rimmed in gold, and opened her palm to reveal a trio of perfectly square sugar cubes. "Shall we?"

I edged closer to the contraption, which, from the accouterments and from the limited reading I had done on the subject, was probably an absinthe fountain. I didn't have the taste for spirits and had certainly never tried absinthe, but I wasn't about to let either of them know that.

De Lafontaine poured an inch or two of luridly green liquid into our glasses from a nearby bottle labeled in French, then placed filigreed slotted spoons over the mouth of our cups. The sugar cubes were arranged on top of the spoons just so, and then De Lafontaine positioned two of the glasses underneath the silver spigots and started dripping icy water over the sugar. The white crystals slowly dissolved, trickling down into the absinthe and turning it a milky pistachio color.

"I love this little ritual," De Lafontaine said in her smoky voice. It made everything she said sound slightly conspiratorial, like she was speaking for my benefit alone.

Mine and Carmilla's, I supposed.

De Lafontaine handed one glass to me and one glass to Carmilla, ever the gracious host, and then fixed herself a drink. She raised her glass in a toast, and Carmilla and I clinked our cups against hers.

"To the pursuit of knowledge undying," De Lafontaine proclaimed, flashing her perfect teeth in a grin.

"Hear, hear," Carmilla said, and downed half her glass in one swallow.

"I picked up my love for absinthe in Paris," De Lafontaine said. "I used to sit in the cafés with the other poets and argue philosophy from dusk till dawn."

"I love Paris," Carmilla cooed. "The Seine under moonlight is breathtaking."

I tentatively sipped my drink, the harsh taste of alcohol and licorice blooming on my tongue along with a saccharine sweetness and surprisingly delicate floral quality. I wasn't sure if I liked the flavor, but I did like the experience, sitting close to De Lafontaine and participating in a social rite that was obviously dear to her heart. I felt like I was being inducted into some kind of secret society, a special social class made up of world-traveling girls and their intrepid guide.

Except I hadn't traveled the world. I had never been further from home than I was now. I wondered if De Fontaine would still want me in her cohort if she knew I was just a dull American with no passport to speak of.

I carefully avoided the topic of international travel and tried my best to participate in the conversation otherwise.

"I very much appreciate being invited over," I said, falling back on my Southern manners. "You're a wonderful host."

"I take hospitality very seriously," De Lafontaine said with a twinkle in her eye. "I was raised in a grander time, a time where graciously opening one's home was the utmost mark of sophistication and status. I try to preserve the tradition, even in the most modest surroundings."

I wondered idly how old De Lafontaine really was. Her face was almost entirely unlined but completely devoid of the plumpness of youth. She was still lovely, still striking and strong. She was the kind of woman I would have liked to grow into; confident and poised and aesthetically cohesive.

Carmilla, I realized, was watching me over the rim of her glass, her carmine lips pursed. There was something half-feral in her expression that I had tried and failed to grasp in poetry a dozen times over the last few weeks. She almost looked ready to bolt, or to bite.

I looked right back, sipping my drink like it wasn't burning all the way down. In the end, she broke first, her eyes flitting away from mine and over to De Lafontaine's.

"Shall we have a reading?" she chirped, all sweetness and light once again.

Carmilla stood and smoothed her short skirt, then sauntered over to one of the packed bookshelves and ran her fingers along the exposed spines. My arms got goose pimples watching her, like it was my skin she was touching, not old leather and hardbound cloth. I was once again struck with fury at what she did to me. How could one girl tie me up in so many knots without even trying?

"No more Donne," Carmilla proclaimed. "I'm tired of his equivocation. Why don't we hear a little Marlowe? His words always cut to the quick."

"A brilliant idea," De Lafontaine said. "Carmilla, you must read from *Faustus*. I cannot imagine a more inspired Mephistopheles."

"Will you play Faust, Ms. D?" Carmilla asked, eyes sparkling merrily. I couldn't fathom being so brave as to invite De Lafontaine into a recitation in class, but it appeared that in the private environs of De Lafontaine's apartments, Carmilla was bolder.

What else had they done together here, I wondered, when no one else was watching?

"Oh no," De Lafontaine said, waving the suggestion away with her glass of absinthe. "Playing that part will just remind me of my age. Laura, you should read for Faustus."

What could I say? There was no arguing with the woman, no matter how uncomfortable public recitation made me, so I dutifully stood on fawn-shaky legs and crossed the room to Carmilla. She didn't snipe at me as I stood beside her, peering over her shoulder at the book. I was taller, I realized with a bit of surprise. She had such a presence that I always assumed she had inches on me.

Carmilla shifted her grip on the book so I could read more clearly, our shoulders pressing together. Heat bloomed from the point of contact, running down my arm like the pins-and-needles sensation one gets from falling asleep at strange angles. She shot me a suspicious glance from under her lashes, and I held her gaze without shrinking from its intensity.

"Any time you're ready," De Lafontaine said, a touch impatiently. Carmilla's eyes fell back to the text, and she shifted into a loose stance, with her free hand hanging down at her side and her feet shoulder width apart. She had theatrical training, then. I wasn't surprised. Everything I had observed about Carmilla suggested that she came from the kind of family who could afford private lessons and conservatory visits. My father worked as a paralegal, making enough to keep us comfortable but never enough that there was much left over.

Carmilla wet her finger with the tip of her tongue and then flipped through the book until she found a section that pleased her. Then she began to read from the scene in which Mephistopheles convinces Faustus to sign his soul over, in blood no less, to the Devil. She delivered the lines with fervor and verve, and her recitation stirred something deep inside me even as I tried to overcome my debilitating stage fright in order to read my own lines.

We volleyed Marlowe's poetry back and forth between us, eyes locked, until we reached the climax of the scene.

"*Lo, Mephistopheles,*" I read, familiar enough with this section that I could lift my eyes from the page and fix them on Carmilla's lovely, cold expression. "*For love of thee, I cut mine arm, and with my proper blood assure my soul to be great Lucifer's, chief lord and regent of perpetual night."*

In that moment, I imagined it. Opening a vein right there in De Lafontaine's living room, bleeding for love. I wondered what it would feel like, to be that abased with desire for someone.

De Lafontaine clapped briskly, a delighted smile on her face. Her glass, I noticed, was now empty.

"Marvelous, both of you. I would tell you to try out for the acting troupe on campus, but I don't want anything distracting you from your studies. Poetry is life, you see. You must throw yourself into the study and creation of it wholeheartedly."

"Yes, Ms. De Lafontaine," Carmilla and I said in unison.

"Now," the professor said, beginning to refill her glass, "you must show me what you've been writing. Only bring me your best, girls."

Carmilla and I dutifully rifled around in our bags, me in my practical tweed backpack, a birthday gift from my father, and Carmilla in a buttery camel-colored leather handbag, until we produced our notebooks.

"I'll go first," Carmilla said, draping herself elegantly across the couch. Everything she did was elegant. It absolutely infuriated me.

Her poem was an ode to beautiful death, strongly in the tradition of Keats or Shelley. I wondered if death had touched her life yet, or if she was too young to know its sting. My grandmother had died when I was nine, two years after my mother had passed away, so I was well acquainted with tragedy.

When De Lafontaine turned her eyes on me, I read from my typewritten pages while doing my best to keep my hands from shaking.

I chose something safe, something conservative in style and content.

After I finished, De Lafontaine fixed me with her flinty gaze.

"Don't tell me you've already peaked, not three weeks into the semester."

Heat flooded my face in a sickly rush of shame. Carmilla mimed a yawn to stealthily cover a smile.

"No, Ms. De Lafontaine," I whispered.

"Because you're capable of so much, Laura," she said, her voice a little softer. Her affect could swing from imperious to nurturing on a dime. I found her mercurial temperament difficult to keep up with. "I've seen greatness in your work. You just need to figure out how to tap that wellspring and let your genius flow."

"Thank you," I said, sitting back down on the sofa so my knees wouldn't give out from under me.

"Shall we have another round?" De Lafontaine said brightly, already reaching for the sugar cubes and slotted spoons.

I must have passed three hours in De Lafontaine's apartment, all said, staying up well beyond my bedtime. We discussed everything we had been reading (Carmilla showed off by discussing the French poetry we had been assigned in the original language, fluent as she was) and the life of the artist.

When De Lafontaine finally released us, my head was swimming with absinthe and new vocabulary. Carmilla and I gathered up our coats and stumbled out into the dark. Bafflingly, she held the front door open for me. I thought she might slam it shut in my face, but she ensured safe passage as I stepped over the sill and onto the grass outside.

"You're really very good, you know, Laura," Carmilla said, her vowels loose from the liquor. I watched, entranced, as her lips formed the shape of my name.

"Am I?" I said coolly.

"Yes," she responded, eyes flashing in the dark. "I hate it."

I wasn't quite sure how to respond to such naked honesty. She just stood there in her slingback shoes and corduroy skirt, looking up at me with a little furrow between her perfect brows. I very much wanted to rub it away with my thumb.

"Happy to be hated by you," I shot back, truth dribbling out of me like the iced water from the absinthe fountain.

"Why ever would that make you happy?"

"Because it's interesting," I said, painfully aware of how close we were standing together in the dark. There were no stars overhead, and our conversation was lit only by the ambient golden glow thrown from the windows of the apartment building. "Because it's the most interesting thing that's happened to me in my whole life."

Carmilla stared at me for a long moment, her face half in shadow. Then she threw her head back and laughed, the pale expanse of her throat exposed to the sharp sliver of moon overhead. She laughed until her eyes watered, and then she put one hand on my shoulder, as though to steady herself.

I froze, turned to stone by the weight of her touch.

"Goodnight, Laura," she said, taking a backwards step away from me, and then another. That infuriating smile was once again fixed on her face. "See you in class."

CHAPTER EIGHT

Carmilla

ctober crept in on quiet stocking feet. I applied myself diligently to my writing, doing everything within my power to create work that would touch even the worldly and hardened heart of Ms. D. I didn't so much grow accustomed to Laura's presence in my academic life as I made space for it, giving her a wide berth and keeping my eyes on my own paper. I tried to internalize what De Lafontaine had said about needing a foil, a challenger. I imagined Laura and me as jousters, racing headlong on sweating stallions and crashing lances into each other until someone was tossed to the ground.

I was determined not to be unhorsed, no matter what Laura threw at me.

Despite this promise made to myself, my stomach still turned during that week's Friday meeting when I walked in to find Laura seated primly on De Lafontaine's velvet couch. Laura, who managed to look saintly with her golden curls arranged around her face in an outdated style, even though she was the devil in my passion play. Laura, who gave me a hopeful little smile like we were anything other than sworn enemies. Laura, who had intruded into my sacred space and now made herself at home there.

"Laura," I said tightly, dropping my bookbag down in the corner. I was suddenly exhausted of her.

"You're late," De Lafontaine said, poking her head out from the kitchen.

"Excuse me," I said, and ducked into the kitchen after her. I clutched the edge of her countertop until my knuckles went white, giving her my most imploring glance.

"Ms. D, does she *really* have to be here?"

She barely spared me a glance, occupied as she was with pouring steaming black tea into china cups.

"She's learning, Carmilla, just like you."

"But," I babbled, panic starting to set in. "But these sessions are *private*."

"And Laura can keep quiet about them, I'm sure. Have you read her work? She's talented beyond her years. Strange to find a young person with such a mature outlook on life and love."

My chest burned just to hear her dole out praise to someone who wasn't me.

"But, *Ms. D*," I whined, and I heard it in my voice, the grating, girlish tone. De Lafontaine gave me a stern look, sucking a stray drop of tea off her thumb.

"No buts, Carmilla. You'll behave yourself without exception. Any complaints you have you can take up with me after the lesson. Now, let's stop neglecting our guest."

With that, she carried the fully outfitted tea tray into the living room, leaving me fuming in the kitchen. I thought about staying there all night, camping out in protest of this infringement on my rights as a student, as the favorite. But the kitchen was small and dim, and I knew there would be nothing to eat in the empty refrigerator. If I pitched a fit De Lafontaine might do the unthinkable and throw me out into the night.

So, I swallowed my pride and stalked back into the living room. I settled down on a plump cushion on the floor and accepted a tiny cucumber and cream cheese sandwich cut into a triangle from De Lafontaine. Laura and I ate delicately with our fingers, passing the plate around in a circle while De Lafontaine mixed burning whiskey into our tea. Laura sipped hers as primly as a puritan. I downed two teacups of the concoction in quick succession, chasing away my rage and indignation with liquor until my cheeks burned with warmth. I reclined on the sofa like a drowsy daffodil wilting under the summer heat, taking up as much space as possible so there was no room for Laura.

"Let's all get to know each other with a little thought experiment," De Lafontaine said, after the snacks had been passed around and the whiskey had been downed. "Why do we write poetry, pupils?"

"To live for ever," I said immediately. There had never been any other answer, would never be. "Art outlives all of us. It makes us immortal."

De Lafontaine turned her cutting green gaze on my rival. "Laura?"

Laura considered the question for a long while, for so long that I began to wonder if she was dim as well as annoying.

"Connection, I suppose," she said eventually.

"Say more about that," De Lafontaine urged.

"When I try to speak about how I feel," she said, pressing her hand over her heart, "I end up stumbling all over myself. But when I write it out, suddenly there's clarity. Life doesn't seem worthwhile without synthesizing my experiences into art, the catharsis of putting it all out onto the page. It's the only way I've ever been able to get other people to understand how I'm feeling."

De Lafontaine hummed in appreciation, taking a sip of her cocktail. I lived for that low sound she made in the back of her throat, indicating her tacit approval. It killed me to hear her give it to Laura.

"Very wise, both of you."

"What about you?" Laura asked shyly.

"What about me?" De Lafontaine echoed.

"Why do you write poetry?"

A strange look flittered behind our professor's eyes. I

realized, with surprise, that the Southern girl had somehow caught the great De Lafontaine off guard.

"Memory," De Lafontaine said finally. "I write to remember the exultations and miseries of my life. To capture certain moments, certain . . . people in amber, so they will never diminish, never fade. When you're as old as I am, sometimes all you have for company are your memories. When everyone else has left you, they remain." She cleared her throat. "Now, Carmilla. A recitation."

That was more like it. I pulled myself to my feet, only swaying slightly, and drew a typewritten piece of paper from my back pocket. I caught Laura staring at my hands as I did so, even though she tore her eyes away the moment they met mine. She was wringing the edge of her skirt between her fingers, which I noticed featured lovely half-moon nails, tipped with stark white. I lost myself for a few tipsy seconds wondering if she painted them herself, or if another girl might kneel at her feet, delicately applying color to her nails with a tiny brush.

Banishing the image from my mind, I cleared my throat and began to read.

Three lines later, De Lafontaine held up a hand, her mouth set into a grim line. I stopped reading with my mouth still open, my lower lip wobbling slightly. Laura sucked in a breath, bracing herself for the criticism.

"That's enough of that, I think," De Lafontaine said, taking a contemplative sip of her drink. The cookies and sandwiches lay untouched before her.

"Enough . . . of what?" I asked, nearly stumbling over my words. My eyes met Laura's momentarily as I frantically threw them across the room, and to my horror, I found sympathy there.

"Enough of the same," our professor said succinctly. "It's always archetypes with you, Carmilla, never specificity. Specificity is the very soul of poetry."

"You've never found fault with my use of archetypes before," I said, a tad defensively.

"It was new before, but now it's tired. Do you want to spend your entire career repeating the same themes over and over again, like some washed-up hack? You have your whole life before you: *innovate*."

"I'll do my best, Ms. De Lafontaine," I said, crumpling the paper in my hands and stuffing it into the pocket of my trousers. Crumpling it didn't feel like enough. I wanted to rip it to shreds and then burn the pieces.

"You'd better not," De Lafontaine said, eyes flashing. "Your best is not good enough, Carmilla, not in the world of art. You must excel or else fade into obscurity."

"I understand," I said, and oh god, now there were hot, shameful tears in my eyes. I would not cry, I would *not*.

De Lafontaine's countenace softened, and for a moment I thought the barrage was over. Laura opened her mouth to speak, but De Lafontaine cut her off.

"Why this obsession with youth, Carmilla? Is this about your mother? Maybe you're trying to recapture your childhood, when she was present in your life and available to you. The mother wound is a deep one, and it will infect everything you write if you let it."

I felt as though I had been struck. One shaking hand drifted up to press against my churning stomach, and for a moment I thought I might be sick. De Lafontaine just watched me, disapproval written in the angles of her face.

"Ms. D," I began, quietly, as though I could cajole some of the old sweetness back into my mentor. De Lafontaine didn't even let me finish.

"Your mother left you because she didn't want you, Carmilla, and you must come to terms with that. You cannot hide for ever in childhood; eventually you must face the facts of life and grow up. I fear that you'll shrink into a sort of perpetual girlhood. I should call you Petra Pan."

I opened my mouth to defend myself, to fight back, to say something, anything, but no words came out. My eyelashes fluttered, and a single teardrop trickled down my cheek.

I couldn't breathe, couldn't think.

I had to get out of there.

"I need some air," I said, voice barely above a whisper. I snagged up my bag and barged past Laura, who inexplicably reached out a hand for me. Her fingertips grazed my wrist, and the touch burned. When I flinched, there was real hurt in her face.

"Carmilla," De Lafontaine sighed, as though only minorly inconvenienced by my outburst. "Don't run off."

If I had been asked mere hours before, I wouldn't have thought myself capable of denying De Lafontaine anything at all. She could have asked me to catch her a wild rabbit from the school grounds and present it to her with a ribbon around its neck, and I would have gone running through the grass to terrorize the nearest warren. She could have asked me to prick my thumb and pen her a haiku in blood and I would have taken up my paper in one hand and a needle in the other. But being so soundly decimated by her, in front of Laura no less, soured my taste for her.

Without another word, I stormed through the front door, slamming it behind me. Inside, I heard muffled voices, Laura saying something low in that shy alto of hers, and then De Lafontaine laughing, like I was a toy she had broken simply because she had grown tired of its tricks.

"To hell with you both," I hissed, and dashed off into the night.

CHAPTER NINE

Laura

caught up with Carmilla halfway to the science building, aptly named for Marie Curie. She was striding with her head dipped down against the cold, wiping at her sniffling nose every so often with the sleeve of her blouse. She had forgotten her coat in the apartment and the tips of her ears poking through her dark hair were red with cold. She cut an inelegant figure, which only made me sympathize with her more. In that moment she wasn't a siren out of a dream, she was simply a girl who had been soundly humiliated by, quite probably, her favorite person in the whole world.

"Carmilla," I said breathlessly, jogging a bit to catch up with her breakneck pace. It seemed illicit, somehow, to say her name out loud, when I spent so much time silently turning it over in my head. "Carmilla, wait."

"Why?" she snapped, forging on ahead and flinging open the door to the Curie building. At this time of night, there was no one else around. "Do you want to have a go at me as well?"

Wondering only momentarily if this counted as trespassing, I followed her into the building.

"Please, will you slow down?" I asked. "I'm not trying to make fun of you. I'm just . . ." *Dangerously preoccupied with you. Bereft of any sense of pride that might keep me away from you.* "Concerned."

"Ha!" Carmilla barked, winding through the darkened corridors. "Well, nobody asked you to be concerned, *Laura.*"

She said my name like she was wrapping her finger around the trigger of a gun, somehow pronouncing the soft syllables like a warning shot. I refused to heed her.

Instead, I picked up my pace, pulling up alongside her. Her nose was flushed, and her cheeks were damp with drying tears.

"Where are you even going? De Lafontaine is going to be asking after you, you know. You'll have to see her next week in class as it is."

Carmilla tossed her hair like a horse refusing to be broken.

"Well, until then, I intend to deny her my presence. She can pickle herself in whiskey and smoke herself to death, for all I care."

She finally came to a stop, turning to face me, and I

found we were standing in the lecture hall, that big bowl-shaped room in the center of the building. We were six feet apart on the stained blue carpet, flanked by a lectern on one side and rows of seats on the other. An ancient model of the human skeleton chaperoned the conversation.

"Carmilla," I said again.

I took one step forward before stopping. I didn't trust myself to get an inch closer to her without touching her, and I didn't trust myself to touch her without giving in to some awful, misshapen tenderness. I had no idea how to speak to this enigma that I had built up into a rival over the last month of classes. Who was she, if not a figment of my feverish imagination? What was Carmilla when she wasn't safely trapped behind the bars of one of my poems?

I didn't know her at all, I realized.

"We're both a little drunk," I lied, knowing full well I had taken only the tiniest sips of my cocktail to be polite. "And it's late. Won't you let me walk you back to your dorm?"

She stared at me with her fists balled up at her sides, and for a moment I thought she might take a swing at me. I held up my hands to show I meant her no harm.

"I just want to make sure you're all right," I said.

"She'll get you too," Carmilla said, acting as though she hadn't even heard my suggestion. "First she's sweet, and then she terrorizes you. It's part of her pedagogy. The strongest among us learn to grow a thick skin. I'm still growing, it would appear."

"That doesn't seem like any way to run a classroom," I said.

Carmilla laughed bitterly.

"What are you going to do, drop her class? No, I don't think so. She's already got her claws into you. I can tell."

I bristled a bit at that. I didn't like being seen so plainly by someone who was as opaque to me as a sheet of frosted glass.

"That's not fair."

"De Lafontaine isn't fair, and the sooner you understand that, the farther you'll get in her class."

"Don't you think it's wrong, though? What she does to her students?"

"Right and wrong don't exist, Laura. They're fairy tales made up by priests and parents. There is only art and ugliness, and I'm willing to suffer any indignity for the sake of art. Even at the hands of Ms. D."

An uncomfortable silence settled between us then. I shifted awkwardly from foot to foot while Carmilla stared me down with her arms strapped across her chest. Her tears had evaporated, and she looked more like the girl I saw in class, beautiful and unbreakable.

I thought about leaving her. I thought about turning around and walking myself back through the dark to my dorm, of brushing my teeth and stripping off my clothes and crawling right into bed to sleep off this entire conversation.

But in the end, I stayed. I had the awful, yawning feeling

inside myself that for her, I would always stay. It felt like standing on the edge of an abyss, looking down at the velvety darkness below and feeling held by it.

I took another tentative step forward, and Carmilla took a step back.

She narrowed her eyes, and I was sure she was going to tell me to leave her alone. Instead, she swung herself up on to the lectern and gripped the edge, looking down at me.

"Why did you come here, anyway?" she asked, cocking her head. "You could have just stayed down South with those journal editors who thought you were the new best thing, and you could have carved out a tidy little writing career. You didn't need to move up to the chill damp of New England and plant your flag in my class."

My class. I almost scoffed. Carmilla didn't own an inch of that classroom, it was entirely Ms. De Lafontaine's domain, and if she thought she was somehow in charge, she was deluding herself.

"I came because I wanted to rebuild myself as a stronger writer," I shot back. "Why didn't you stay in Austria? I'm sure they treated you like a princess there, with the way you act."

It was a pointed sentiment, bordering on cruel, but Carmilla didn't seem to care. She just flipped her hair like I had read her right.

"I left because my mother abandoned me and my father locked himself in his study and drank himself to sickness, and because all my tutors were boring me to death. I came to Saint Perpetua's *for* De Lafontaine, Laura. I read her work in an international review of poetry, saw her picture, and knew I had to be her student. Teachers like Ms. D only come along once in a lifetime. I would move mountains just to be close to her."

The raw adoration in her voice almost embarrassed me, as though I was seeing her slowly stripped naked under white-hot stage lights. This burlesque of a conversation was not going the way I thought it might. I thought she would bare her teeth at me, swear and spit and tell me to never speak to her again, but her pupils were blown in the dim room, round with hero worship and whiskey.

"Is she really so wonderful?" I challenged. "This woman who brought you to tears not ten minutes ago?"

Carmilla let out a brittle bark of a laugh.

"You tell me, Laura. You're still here, aren't you, still enrolled? You try walking away from her, then come back and lecture me about how easy it is."

There was so much more I wanted to say, but in the end I bit my tongue. Carmilla looked down at me through her curtain of black hair, as imperious as a fire-and-brimstone preacher, and then something in her demeanor softened.

"You wouldn't do it, though," she said, her voice nearly a whisper, like she was talking to herself. "You wouldn't leave her. You can't. No one ever does."

I got the distinct feeling that Carmilla knew more about

Ms. D than she was telling but I felt even more strongly that it wasn't my place to ask about it.

"You want some advice, frosh?" she asked, hopping down from the lectern and walking right up to me, until she was a scarce few inches away. Her breath stirred the collar on my shirt, the tiny baby hairs escaping my face. "You should strap in for a long, hard semester. Because I'm not going to go easy on you, and neither will De Lafontaine."

I wanted so desperately to wrap my hands around the collar of her blouse and yank her closer, but I resisted the urge and just stood there, letting her look at me. I felt, somehow, that she was seeing me for the first time.

"You're really not going to back down, are you?" she asked, eyelashes fluttering.

I shook my head solemnly.

"Fine," Carmilla sniffed, haughty once again. "We'll let Ms. D decide who's the better poet, then. To the victor the spoils."

She thrust out her hand to me, and it took me a moment to realize she was offering it for a shake. I slotted our fingers together and squeezed mercilessly, making her a vow. Carmilla smiled faintly.

"Things were so boring before you arrived. I'm almost happy you're here, Laura."

Then, impossibly, she brought our laced fingers to her mouth and kissed my wrist, as though she were sealing a pact.

My lips parted in surprise.

We stood there in the dark for a long moment, just looking at each other. Carmilla's eyes glittered with otherworldly fervor.

It took all my restraint not to seize her face in my hands and kiss her until her lips were bruised.

"You should get some sleep," she said finally, taking a few steps away from me. "Tomorrow will be here sooner than you think."

And with that, she turned from me as though I wasn't even there, examining the skeletal model with a scholar's focus. I got the sense that I was being dismissed and said nothing in response, merely slipped out of the science building and into the night. I decided that too much time had passed to return to De Lafontaine, certainly not alone, so I trekked back across campus to my dorm.

After I reached my room, I lay awake in the darkness, my skin feeling too hot and too tight.

When I closed my eyes, all I could see was Carmilla's tearstained face.

CHAPTER TEN

Laura

———◆———

"What's going on with you and Carmilla Karnstein?" Elenore asked one night during one of our marathon study sessions. It was half past midnight, and we were propped up on pillows on Maisy's dorm-room floor, sharing a carafe of pour-over coffee and a big box of Sugar Babies. The candy was stuck in my molars, and my head buzzed with caffeine. I had been taken under Maisy's wing, and that meant spending plenty of time with Elenore, who had become something close to a friend in the insular and cliquey seminar group.

My skin prickled at the sound of Carmilla's name. It was a physiological reaction, uncontrollable and undeniable.

"What do you mean?" I asked. I had told no one of my strange fixation on the vexing young woman. I liked

S. T. Gibson

to play my cards close to my chest, especially where my erratic and devastating crushes were concerned.

"You two are always shooting daggers at each other during class," Elenore went on. "Is she your nemesis or something?"

"I don't have a nemesis," I scoffed.

"Everybody's got a nemesis," Maisy put in. "Mine is Sasha Hoffman. She beat me at the spelling bee in fourth grade, and I've never forgiven her. Every time I visit my hometown and run into her, it's nothing but one-upmanship."

"And I can't stand Lucy Rourke in Ms. De Lafontaine's seminar," Elenore put in. "Her father's a senator, and he voted against integration. I know she agrees with him; I can just feel it."

"That's vile," Maisy said, wrinkling her nose. "Say the word and I'll smuggle tadpoles into her bed."

"I wouldn't wish that on the tadpoles," Elenore replied, her lips quirking into a smile. "But seriously, Laura, what's your problem with Carmilla? Outside of the fact that she's stuck-up, obviously."

"I don't think she's stuck-up," Maisy said, saving me from answering. "I think she's lonely."

Elenore scoffed, popping another Sugar Baby into her mouth.

"Don't tell me you're joining the cult of Carmilla. You've seen her with her half a dozen hangers-on."

"Sure, but have you ever seen her with any of those

girls at meal times, or playing sports, or hanging out on the quad? She keeps to herself. I think she knows she's strange, and she doesn't want to let anyone get too close in case they don't like what they find."

I mulled this over silently as I chewed on the end of my pencil. The astronomical equations in my notebook had long ago started to blur together in my eyes, and I wasn't really paying attention to my homework anymore. I was carefully cataloging everything my new friends were saying, weighing it against what I knew about Carmilla. I felt like a detective, piecing together clues about an elusive suspect.

Was there more to Carmilla than her glittering talent, her cutting remarks? Was I looking in the wrong place, trying to riddle her out through her writing?

"I don't know why I don't like her," I lied finally, giving a milquetoast shrug. "I just don't."

"All right then," Elenore said, giving me a look that told me she didn't believe me for a moment.

———◆◆———

In the middle of October, there was an unseasonably hot day, and Elenore cajoled me into joining her for a picnic on the quad. At first I resisted, insisting that I simply couldn't leave my typewriter, but I folded under her insistence.

Elenore reclined on a petal-pink blanket, eating strawberries and sunning her shoulders in a white dress trimmed with cheery eyelets. I was laying on my stomach, soaking up the heat like a tropical lizard. Perhaps emboldened by the compliments Elenore had given me in my dorm room as we plotted our picnic, I had opted to wear my shortest shorts, the ones that showed off the dimples in my thighs. The reading for De Lafontaine's seminar lay open and forgotten between us, a slim tome of sonnets that I had found cloying and a little dull.

"I can't stand New England winters," Elenore said, tilting her face up towards the sunshine. She was wearing heart-shaped sunglasses, and she reminded me of the poster for Kubrick's *Lolita* movie. Elenore and I had bonded over our love for the novel, commiserating over how the dreamy film had glossed over the horrors of girlhood, the sinister ubiquity of society's obsession with youth, the grinding demands of American capitalism. I suspected privately that Elenore was a socialist, but I was too polite to ask her outright.

"It's not winter yet," I reminded her.

"I just wish the weather would hold like this for ever."

"Where are you from, anyway?" I asked. "Some place sunny?"

Elenore smiled widely, flashing her slightly gapped teeth at me.

"San Francisco. Not exactly sunny, but one of the greatest cities in the world. Have you ever been?"

"No," I mumbled. Elenore should know better than to ask me that; she was the one who always teased me for being such a homebody and never emerging from my room.

"You would love it," she said. "It's so full of life. Young people from all over the country are flooding in right now, bringing their music and their art with them. It's the perfect city to be a writer in."

"I'd like to go sometime," I said thoughtlessly, popping a strawberry into my mouth.

"Are you doing anything over Thanksgiving break? You should fly out and visit for a few days. Both my parents work, so we'd have the apartment to ourselves. I could introduce you to my friends and we could go to Haight-Ashbury and listen to slam poetry."

"Are you serious?" I said, lifting my head up off the blanket. I didn't think I would survive it if Elenore was just pulling my leg. But she glanced at me over her sunglasses and nodded, giving a little shrug.

"Sure. It gets boring over the holidays. You would be keeping me company. And I'm sure my parents wouldn't mind having somebody new over for Thanksgiving dinner. They're real hospitable types."

Just as I was opening my mouth to tell her how phenomenal that sounded, to let her know I was grateful and would behave myself exceptionally around her parents, a shadow fell over my face. I turned around and looked up to see Carmilla Karnstein standing at the edge of the blanket, blocking our sunlight. Despite the heat, she wore a long-sleeved dress with a stiff white collar.

"Hello," Elenore said, a little taken aback. From what I could gather, there was no animosity between Elenore and Carmilla, but they weren't exactly friends either.

"Hi yourself," Carmilla said, bending down to pluck a strawberry from the bowl and put it into her mouth. I watched her chew, my overactive poet's brain idly spinning the metaphor that it could have been my heart she was masticating, for all the effect it had on me. "Did you do the reading?"

"We're slogging through," I said.

"Sonnets are so predictable," Elenore put in.

"Ms D doesn't like them either, but the dean insisted they be part of our curriculum. I doubt she'll quiz us too ruthlessly on them."

I once again wondered at her strange closeness with our teacher, who I hadn't spoken to since the meltdown during our last meeting. De Lafontaine was scarce during the days and held all her classes in the evening, so I assumed that she moonlit at another job during daylight hours. Not that I was particularly looking forward to seeing her again, after how I had run out on our last meeting. Would she be angry with me? Would I have my privileges as one of her special students revoked?

Carmilla toed at the grass with one of her ballet flats, sticking her hands deep into the pockets of her dress. She almost looked uncomfortable.

"De Lafontaine sent me, actually. She wanted me to check on you, Laura."

This seemed odd to me. Why would she need to check on me when Carmilla was the one she had reduced to tears with a few well-deployed sentences?

"I'd be happy to talk to her myself and let her know I'm all right," I said, casting a wary glance Elenore's way. She was flipping through the book of sonnets, pretending not to listen. I liked Elenore immensely, and trusted her in theory, but in practice, I wasn't sure I was supposed to share details about my late-night meetings with De Lafontaine with anybody but Carmilla.

"I'll tell her. No need to worry."

"Where is she, anyway?" I asked, craning my neck to look around the quad. It seemed like half the school was out enjoying the weather, and I spied a dozen professors sipping lemonade while they graded papers at the benches outside the academic buildings, or leading their students in discussion while seated cross-legged under trees.

Carmilla gave a shrug that was probably supposed to be blasé but came off too theatrical. She was, I realized, a bad liar. She was covering for De Lafontaine, for some reason.

"I don't know where she is. But I'll tell her you're all right when I see her again."

I wondered if De Lafontaine was playing a mind game, if sending Carmilla to check up on me was just another way of humbling her. Was speaking to me really so terrible? I hated the idea of being anyone's punishment, and I felt my mouth twist into a frown.

"Fine by me. See you in class, I guess."

Something behind Carmilla's gaze shuttered, and she looked at me with the hatred I had come to expect. This was familiar territory, and somehow more comforting than the interest she had shown in my wellbeing moments before.

"See you there, Sheridan," she said, making it sound like a threat.

With that, she turned on her heel and started to stalk back through the crowds thronging the quad. She was walking, I noticed, in the direction of De Lafontaine's apartment. I watched her until her silhouette disappeared behind an assortment of trees.

"I don't know what you see in that girl," Elenore muttered, letting the wind ruffle the pages of her schoolbook.

"What's that supposed to mean?" I snapped, too defensively, as heat flooded my face.

"Mm-hmm," Elenore hummed, as though all her suspicions had been confirmed. Then she turned back to her book, a small smile playing at her lips.

"Come on, now what's *that* supposed to mean?"

"You're about as transparent as a glass of water. It's true what they say: there's no accounting for taste when the heart is involved."

I must have turned white as a sheet, because Elenore gave a little laugh and snapped her book shut.

"Oh, come on, Laura, let's not pretend you don't have a little crush. Don't worry, I won't tell. My cousin Vivienne's got herself a girlfriend; I know how these things work. Personally, I can't fathom how you live without men, but I'm nobody's judge."

My world tilted on its axis. The sense of being suddenly unsafe flooded my system, mingled oddly with bone-deep relief that Elenore wasn't disgusted by me.

"Good God, does *everybody* know?"

Elenore shrugged. "Can't say. Maisy knows."

"Maisy knows!?"

Elenore reached over and patted my knee.

"Maisy's the least discreet lesbian I've ever met, Laura, and if you didn't notice that right away then there's simply no hope for you."

Lesbian. She threw the word out so casually, as though anyone might hear her. She seemed completely unbothered by it, as though it were any other noun, and not a total bombshell. I didn't even use the word to describe myself in my own diary; it seemed too damning.

But if Elenore wasn't ashamed of it, maybe I shouldn't be either.

"But," I stammered, still gobsmacked that we were having this conversation at all, "you invited me home with you for break. Weren't you afraid that I would . . . I don't know . . . make a pass at you or something?"

Elenore snorted, as though I had suggested we fly to the moon together.

"Come on, Laura, you're not the type. And we're friends, aren't we? Friends don't make unkind assumptions about their friends."

To my great embarrassment, my eyes started to water.

"Oh no, no," Elenore tittered, producing a silk hand-kerchief from somewhere on her person and pressing it to my cheeks. Her fingertips were warm and steadying, and I was grateful for the coddling, even if I was a little embarrassed to be fussed over. "Eat a strawberry. You'll feel better."

I let out a relieved laugh and did as she said, sucking the sweet juice from my fingers. And then, that was that. Neither of us harped on the subject or even brought it up for the rest of our study session, overcome as we were by the poetry at hand.

CHAPTER ELEVEN

Carmilla

e Lafontaine waited a week after my melt-down to call on me again. She probably thought she was giving me time to cool off, but the neglect just made me even more furious. I had never, not even when I had strep throat, missed one of De Lafontaine's seminars, but I flagrantly skipped two in a row, just to show her two could play the cold shoulder game. To tell the truth, I wasn't keen on the idea of sitting across the Socratic circle from Laura either. Laura who ate me up with those downturned blue eyes every time I caught her looking my way; Laura who had burrowed so far under my skin that I probably couldn't dig her out with a knife. I hated her, no two ways about it, but there was also something about her that made my stomach tighten every time she walked into a room, something that made me want to push her just to see what would happen when she broke, and that unsettled me.

So, I avoided the situation entirely, spending the time I would usually pass in De Lafontaine's class reading comics on the quad. In full view of Seward's lecture-hall window, of course, just in case De Lafontaine happened to glance outside.

When I finally got her note in my school mailbox, it was terse and to the point.

> C,
>
> *You're expected.*
> *Thursday night, 10 p.m.*
> *The usual place.*
> *Sincerely,*
> *D.*

I crumpled up the note, but come Thursday night at quarter till ten, I was standing outside her apartment building, shivering from both the autumn chill and pure anticipation.

She looked half famished when I arrived, her eyes dull and gleaming like a shark's. She was wearing flimsy black cotton pajamas and a silky robe sashed loosely at the waist. I noticed for the thousandth time how long her fingers were, how pronounced her collarbones, how stark the sinews of her neck. She looked like a predator wearing the strained skin of a woman, which, I suppose, is what she was.

"You came," she said, sounding relieved.

"I always come when you ask," I said, and already, everything was all wrong. I had promised myself that I would swan in here like a queen and demand a formal apology before giving her a drop of myself, but instead there I was admitting to my naked need for her.

"Have a seat," she said, ushering me over to the couch. I let her take my coat and gloves like she had done so many times before, then sat on the velvet waiting for her to begin. She didn't have the patience for pleasantries or the strength to wait to imbibe tonight, I could tell that much.

Sure enough, she sank down next to me and pulled my long hair away from my neck. I tilted my chin to give her better access, assuming a familiar position.

"Recite for me," she said, her breath hot against my skin.

I closed my eyes and let lines of poetry spill from my lips as De Lafontaine sank her teeth into my neck.

There was always pain at first, sharp and stinging, then a sort of tingling warmth that spread from the wound down my neck and across my chest. It wasn't exactly pleasure, but more like a sweet ache. I winced as she bit me, focusing on the poetry to distract me from the discomfort, but then I grew accustomed to the sensation of being pierced, and I relaxed into her touch. De Lafontaine's hands drifted up to hold me gently by the shoulders, steadying me just in case I swooned. I had lost consciousness a few times, in the beginning, but I had grown stronger as our unorthodox lessons continued.

That night, especially, I welcomed the soreness. It had been so long since she drank from me, an impossible two weeks, and I worried that our private sessions of poetry and pain had come to an end. But she needed me, just like I needed her, and she couldn't keep away from me for ever.

I kept reciting until I started to get lightheaded, but De Lafontaine didn't let me go. She just pulled me in tighter, pressing our bodies together as she drank from me, making up for lost time. My body responded to her closeness, warming and becoming pliant. Need thrummed between my legs, beating in time with the pulse in my neck.

I tilted my face to hers, trying to capture her lips in my own.

"Carmilla," De Lafontaine warned, pressing two fingers to my mouth and holding me in place. Her own lips were slicked with my blood, and I would have kissed it off her if she'd let me. I would have done so much, if only she would let me.

"One kiss," I begged, feeling delirious from the blood loss and her nearness. "There's no point denying ourselves one kiss."

"That's a line I won't cross," she said, her voice chilly despite the naked desire shining in her eyes. For my blood, or for my body, I couldn't tell. I don't think it really mattered. "You're my student. I have a sacred duty to protect you."

"I don't need protecting."

De Lafontaine wiped her mouth with a handkerchief. Already, the color was coming back into her face. I wondered how long she could go without feeding. Since we had met, she had never gone more than two weeks without drinking from me. During the summer term, when there was less oversight from other members of the faculty, she took her fill of me after all of our weekly independent study sessions. Some of my fondest memories were lying with De Lafontaine in the blue violets on the banks of the river that ran behind the school, dozing in the sun while she sank her teeth into my wrist.

"You're sweet," she said. "But you're young. You don't have a sense of consequences, of the way one moment of indulgence can haunt you for a lifetime."

"That isn't fair," I said, taking the handkerchief from her and pressing it firmly against my neck to staunch the flow of blood. When we had first started down this path together, I had grown queasy at the sight of my own blood, but I was used to it now.

"I'm not interested in fairness," she said airily, reclining on the couch next to me. "I'm interested in being right. And I am right, Carmilla. You'll understand in time."

She reached out a hand for me, inviting me to recline against her breast as I had done so many times before, but I flinched away from her.

"Are you still cross with me for putting you on the spot?" she asked.

I crossed my arms over my chest, keeping my knees pressed tight together.

"That's putting it lightly. You humiliated me."

De Lafontaine sighed extravagantly, as though I were a child crying for a lollipop in the store instead of a grown woman expressing justifiable anger.

"If you want to succeed as an artist, you're going to have to toughen up. It was a professional critique, not a personal attack."

I fumed in silence, knowing full well that a personal attack was exactly what it was. She had never been so callous to me, so cruel without cause.

De Lafontaine's fingers encircled my wrist and pulled me gently closer, and I pressed my lips tight together as I sidled up against her.

"What can I do to convince you I'm not your enemy, Carmilla?"

"You might start by sharing more with me about your condition, your history," I muttered, my eyes fixed on the floor. "You hardly tell me anything these days."

"Where shall I begin, then?"

"Were you always a professor?" I asked carefully, knowing I was stepping on thin ice. I could practically hear it groan and splinter beneath me as De Lafontaine fell silent. Deliberating how much she wanted to share with me.

"I was always a teacher. Even before I changed, I worked as a governess. I enjoyed the mental stimulation of it, the freedom to travel, the release from the obligation to marry. I've never had a taste for men, or for marriage."

"How did it happen for you? The change."

De Lafontaine dropped a kiss to the top of my head, and the sensation jolted down my spine like electricity. I swallowed hard and willed my racing heart to still.

"I met a high-born lady in Paris, at a benefit dinner for some charity. The year was 1818. I was there with my charges, two little boys still in short pants, but I forgot all about them when I saw her. She had traveled all the way from London to study French, and I immediately offered her my services. We were inseparable after that. I traveled with her, I was taken into her confidence, and I helped her lure the young women she desired. No one suspected that we were murderers, or lovers."

Twin shudders went through me at her casual mentions of violence and sex. I held my breath, hoping that she would go on, that she wouldn't shut me out again.

"We were happy, for a time. But love rots and spoils, it disintegrates with time like a rose in a vase, and soon there was nothing between us but animosity and arguments and the resentfulness of having to rely on each other. I awoke one night to find her side of the bed empty, all her dresses gone from the closet, her silk slippers and her ruby earrings disappeared from the chest. I have not received a single letter or telegram from her since, not one call, not after all these years."

"Your sire abandoned you," I said quietly. I couldn't

imagine anything more terrible than to be discarded by the very person who had promised you everlasting life.

De Lafontaine stood, wrapping her robe tighter around her body as she padded over to the window. She looked out in the direction of Seward Hall with a pensive line between her brows.

"Love gone sour is still love, and I still think of her every day, the moment I open my eyes to find the pillow next to me empty. But the past cannot be rewritten, Carmilla, except under exceptional circumstances."

"Circumstances like what?" I asked, entirely rapt. It was so easy to get caught in De Lafontaine's shimmering web of words. She turned to me, her face softening into a smile.

"Listen to me, rambling on about old torches long since extinguished. I must be boring you, darling."

"No, I find it fascinating."

Despite myself, I yawned, my pulse pounding in my head. I was feeling a little faint, and it occurred to me that in her ravenous hunger, De Lafontaine might have taken more from me than I had to give. The tips of my fingers and toes were numb despite the fact that I was bundled up against the October chill, and my mouth was dry.

My professor laid her palm against my forehead, frowning.

"You're cold. I'm afraid I drank too deeply from you. You should lie down, Carmilla."

Never one to argue with De Lafontaine, I slipped out

of my shoes and reclined on the couch. She draped a fluffy afghan over me, tucking it in around my shoulders, and for a rosy, secretive moment, I let myself pretend.

That we were friends or lovers or family.

That she cared for me just as deeply as I cared for her.

"Get some sleep," De Lafontaine said, dimming the living-room lamps. "I'll be awake all night if you need me. Goodnight, Carmilla."

"Goodnight, Ms. D," I murmured, and then let sleep claim me.

I woke to the sound of rustling cloth and jingling keys. A quick glance out the window told me it was a few hours to dawn yet. I stretched languidly under the afghan and then pressed two fingers to the pulse in my neck. It felt stronger than before, and I was warm and reinvigorated.

"Are you going out?" I asked. In the dim of the unlit apartment, I could make out the silhouette of De Lafontaine by the door. She turned on one of the lamps (for my benefit, not hers, since she could see perfectly well in the dark) and smiled down at me. She was dressed in paint-splattered jeans, and a pair of gardening gloves were sticking out of the pocket of her canvas coat.

"Just to the greenhouse. Would you like to come with me? The blooms are sure to be beautiful at this time of night."

"I'll come," I said, hoisting myself eagerly to my feet. The night-blooming garden was De Lafontaine's private oasis, and one I was rarely invited into. If she was feeling magnanimous enough to share her flowers with me, I wouldn't pass up the opportunity.

Careful not to make too much noise on the stairs, I followed De Lafontaine out of the apartment building and trekked dutifully behind her to the edge of campus and then beyond. The rolling hills just beyond Saint Perpetua's manicured green lawns were mostly undomesticated, but they were owned by the school, miles and miles of them. De Lafontaine had laid claim to a tiny parcel of land about a half-mile from her apartment, and it was there she had sown her seeds of wonder.

We eased carefully through the glass doors of the small greenhouse, navigating our way through vines, potted plants, and bushy green growth. She had imported and carefully cultivated nicotiana, evening primrose, datura, and so many more nocturnal beauties, and tended to them over the five years she had been teaching at Saint Perpetua's. But that night, we were on the hunt for the *pièce de resistance*, the rarest bloom of all.

"There she is," De Lafontaine breathed with a toothy grin. Outside of poetry and cigarettes, gardening was one of her only passions, and I always enjoyed seeing her swept away by such fervor.

I knelt at her side as she crouched beside a leafy plant that boasted a pair of moon-white flowers. The petals were delicately curled and accented by a halo of pointed fronds. It was one of the prettiest things I had ever seen, and it was all the prettier because De Lafontaine was sharing it with me.

"Queen of the night," she said wistfully, reaching out to stroke one of the petals. "She only blooms once a year, and always at night. They usually don't grow in these conditions, but I got very lucky in finding the perfect greenhouse atmosphere."

She leaned forward to smell the flower, then gestured for me to do the same. My nostrils were filled with a strong, sweet scent very much like jasmine.

"You must be so proud that you got it to flower," I said, keeping my voice hushed. I felt as though I should be reverent in the presence of such a miraculous plant.

"There's a special pleasure in cultivation," she said, cradling the bloom in her hand. She turned her head this way and that, inspecting it for imperfections. "In helping things grow. I love knowing that I was the force behind such beauty, that, in the end, it couldn't exist without me."

In one fluid motion, De Lafontaine picked up a silver sickle from the ground and severed the flower's stalk. I let out a little cry.

"But it will die!"

"It will die either way," De Lafontaine said, her voice a soothing lull. She tucked the flower into my hair, securing it behind my ear. "I'd rather it be enjoyed by you for the rest of its short life than for it to sit unappreciated in my greenhouse."

I delicately touched the silky petals.

"Thank you," I said quietly.

Sometimes, it was easy to convince myself that De Lafontaine was entirely self-interested, that she only kept me around to feed her ego or keep her in a steady supply of blood. But then, other times, she was so tender to me, so generous and kind, that proof of her love seemed undeniable.

It was almost worse that way.

CHAPTER TWELVE

Laura

———◆◆◆———

made the mistake of taking a late-afternoon nap one cloudy evening, and so woke groggy and disoriented as the sun was setting behind the Massachusetts mountains. I gasped as I spied the clock, which told me it was mere minutes until the poetry seminar started. Rain pattered down on the roof, but I was in such a tizzy, yanking a brush through my hair and wiggling into my sweater, that I didn't think to grab an umbrella. This proved nearly disastrous, as I was drenched on my brisk walk across the quad to De Lafontaine's seminar. Fearing that the rain would soak through my bag and corrupt my notebooks if I stayed outside a moment longer, I took a sharp left and sought refuge in a gazebo nestled among some bushes.

However, I realized instantly that I might have to change my plans.

Someone was huddled beneath the gazebo roof, their face illuminated only by the burning embers of a cigarette.

Carmilla.

I stopped outside the gazebo, hot to the touch with embarrassment despite the drenching fall downpour. When Carmilla turned to me I saw that her hair had been flattened by rain, and the shoulders of her blazer were dark with damp.

"Keep moving," she said, shooing me away with her cigarette. "This is my gazebo."

"I think, strictly speaking, it belongs to the university," I said, putting one foot up on the steps to the gazebo. A shiver racked my frame. I would catch my death of cold if I stayed out in the rain much longer.

Carmilla looked me up and down, noting the sorry state I was in.

"Fine," she said, waving me in. "But only because you're half-drowned."

I stomped up the steps, and stood at the opposite side of the structure so as not to infringe on Carmilla's space. She watched me with those dark eyes, as though daring me to say something.

"Awful weather out," I attempted weakly.

Carmilla let out a little scoff.

"Are you really trying to strike up a conversation about the weather? With me?"

"It seems better than standing around in silence," I muttered, stepping from foot to foot to try to shake some feeling into my toes. Massachusetts autumns were unpredictable, I was learning; some days were downright balmy while others, like today, were miserably cold.

Carmilla merely sniffed, taking a pensive drag off the cigarette burning down to ash in her fingers. It smelled strongly of cloves.

"I suppose you're right," she said, flicking the cigarette on the ground and crushing it under her boot. Despite the weather, she was wearing knee-high riding boots with a short skirt. Carmilla always insisted on wearing the shortest skirts imaginable, even during the icy rains of autumn in New England, and she wasn't a fan of umbrellas, either. They either ruined her aesthetic or she was simply too scatter-brained to ever remember to grab one on gray days. I was often entranced by the sight of cold droplets skittering down her thighs as she shook the water from her hair upon entering one of the academic halls.

"Did you do the reading?"

"Of course I did the reading," I shot back. "Did you write your poem for the week?"

"Of course I did," she responded, and we stood there for a moment in simmering silence. We merely watched it rain from our respective sides of the gazebo. Then Carmilla glanced down at her bulky watch. It was a miracle the thing was still ticking after her walk in the rain.

"Damn," she hissed. "We're going to be late for the seminar at this rate."

S. T. Gibson

"Not if we run," I said, thoughtlessly, for no reason at all.

Carmilla quirked an eyebrow at me, mischief sparking in her gaze. I understood her meaning at once.

"Carmilla," I said, a warning in my voice. It was too late. She was already tying her hair up with that blue ribbon, her mouth set into a determined line. Against my will, every muscle in my body tensed, suddenly alive.

"Loser has to explain themselves to Ms. D," Carmilla said, and then without another word, she bolted out of the gazebo.

What else could I have done?

I tore off my shoes and ran after her.

The rain lashed my face as I sprinted across the slick grass, nearly slipping not once but twice. Carmilla had a head start and she was fast, cutting across the quad with merciless precision, but my legs were longer, and my lungs were healthy and strong from long summers swimming laps in the lake behind my father's house. I overtook her quickly, coming into the lead just as we rounded the corner towards the seminar building. Carmilla, ever the dirty sportswoman, tried to trip me up as I passed, but I swatted her with one of my shoes and managed to pull ahead.

I careened around the final corner and burst into Seward Hall, hurling myself up the stairs. I could hear Carmilla's heavy footfalls behind me, getting closer and closer. By the time I reached the third-floor landing, I thought my heart was going to burst.

I stumbled through the doors of the seminar room, my chest heaving for breath. Ms. D was sitting on the edge of her desk, deep in a lecture about Allen Ginsberg.

De Lafontaine's eyes cut over to me, twin shards of green glass, as I stood panting and dripping in the doorway. Carmilla barreled through the door moments later and collided with me, nearly sending us both sprawling onto the floor. We both burst into endorphin-spiked laughter, clutching at each other as though we had known each other all our lives. Carmilla's skin was rain-cooled and slick beneath my fingers, and she gripped me tight.

"Laura." De Lafontaine's voice was toneless. "Carmilla. Have a seat, please."

I stood frozen in the doorway for a moment, staring at my professor like a doe in headlights. It was apparent that something about our dishevelment, or perhaps our closeness, irritated her immensely. Hurt and confusion coursed through me. Shouldn't she be happy that we were finally getting along, that something like collegiate companionship was starting to peek through the rocky soil of our acquaintance? Why wouldn't she be pleased that we were finally warming to each other?

Unless keeping us starved for her approval, fighting over scraps of her love like neglected puppies, had always been her aim.

Carmilla strode past me, heading for her usual seat in the center of the circle of chairs crowded around Ms. D, but the professor held up a hand, freezing Carmilla in place.

"Not there."

My cheeks flared. The only other open seats in the room were the stadium-style seats of the lecture hall itself. Carmilla stomped over to a seat, slamming it down, and dropped herself into place. I followed suit, albeit with less of an attitude.

We sat shoulder-to-shoulder for the duration of class, my stomach tense from cold and Carmilla's closeness. De Lafontaine barely looked at us during her lecture, and ignored Carmilla every time she raised her hand. We were both being punished, that was clear.

After class, Carmilla waited with her arms crossed for every other student to leave. De Lafontaine continued to act as if we weren't in the room, simply gathering her notes and flipping through papers. I sat awkwardly with my knees pressed together, wondering if I was supposed to stay after for a talking-to or get out of that classroom as soon as I could.

Carmilla pressed to her feet the moment the door swung shut behind the final student.

"What was that about?" she asked. I could tell she was trying to sound nonchalant, but her voice was strained. De Lafontaine didn't look up from the notebook she was writing in.

"If you're going to act like a child I'm going to treat you like a child."

"Funny how you've never seemed to consider me a child before," Carmilla shot back.

Now De Lafontaine looked at her, pinning her in place with that merciless gaze. "Watch your mouth, Carmilla."

"I'll see myself out," I said, fumbling for my bag and making my way towards the door.

"Not so fast," Ms. D said, her voice stopping me in my tracks. I turned to face her, swallowing hard. The disappointment in her eyes gutted me like a fish.

"Antics from Carmilla I've come to expect," De Lafontaine said. "But you, Miss Sheridan? I thought you were the mature one."

She had never called me by my last name before. It was always Laura, Laura when she called on me in class or Laura when she refilled my glass at her apartment or Laura when she passed me a smoldering cigarette still damp from her mouth. She made something as simple as two syllables sound like sun-warmed honey, luscious and rich, but now my family name was frosty on her lips.

"I'm sorry," I said quietly, wishing that the floor would swallow me alive.

"I expect better from the both of you," she went on, gathering up her personal belongings and slinging her purse over her shoulder. The keys to the lecture hall jangled in her hand, telling me that this conversation was coming to an end. "To make up for your rudeness, I expect two extra poems from each of you ready for recitation by the end of the week. And I'll know if you phone it in, so do try for me, girls."

"Yes, Ms. De Lafontaine."

"As for you," the professor said, turning towards Carmilla, "I think we need to discuss your little outbursts."

I took a step forward, opening my mouth to explain myself, to take on the blame, anything to smooth over the cracks that had erupted between me and Ms. De Lafontaine. But she merely looked affronted, raising one elegant eyebrow as though daring me to utter a word. At that moment, it was as if she didn't even know me, like I was no better than any other fawning freshman desperate for her attention. I closed my mouth, blinked back tears, and made a beeline for the exit.

I let out a muffled sob as the heavy door clanged shut behind me, covering my face with my hands. This had to be my fault, somehow; I was the one who had interrupted Carmilla's smoke-break in the gazebo, and I was the one who had suggested that we run through the rain. But underneath my shame and fretting, there was very real anger. How could De Lafontaine speak so harshly to us for an infraction as small as showing up late? It was like I had personally injured her in some way. Like she took offense at Carmilla and me laughing together, touching each other in her classroom.

Maybe she liked us better when we were at each other's throats. Maybe, in her infinite wisdom, she knew that animosity made better poets out of both of us.

Rationally, I knew I should go back to my dorm room and get started on those poems, but anger and curiosity proved a stronger cocktail than reason. Perhaps through providence or some sort of devilish temptation, the door with its faulty deadbolt was still cracked. I could hear voices filtering out from inside the classroom, rising in volume and intensity.

"You get off on making an example out of me in front of everyone." This was Carmilla, speaking in a tone tipped with rage.

"Don't be so dramatic," De Lafontaine replied, her voice as smooth and even as ever. "You know I hate it when you work yourself into hysterics."

"I am not being hysterical. Hysteria is a made-up patriarchal tool of oppression, you know that?"

"Well, aren't you clever? Shall you teach the class while I sit in the student section?"

"Why are you being so cruel to me? Have I done something to you I don't know about? Denied you anything at all?"

I heard agitated footsteps inside the lecture hall, and when I peeked through the crack, I saw that Carmilla was pacing, her long fingers tangled in her still-wet hair. She looked ready to tear it out in clumps. De Lafontaine watched her with arms crossed.

"You're exceptionally bright, Carmilla, no one is disputing that. But you squander your potential on distractions. Like the Sheridan girl."

"I am not distracted."

"Aren't you? You're always staring at her during class, and she derails you during our Friday-night meetings. I thought having someone keeping pace with you might push you to be better, but you're losing yourself in a fleeting connection that won't last the semester."

I blinked, a little bit stunned at De Lafontaine's words. I was so rapt in my eavesdropping that the tears were drying on my cheeks, my sadness all but forgotten. I was intruding on something private, I knew that much, but I couldn't force myself to walk away.

"Laura and I aren't connected; we're classmates, that's all. Any interest I feel towards her is purely academic."

"So now we're lying to each other? I thought there were supposed to be no secrets between us, Carmilla."

"There aren't," Carmilla said, her voice almost a whine. In her righteous indignation, she had seemed like a wrathful goddess, but now she sounded very much her age, a child chasing after the approval of her mentor. "I would never lie to you, Ms. D. Your secrets are safe with me. All of them."

Ms. D made that humming sound in the back of her throat, the one that, like Caesar's thumb, could signal her ultimate approval or disapproval. Now, she sounded displeased. "I'm not so sure about that anymore, darling."

My breath caught in my throat at the endearment. It seemed searingly intimate. Inappropriate even. That word had never occurred to me when it came to De Lafontaine's conduct, but now it floated to the surface of my mind. The entire situation suddenly seemed charged with an electricity I couldn't name and didn't dare to.

Tears sprang to Carmilla's eyes, and began to course freely down her cheeks. It was almost frightening, to see her so undone. She took a few steps towards De Lafontaine, her fingers trembling at her sides.

"I promise I'll shape up. I'll be whatever you want me to be, Ms. D. Just don't toss me aside."

"Oh, sweet girl." De Lafontaine sighed, approaching Carmilla and cupping her face in her hands. My pulse pounded in my jugular. I was sure that I should tear my eyes away and leave them to each other, but I couldn't stop watching.

De Lafontaine circled Carmilla's cheeks with her lacquer-tipped fingers, murmuring something indecipherable to me.

Then, my professor parted her lips and lowered her mouth, lipsticked and undoubtedly hot, to Carmilla's neck. The kiss turned violent in an instant, De Lafontaine bending Carmilla backwards and digging her teeth – suddenly so sharp – into her throat. Carmilla let out a little cry, clutching De Lafontaine close, and De Lafontaine's throat bobbed.

My heart raced in my chest, adrenaline scorching through my veins, but still I couldn't look away. Not even when Carmilla's legs gave out from under her and De

Lafontaine crouched over her body like a lion tearing into gazelle flesh, cradling her in her arms.

The professor's gaze suddenly cut across the room, finding the crack in the door, and we made eye contact for one awful second.

I jolted as though I had been physically struck, shoving myself away from the door. Nausea roiled in my gut and my heartbeat thudded in my head. I had witnessed something unspeakable, something inconceivable. There was no way I had seen what I thought I had seen, was there? I must have been hallucinating; otherwise I must face the undeniable fact that there was some sort of twisted intimacy between professor and student that I could have never even imagined.

I wondered how long this had been going on. I wondered if I should have noticed sooner, if there was some sign or suggestion that I had missed.

I turned to go, but it was at that very moment that the door to the lecture hall swung open, and De Lafontaine stood glowering in the doorway. Carmilla peeked over her shoulder, looking shaken.

"My office," De Lafontaine ordered. "Both of you. Now."

CHAPTER THIRTEEN

Laura

t seems like you've all been keeping secrets from me," De Lafontaine said, sinking into the black leather chair behind her impressive mahogany desk. Carmilla and I were sitting shoulder-to-shoulder on a bench in her office, the space suffocatingly warm with body heat and accusations unspoken. De Lafontaine steepled her fingers, looking at us squarely with that burning green gaze.

The gaze of a serpent transfixing its prey.

The gaze of a predator.

"I don't appreciate being kept in the dark," she said. "And I suggest you take this opportunity to come clean. Would anyone like to go first?"

We sat in shameful silence, looking anywhere but at De Lafontaine. I tried to keep quiet, but the truth clawed its way out of me all the same.

"I'm sorry for spying on you," I blurted.

"And what, exactly, do you think you saw?"

"I saw . . ." The words dried up in my throat. How could I put the impossible into words? "An . . . indiscretion."

De Lafontaine threw her head back and barked out a laugh, actually *laughed* at me.

"You'll learn quickly that I hate coyness. You saw me bite your classmate, feed from her very lifeblood. Isn't that right, Laura?"

I shifted uncomfortably in my seat. In the span of minutes, my perception of reality had been shattered, and I was still scrambling to pick up the pieces.

"I don't know what I saw," I said hoarsely.

"Suit yourself," De Lafontaine said, then turned to Carmilla. "And someone has been running around behind my back, stealing books from the library."

Carmilla chewed on the inside of her mouth, her fingers tangled together in her lap.

"I just wanted to see what was so important that you wouldn't share it with me," she muttered. Unlike me, she didn't sing like a canary when the pressure was on. She tried to hold her ground, to insist that she had somehow been in the right. I found her stubbornness charming, despite the situation.

"If I don't choose to share something with you, I have my reasons, do you understand?"

"Yes, Ms. D."

"I'm not following," I said, wondering if this was all

some kind of fever dream. Had Maisy slipped something into my morning tea as a hazing ritual? Was I succumbing to some sort of early-onset mental delirium, exacerbated by stress?

"De Lafontaine is a vampire," Carmilla said, as though it was as apparent as the color of the sky. A thousand questions bubbled to the forefront of my mind, but only one managed to surface.

"I beg your pardon," I said, pressing a hand to my chest as though I could still my overworked heart. "A *vampire*?"

"That's the contemporary term, yes," De Lafontaine said, looking bored with my incredulity. "I assume you're familiar? Literature doesn't always get us right, but it isn't a poor place to start. Perhaps you've read Polidori? Surely you've encountered Stoker?"

"I don't believe it," I said with a high laugh, pushing up from my seat. "You're both playing a trick on me. Prank the provincial girl, is that it? Well, I don't appreciate it at all."

"Does this seem like a trick to you?" Carmilla asked, yanking the collar of her shirt back to show off the two angry red marks on her neck. "Sit back down, Laura."

"Carmilla," I begged. "Come on, say this is a joke."

"It's no joke, Laura," Carmilla said, looking, to her credit, almost apologetic.

I blinked back baffled tears. It was all too much.

"So you're some kind of ancient creature, is that what I'm supposed to believe?" I asked De Lafontaine.

"Ancient is reaching," De Lafontaine said. "I'm barely two hundred. The young ones can pass for human more easily than the older set. As we age we . . . change."

"I don't believe it," I said, refusing to sit down, to accept any of this. "If you're a vampire, prove it."

"How is she supposed to prove it?" Carmilla said with a nasty laugh. "Bite you?"

"I suppose that would work," De Lafontaine mused. "But I don't have to take it to that extreme, because you've already seen everything you need to see. Think, Laura; use that bright mind of yours. You know what you saw. Don't lie to yourself now."

I seethed in my seat. I had seen *something*, that much was true. And from the outside, it had looked very much like a bite.

I believed in things like angels and prophecies and divine revelations, I thought, trying to rationalize the situation. I could even be convinced to entertain the thought of ghosts. Perhaps vampirism wasn't entirely beyond the pale.

Or perhaps I was losing my mind.

"Are those things in your mouth all the time?" I demanded.

"They retract," De Lafontaine said.

"And what else can you do? Summon swarms of bats, hypnotize unsuspecting victims?"

"You can't believe everything you read in books," Carmilla muttered.

"Neither of us is lying to you," De Lafontaine said, steering the conversation back on track. "This is real, Miss Sheridan. And the sooner you adjust your worldview, the better."

I looked from De Lafontaine to my classmate, feeling a little breathless. I wanted, possibly for the first time in my life, a stiff drink.

"All right," I said, forcing my voice to steady. "All right. But I have questions. And I'm not going anywhere until you answer them."

De Lafontaine grimaced down at her watch but didn't stop me.

"Why Saint Perpetua's?" I asked. "If you are what you say you are you could go anywhere in the world, be anyone you wanted. Why teach college poetry? For that matter, why drink from a student?"

"I'm here on academic business," De Lafontaine said, in a tone that told me that was all I was going to get out of her. "Carmilla is my chosen companion. She sustains me."

"So, you lied to me," I said flatly to Carmilla, still feeling wounded about the whole thing. "About you and her. You just pretended like she was your professor and nothing more."

"It wasn't personal," Carmilla said. "I lie to everyone."

De Lafontaine leaned back in her chair, surveying us both. "Well, what a miserable little band we all are. Bound by blood and secrecy, with no recourse to anyone but each other. It would almost be romantic, under more advantageous circumstances."

"I'm not going to tell anyone anything, Ms. D," Carmilla said quickly.

"I know, Carmilla. It's not you I'm worried about." She turned to me, surveying me like she was calculating how many liters of blood were in my veins. "You're complicit in our secret now, like it or not. The only question is: can you be trusted to keep it?"

"It doesn't sound like I have much of a choice," I said.

"No," De Lafontaine said, almost sadly. "You don't. I had hoped to bring you into my world slowly, to keep from frightening you, but this works just as well, I suppose."

"You were going to tell me?"

"Of course," she said, her gaze softening. "I chose you, Laura. And I'd choose you again, no matter the consequences."

A lump formed in my throat. I had never been chosen for much of anything in my life, not for friendship or academic acclaim or love, and what De Lafontaine was offering felt a little bit like all three tangled up together. In De Lafontaine's eyes, I was a once-in-a-lifetime talent, and in Carmilla's eyes, I was a worthy opponent. I had never been any of those things to anybody before.

"Nothing has to change," De Lafontaine went on. "All three of us can continue our studies together, and we can protect each other. We can go even deeper, ascend to new heights. There's so much I want to show you, so much I want to share. Would you like that, Laura?"

This was my last chance, my final opportunity to go back to my mundane little routine and forget everything I had seen and heard.

A sensible girl would leave.

A good girl most certainly would.

But I was tired of being sensible, and I was tired of being good. I couldn't walk away from what I was being offered: the chance to live an exceptional life.

"Yes," I said, my voice so quiet it was almost a whisper. "Yes, please."

A thin smile of approval tugged at De Lafontaine's coral-colored lips. I would chase that approval until the end of my days, into hell and back if I had to.

"I was hoping you would say that." She opened a file of papers on her desk, clicking open a red pen. "That's all for today, I think."

"You're not . . . going to kick me out of the cohort?" I asked as we stood.

"For now, your spot is safe. I don't turn away talented students. But I expect nothing but excellence from you from here on out. And no more sneaking around, Carmilla."

"Yes, Professor."

"You are both dismissed."

With that, we were tugging on our coats and filing out of the office in dumbstruck silence. We walked down the stairs and spilled out into the dreary night. It was still drizzling, and we stood in the arching stone doorway of Seward Hall, watching the silver droplets fall from the sky.

Carmilla produced her tin of cloves and held it out to me. I wasn't a big smoker, but I accepted a cigarette all the same. Then she pulled out an ornate gold lighter, and we both bent towards the flame, our heads close together.

"I think," I said, after taking a few ponderous puffs, "this would all be immensely easier if we were friends."

"You might as well try getting blood from a stone," Carmilla scoffed.

"I don't think you're as mean as you make yourself out to be." I had never been a bold person, but something about the brush with De Lafontaine made me brave. "I think you're lonely."

Carmilla didn't have anything to say to that. She just stood with her back to the door, smoking down her cigarette and watching the sky with a serious expression.

She was, I realized after a moment, thinking.

"I suppose we could try," she said, flicking her cigarette into a puddle. "But I'm not making any promises."

"Don't tell me there's a heart under all that ice."

Carmilla shot me a hard look, but her lips quirked as though she were fighting back a smile.

"Let's not get carried away. I'll see you on Friday."

Then she turned the collar of her coat up and started her long walk across the quad.

CHAPTER FOURTEEN

Carmilla

ctober slipped by quickly, rippling through time like the pages of a book ruffling in the wind. The nights got darker and colder, and the quad was soon blanketed with crunchy brown leaves. Soon, Halloween was banging down my door, demanding that I plan my costume and get my affairs in order for Saint Perpetua's biggest party of the year.

My Friday-evening sessions with Laura and De Lafontaine continued with renewed vigor, the good professor leading us by the hand into ever more arcane literary wonders. We fell into a strangely companionable sort of competition, trying to one-up each other every week with new poetic forms, new metaphors, new turns of phrase. Laura burned like a fiery beacon, igniting the page with her passion and verve.

I grew to appreciate her, slowly and against my will.

Laura, who had so agitated me since the moment I had first heard her recite, became a familiar presence in my life. I saw her probably more than I saw any of my other friends, not that I had many to begin with. She wasn't so bad, especially when she wasn't looking right at me. When we made eye contact, I always became antsy and irritable, ready to crawl out of my skin. I told myself it was because she was De Lafontaine's newest pet project, a direct competitor for her time and attention.

Every Halloween, the upperclassman girls hosted the party to end all parties in our four-story dormitory. This year was Dante's *Inferno* themed: the top floor was outfitted like Paradise, the third floor like Limbo, the second like a fiery inferno, and the first floor like the icy inner circle of Hell. I got roped into decorating by the RA on my floor, and spent much of the week leading up to the party stringing paper fig leaves and gauzy white fabric from the eaves of the top floor.

The night of the party, I squeezed into a drop-waist dress I had stolen from the theater department and tweezed my eyebrows razor-thin. I applied brick-red lipstick and piled my hair up, completing the look with a sheaf of silken fabric draped over my shoulders and around my head. I threw back a shot and a half of vodka from the stash in my closet, looking at myself hard in the mirror for a long moment. I tried to silence my mother's voice in my head, the one that told me I was trying too hard, and I was destined to make a fool of myself.

I looked fine, I assured myself. I looked better than fine.

The hallway was already swimming with girls when I slipped out into the milieu. Juliets and Joans of Arc and Twiggys pressed past me, plastic chutes of champagne and party punch in their hands. I made my way through the crowd, seeking a familiar face.

Laura was wearing a white dress belted at the waist with a golden sash, with glitter on her cheeks and a pipe cleaner halo nestled into her hair. She looked like something out of a small-town Christmas play, and my heart constricted at the sight of her.

"An angel?" I asked, pouring myself a double helping of party punch. It tasted like cheap wine, carbonation and cranberry juice. "Isn't that a little obvious?"

"What are you supposed to be, Carmilla?" Laura asked in a way she probably thought was friendly, but I reared back in offense.

"Isn't it obvious?" I said. "I'm Anaïs Nin, the greatest diarist of the modern era."

"Didn't she have two husbands at the same time?"

"Well, nobody's perfect."

"I think you look grand," Laura said in that stiff, overly polite way of hers. She was obviously in the mood to extend the olive branch tonight, despite our ongoing rivalry.

"Thanks," I said, a little wary of her goodwill. I couldn't let my guard down around Laura, I reminded myself. No matter how friendly we might act around each other, we could never be friends, not really. One of us would always come out on top and that would ruin everything, so best to keep an emotional arm's-length distance for the time being. "Shall we descend into the flames together?"

I plucked a shining red apple from a nearby bushel prominently displayed by the elevator. An upperclassman girl dressed as St Peter, beard and everything, guarded the sliding metal doors. Saint Perpetua's girls had a taste for the dramatic, and every partygoer had to partake of forbidden fruit before they were allowed to advance through the levels of the building.

I took a brisk bite out of the apple. Sweet juice spurted into my mouth.

"Your turn, Laura."

When I passed her the apple, our fingers brushed. She considered the apple for a moment, then took a big, unrepentant bite.

"Descend, sinners," St Peter intoned. She pushed the elevator button and ushered us inside. We were pressed against a gaggle of giggling girls dressed in matching black cat costumes, and I got pushed into a corner up against Laura.

"Sorry," I muttered, unable to look her in the face.

"S'fine," she responded, clutching her fingers tightly together in front of her.

We rode the hot box down to the third level, all filing out on to the floor the moment the doors dinged open.

The Purgatory level was part graveyard creepfest and part Elysian fields, with cut grass and straw strewn on the ground, thick spiderwebs hung from the ceiling, and attendants in corpse paint handing out bubbling black brew to partygoers. The cocktail tasted like blueberries and the cold kiss of dried ice, but it went down smooth.

I waited patiently while Laura availed herself of the bathroom. I might not like her very much, but I knew the iron-clad rules of girlhood: when you showed up to a party with someone, you stayed at their side all night.

Just about the time I was getting antsy, Laura returned. She looked pale.

"You didn't lose your lunch in there, did you?" I asked. "I won't babysit a messy drunk."

"I'm fine," Laura said, adjusting her halo. "I'm just not the biggest fan of crowds."

"And yet you came to a party."

"There were people here I wanted to see," she muttered into her glass, and I couldn't tell if she was talking about me or somebody else. Surely, it was somebody else. Why in the world would she want to see me?

We rode the elevator down to Hell, squished together in the overfull contraption. Laura's hair brushed against my face, filling my nose with her pressed powder and vanilla scent, which irritated me unspeakably. When we spilled out on to the second floor, a silver-bright smile lit up her face.

Crepe paper fluttered down from the ceiling, and a red

carpet had been rolled out under our feet. The floor had been decorated in charmingly tawdry shades of orange and red, and the girls handing out drinks were dressed in short, scoop-necked dresses with flames for skirts.

"Oh but this is fun, isn't it, though?" she asked, with that earnestness that I could never quite wrap my head around. I don't think I had ever met someone quite as straightforward as Laura Sheridan, and I wasn't entirely sure how to respond to her. I had been raised among an echelon of people who spoke mostly in double entendres and backbiting compliments. Earnestness was considered passé among my set. "My friends back in Mississippi . . . Well, I didn't have many, but they weren't big partiers."

"Is this your first party?" I asked incredulously.

"I don't suppose birthday parties when I was a girl count?"

"No, Sheridan," I said with a laugh, "they don't. Oh goodness, what are we going to do with you?"

"Whatever you want," she mumbled, so quietly the noise of the party almost snatched her words away.

The RA hosting the Hell floor's party bounded up to us, three tiny cups of red liquid balanced in her hands. Her golden skin was dusted with red glitter, and her jet black hair was piled on top of her hair in a beehive.

"You've got to throw it back quick," she said, handing out the shots. "They're called fireballs. And man alive, do they burn."

We dutifully clinked glasses and swallowed down the

sticky sweet cinnamon concoction. It felt like flames slithering down my throat, and I coughed a little.

"Laura's never been to a party," I said to distract from the distinctly uncool spectacle of me choking on my liquor.

"Oh, no kidding!" the RA chirped. "Well, happy Halloween, chickadee! You two are gonna have a great time tonight."

If I was smart, this was about the time when I should have feigned a headache and excused myself, leaving them to each other. But the alcohol had started to take the edge off my mood, and I was feeling devil-may-care. It wasn't like I had anything better to do that night than get royally sloshed with the only person in the school I could trust to keep my secrets, when it came down to it.

"Of course we will," I said, hooking my arm through Laura's like we were old school friends. She stiffened but didn't pull away. "First course of action: a cigarette break. Then, dancing. It's not a party unless you dance."

Laura smiled at me shyly, and I found, to my great surprise, that I smiled back.

We popped a window and crept out on to the fire escape, seeking refuge from the sweltering heat of the party in the cool night air. I only had one clove left in my tin, so we shared it round-robin style, passing it back and forth like a joint and making fun of each other's attempts to French inhale. A pleasant buzz built in my brain, part liquor, part nicotine, and part companionable closeness.

When we crawled back into the party, Laura laced her fingers through my own for stability. Being held by her felt like being electrocuted, and my stomach did the strangest flip at the sensation.

The dance floor was on the first level of the dorm in the common area, along with blue halogen lights stolen from the theater department and huge fans that kept the room as icy as the ninth circle of Hell. There was a live band squeezed into a corner, playing rock and roll and the occasional Motown standard. Laura didn't dance, but she watched the proceedings with round, delighted eyes, a glass of frosty blue Curaçao in hand. She waved at Maisy, who was grooving near the band with a few girls from her rowing team, and Elenore, who was draped around her off-campus boyfriend, shipped in for one night only of drinking and dancing.

Someone snagged my hand, and before I had a chance to protest, a boy was tugging me on to the dance floor. He was handsome, in a sort of angular way, and he was dressed as a devil, with red ram's horns in his curling blond hair and a red sparkling bowtie displayed prominently above his open collar. The band had transitioned into a cover of "House of the Rising Sun", and the boy, undoubtedly a townie who was here as someone's date, grinned from ear to ear.

"I dig this song, don't you?"

"Get another partner," I said, but laughter was bubbling up in my voice.

"Don't go all wallflower on me now. I know your parents must have paid for dancing lessons."

"Maybe a few."

"Show me what you can do, then."

I snapped into position, holding my arms out expectantly for my devil. He gave me a boyish smile but stepped up to the plate admirably, molding his hands around my back and hand.

We waltzed together in the icy blue glow of the theater lamps, barely able to keep from laughing, while the other couples swayed around us. I kept my back arched and my neck long, remiss to forget any of my training despite how drunk we both undoubtedly were. He moved with assurance despite the fact that I was leading. I held him tightly, anchoring myself to the solid, warm weight of him.

"You aren't half bad," he said, smiling down at me.

"I could say the same for you."

"Aw," he said, pulling me closer than the dance strictly demanded. "I'm touched."

I brought one hand up to rest on his chest, the tips of my fingers slipping beneath his open shirt.

It would have probably been wise to get off the carnival ride at that point, to laugh haughtily and disentangle myself from his arms, but the hedonistic atmosphere of the party had long ago gone to my head. It felt so nice to be touched by him. I shifted closer, breaking the prim and proper format of the waltz to slide my arms around his neck in a more casual and altogether more intimate position.

"Are you coming on to me, Mr. Whatever-your-name-is?"

"You can call me whatever you want," he said, with an inflaming smirk.

"What if I call you a libertine playboy of the worst variety?"

"Then at least you wouldn't be lying. Come on, let me kiss you."

His words were halfway between an order and a plea, and my stomach flooded with heat. I had long ago begrudgingly accepted being the initiator in so many of my relationships; the role was as well worn to me as a monologue from my favorite play. Despite my taste for being chased, people always beat around the bush so much that I got impatient and started chasing them instead. It had been ages since anyone had wanted me like this, so openly and unashamedly. I had forgotten what it felt like, to be wholly desired without qualm.

I all but melted in his grasp.

He slid his arm around my waist and pulled me into a deep, exploratory kiss. My lips parted for him instinctively, and I could taste the burn of liquor and another woman's lipstick on his mouth. Something about the thought of sharing him with an anonymous third party stoked the fires of my lust even brighter, and I tangled my fingers in his hair.

We carried on without shame for a few long moments,

then he broke away, looking at something over my shoulder.

"It seems someone's feeling a little left out," he said with an unkind laugh.

I turned to see Laura staring at us from the sidelines, her glass clutched so tightly in her fingers that her knuckles went white.

"Laura," I said, taking a step towards her.

That seemed to break whatever rageful spell she was under, and she dropped her eyes to the floor. Before I could say anything else, she pushed her way through the crowd and to the door and disappeared.

"You should go patch things up," he said, already eyeing another girl across the room with a cloth iris pinned to her kinky black hair. "I'll entertain myself until you get back, sweetheart."

If I was another sort of girl, I might have been offended at his ability to move so quickly from one dalliance to the next. But I wasn't in the market for anything permanent or committed, so I was unbothered.

I pressed past countless dancing couples and slipped out into the hallway, which was only marginally cooler than the sauna of the common room. I caught a glimpse of white trailing out the door as Laura dashed through the front entrance, and I followed her with a determined stride.

Damn her for making a scene in the middle of a perfectly pleasant night. And damn her for making me chase after her.

"Laura," I said long-sufferingly, pushing open the door. "This is ridiculous. Come back inside."

She was leaning against the side of the building, just outside the glow of the lamplight. She dabbed at her eyes with a lacy handkerchief she had procured from somewhere, her Southern manners still intact despite her distraught state.

"Go away, Carmilla," she said, her voice, usually the gentle melody of morning birdsong, rough with emotion.

"That guy is not worth crying over," I said, leaning up against the wall next to her in the shadows. Her mascara was smeared across her cheek, and I was tempted to lick my thumb and scrub her face clean. "If you ask him to kiss you, I'd bet he'd do it. We've got a name for boys like that in German, but it isn't polite to say out loud."

She shot me a hateful look, her blue eyes tempestuous. It nearly took my breath away, how ferocious she looked.

"For somebody so smart you really are stupid," she said.

Anger flared to life inside me. I felt, perhaps for the first time, that I was on the verge of seeing beneath her civility and manners to the feral creature underneath, and I craved the conflict.

"What's that supposed to mean?" I demanded, leaning in closer to look her in the face.

I expected her to draw back, but she just stared me down.

"Do I need to spell it out for you?" she said.

"Put it in a poem, why don't you? Maybe you'll feel better."

Moving with astonishing swiftness, Laura slammed her hands on either side of me against the brick of the building. She was close enough that I could feel the heat radiating off her body and smell the scent of skin beneath her perfume.

I froze, my stomach tightening instinctively. I felt cornered, like a little prey animal caught by the throat in the strong hands of the hunter. Part of me wanted to fight back and writhe away from her, but another, quieter part of me wanted to capitulate to whatever she had in store.

I've always had a strange proclivity for being subjugated. It tended to rear its head at the most inopportune times.

That didn't mean I wanted Laura to know about it, however.

"You lay a single finger on me and I'll bash your pretty face in," I snarled, my heart beating like a war drum in my chest.

If anything, Laura just drew closer to me, until our bodies were almost flush together. Her breathing was uneven, as though she was fighting a terrible onslaught of nerves, but she was here with me, real and forceful and undeniable. I was so close to trapped, so very nearly pushed up against the bricks. In a heady flash, I wondered if they would scrape and chafe my delicate skin through my dress, what they might feel like against bare skin if someone hiked up my skirts.

"Go inside, then," she challenged, voice only a little shaky. "Go inside and pretend like this never happened."

"I'm not going to give you the satisfaction."

She opened her mouth and then closed it again, abashed. Triumph flooded my veins. I was winning this little tete a tete, and I could probably have broken her hold on me right then and walked away. But I was possessed with a need to know what she had in mind for me.

"Go on," I said. "Say it. Whatever it is you're thinking."

"This is your last chance to leave."

"Or you'll do what?" I said, my chest rising and falling with rapid, shallow breaths. I was transfixed by her aggression and nearness, and I had no intention of going anywhere. I couldn't tear my eyes away from the perfect cupid's bow of her mouth. "I'll bet you've never even had another girl. I'll bet you've just read about it in books is all."

"You'd be surprised what you can learn from reading books," she said, and slid her knee between my legs.

I gasped, my hands coming up to grasp her shoulders of their own accord. We were tangled up in darkness and the skirts of my dress, but I could still feel her pressure against the throbbing heat between my thighs.

"Fuck," I whimpered.

Something about that simple explicative broke her, and she surged against me, crushing our mouths to each other.

She kissed me with a martyr's agonized desperation, like I was the only sword she ever wanted to fall on. I kissed her right back like the cutting edge of a blade, trying to inflict as much damage as possible.

I wanted her to be able to think of nothing but this kiss when she was alone in her bed at night. I wanted her to feel just how much I reviled and desired her, to what maddening brink she drove me.

I wanted her to want me so badly it hurt.

Laura clutched me close, rocking her thigh into me. The angle was awkward and inexpert, but it sent a pulse of pleasure shooting through my body nonetheless. I moaned into her mouth, not caring if she heard me.

"I still hate you," I said, nipping at her plush lower lip. I canted my hips against her knee, chasing the friction.

"And I find you intolerable," she said, her lips tracing the word against my mouth. She made it sound filthy, and a shudder ran down my spine.

In that moment, I would have let her eat me in two bites.

"Am I interrupting something?" a cool voice asked from behind us.

Laura let go of me like I was a hot stove. She wiped the lipstick from her mouth with trembling fingers. Instantly, the domineering affect evaporated, leaving behind the anxious girl I was used to seeing in class.

I turned to face the interloper, ready to snap at whoever it was to clear off and mind their own business, but then the words dried up on my lips.

De Lafontaine stood under the glow of the lamplight, just outside of the anonymous shadows Laura and I had retreated into. In the dim yellow light her skin was like parchment, her eyes dull and gleaming, and she looked about a hundred years old. Her mouth was screwed up as though she had tasted something sour, accentuating the frown lines around her lips. I saw her in the moment for what she truly was: a refugee from a more ancient age who only kept up the barest facsimile of youth and modernity, and even then only a smokescreen to draw in prey.

I was, all of a sudden, a little bit afraid of her.

"Ms. D," I said stupidly. "What are you doing here?"

"Chaperoning," she responded. Every syllable was crisp as shattered ice. "All this time I was worried about the girls with boyfriends, but I see now my suspicions were misplaced."

Laura's cheeks were tinged pink with embarrassment as she patted her hair back into place. She probably wanted as few witnesses as possible to her indiscretion.

Mere moments ago, the thought of Laura being indiscreet would have been laughable to me, but now I saw that she was actually like a shaken-up bottle of champagne, ready to pop at any moment. If she was capable of half the things I read about in that book of poetry she had slipped me in the library . . . The thought made my stomach tighten.

"Both of you, come with me," De Lafontaine said, already stalking off into the dark.

"Where are we going?" I asked, trotting after her. Laura skulked behind me, keeping a safe distance between us.

"You've always asked me about my condition," De Lafontaine said, her tone magnanimous, indulgent. "I think it's time I shared more about it with you."

My heart fluttered in my throat. All I had wanted for so long was to be brought into De Lafontaine's confidence, and now she was offering me the answers to all my questions. It was a Halloween miracle.

"Right now?" Laura asked, sounding a little put out. I wondered if she would rather be left to her own designs for me, and the thought sent a pleasant shiver through my body.

"Yes, Laura, right now."

CHAPTER FIFTEEN

Laura

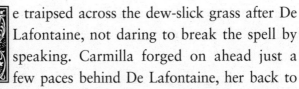

e traipsed across the dew-slick grass after De Lafontaine, not daring to break the spell by speaking. Carmilla forged on ahead just a few paces behind De Lafontaine, her back to me despite the closeness we had shared moments ago. De Lafontaine had come calling and she had dropped everything to follow, but I supposed I shouldn't be surprised by such behavior. She was the professor's pet, bound to her body and soul by a dark, ancient rite I still couldn't quite wrap my head around. I wasn't sure what I had to offer her that could compete with something like that.

In the breeze of the early morning, my lips tingled, still dripping with the taste of Carmilla. Cloves, rosewater, and cheap liquor. I was intoxicated by it, and wondered if I would get the chance to taste her again, or if we had stolen the only moment we would ever share together. She still hated me, after all, she had told me so herself.

We walked half the length of campus until we came upon Seward Hall, looming shadowed by the moonlight. De Lafontaine let us in through the side door with her faculty keys, and I thought perhaps she was leading us up to the third-floor oratory for a spontaneous lesson. But to my surprise, she led us down the stairs into the basement, a dark and dank space used mostly for storage, and occasionally for overflow classes when all the other rooms in the building were occupied. We squeezed past desks latticed with spiderwebs and large crates of mysterious school property, Carmilla and I banging our knees a number of times on pieces of furniture we could barely make out.

"Everything all right back there?" De Lafontaine asked.

"We can't see in the dark," I responded, as though it weren't obvious.

Carmilla huffed in irritation, probably gearing up to declare that she was just fine, thank you, but then she nearly toppled over in the dark. My arms shot out of their own accord, steadying her with a firm grasp on her shoulders. I full expected her to wrench away from me, but instead she just muttered, "Thanks."

As my eyes adjusted to the dark, I saw we were making our way towards the most remote recesses of the basement. When we hit a dead end, De Lafontaine stooped down to haul a crate away from a trapdoor so subtle I almost couldn't see it. When she pressed down on the door, it popped open with a puff of dust.

"Abandon hope, all ye who enter here," Carmilla murmured to herself. Then, a little louder, "Ms. D, what is this?"

"Don't you trust me, Carmilla?" our professor asked, then began to descend the narrow ladder into the bowels of the school. How could we argue with her? She was our intrepid leader, our burning north star. She had never led us astray before.

Carmilla followed first, then me. We navigated down into a cool dirt-floored chamber, hewn from the same stone that had been used to build the campus's oldest structures. Rainwater dripped down from the ceiling and splashed against my scalp.

"Why now?" Carmilla asked, pressing closer to De Lafontaine. "Why tonight, after telling me no so many times before?"

Another question hung unspoken in the air. *Why bring Laura, who doesn't deserve a full share in your secrets?*

"Perhaps I'm feeling magnanimous," De Lafontaine said, although she didn't sound it. She sounded bitter, and brittle besides. As self-centered as it seemed, I could only conclude that something about finding Carmilla and me in flagrante had cemented her decision. That she was bringing us deeper into her world not out of the goodness of her heart, but as some sort of punishment.

The thought sent a shudder up my spine.

"I've spent five years looking for this place," De Lafontaine said. "The records left behind deliberately obfuscated its location. But it was under my nose the whole time. Watch your step."

We followed her deeper into the school, navigating mostly by touch through a narrow passageway. By my estimation, we were no longer beneath Seward Hall, but rather deep underground somewhere else on campus, and I wondered how far this labyrinth of tunnels extended. I was sure that without proper guidance, I would be hopelessly lost.

"Is this some sort of hiding place?" I asked, pressing my hand against the slick walls of the passageway. The ground was slightly sloped underneath our feet. We were going deeper. The air here was thick with the scent of lichen and rot, and it sat heavy in my lungs. "Like a bomb shelter?"

"No," our professor said, producing a match from her breast pocket and setting it to blazing. "It's a crypt."

A stone coffin stood in the center of an octagonal room, completely unadorned except for a border of thorned roses carved around the lid. All the breath left my lungs in a whoosh, and I heard Carmilla give a little gasp beside me.

"Are you serious?" I demanded.

De Lafontaine simply gave me a blasé look. I don't think I had ever heard her joke about anything in the entire time that I had known her.

"Whose coffin is that?" Carmilla asked, her voice breathy. She took one tentative step forward and then paused, as though unsure if she was allowed to move any further.

"Go ahead," De Lafontaine said, with the strangest sort of gleam in her eye.

My heart pounded in my throat as Carmilla approached the coffin. The idea of death made me queasy, but Carmilla seemed compelled by lurid curiosity. Her mouth parted slightly as she curled her fingers around the lip of the open coffin and peered inside. De Lafontaine watched her from the other side of the coffin, as comfortable around a dead body as a mortician.

"This is what you've been researching, isn't it?" Carmilla asked. Her voice was hushed and reverent. "Who was this?"

"My sire," De Lafontaine said, the words falling from her lips like a stone. She and Carmilla shared a glance, and I intuited that there was more to this conversation than was being spoken aloud.

"Your sire?" I echoed, taking another step forward.

"Is she dead?" Carmilla asked.

"Not dead," De Lafontaine said, gazing down. "Merely sleeping. Waiting until the right moment to be awoken. I come down here sometimes just to watch her, just to dream about what it might be like to hold her one more time. Come here, Laura. I want you to look at her."

I swallowed hard and took one jelly-kneed step forward,

then another. I stopped right at Carmilla's side, curling my fingers over the lip of the coffin next to hers. Our pinkies brushed, her skin hot in the cold of the basement chamber.

I wondered if I was being hazed, if at any moment Elenore and the other girls from the seminar were going to jump out of the shadows to frighten me, then reveal with raucous laughter that the body was only a dummy, a little Halloween prank. But there was no explaining the labyrinthine corridors underneath the school. There was no faking the scent of rot in the air, sweet and putrid like a kitchen sink full of dirty dishes gone sour.

Taking a deep, bracing breath, I forced myself to look inside the coffin.

Despite the damp, the body seemed almost mummified. Wrinkled, paper-thin skin stretched over high, hollow cheekbones, and the grimacing lips revealed a few yellowed teeth still stuck valiantly to corroded gums. There was enough hair left that I could tell it had once been long and dark, and the wizened body was dressed in mourning black from head to toe.

I retched instinctively, turning away from the coffin to hack up foamy bile. Carmilla, perhaps motivated by pity or some lingering warm feeling from our kiss moments ago, rubbed her hand on my back in a soothing circle.

"What," I rasped, wiping my mouth with the back of my hand, "in hell is going on here?"

I usually refrained from swearing, especially in front of my teachers, but these were extenuating circumstances if I had ever encountered them.

De Lafontaine looked mildly irritated.

"I trusted the both of you to show you this place. I thought you would be brave enough to look in the face of death and not shrink from it. Don't tell me I misjudged you."

Her words pricked at me like needles. I might be shy, and I might be green, but I was no coward. If Carmilla could keep her wits about her in the face of this creeping horror, so could I.

I straightened myself up, standing tall. My gut gurgled in protest, but I managed to keep the contents of my stomach down.

"No, Ms. De Lafontaine."

"What is she doing down here?" Carmilla asked. She seemed entranced by the gruesomeness of the experience, rapt in the face of the macabre. I wanted with every ounce of will to yank her down the corridor by the wrist and not stop running until we were above ground again.

De Lafontaine reached into the coffin and tenderly brushed a lock of lank hair out of the corpse's face.

"She grew weary of the world, of its inhabitants. So, she beguiled a brilliant architect and convinced him to build her a resting chamber underneath one of his greatest achievements, this very school. I chased her through centuries, piecing together her whereabouts from letters and hearsay, until finally I found her." De Lafontaine's voice dropped to a murmur, and I wasn't sure if she was talking to us anymore. It was like we weren't even in the room. "Diminished. Wasting away in the darkness, alone."

"Ms. D?" Carmilla asked uneasily.

De Lafontaine's eyes snapped back to her, illuminated with a fervor I had never seen before or since. It made her eyes burn like green fire, bright and clear as undiluted absinthe.

"Come here, Carmilla," she said, extending her hand to my rival and the object of all my affection.

Carmilla did as she was told, drawn forward as though by some bewitchment. My heart thrummed a battle rhythm in my chest, beating out a warning.

Wrong. Something was wrong.

"What would you do, if I asked you?" De Lafontaine asked.

"Anything," Carmilla said, her eyes jumping from De Lafontaine to the body and then back again. "You know that."

"Then bleed for me, darling, one more time."

Carmilla dutifully reached up and pulled her hair away from her neck. De Lafontaine shook her head, retrieving a gleaming silver pocket knife from her trousers.

"The blood isn't for me, Carmilla. It's for Isis."

Without another word, De Lafontaine grasped Carmilla's wrist, pressed the cutting edge of the blade into her palm, and opened a bright red incision. Carmilla hissed through her teeth, but she didn't flinch.

Brave girl, I thought.

I crept closer, my pulse pounding in my ears. The sharp scent of iron cut through the air. De Lafontaine locked eyes with me as I stepped up to the side of the coffin opposite her and Carmilla.

"Watch," she ordered, like she was giving me a class assignment.

In that moment, I understood. I was here not as a participant, but a witness. I wasn't supposed to understand what was going on, because this whole scene served only to remind me of my own humanity, my mortality, my smallness. It served to show how Carmilla and I were different, and more important, to demonstrate the claim De Lafontaine had laid on her long ago.

Without another word, the professor tilted Carmilla's wrist and poured the blood pooling in Carmilla's palm into the parted, mummified lips of her sire.

The only sounds in the room were the sounds of our breathing and the steady dribble of blood against the cracked lips of the corpse. The blood trickled down her chin and stained the collar of her dress. I almost felt bad about this desecration of the dead.

Then, impossibly, the corpse dragged in a heaving breath.

I gasped and staggered back, unable to believe my own eyes. Carmilla went white as a sheet, but she didn't run, she couldn't, De Lafontaine still had her wrist in a vice-like grip. The sound coming from the corpse was horrible, an ugly wheezing whine.

I watched in horror as the body lurched, becoming something not quite dead yet not quite alive. The corpse's eyelids cracked open inch by inch, revealing rheumy eyes.

De Lafontaine's entire body was tense, and she clutched the edge of the coffin tightly Her lips were parted, revealing the pointed edges of her teeth.

"Isis," she breathed, leaning low over the coffin and bringing her face close to the corpse, almost close enough to plant a kiss on those dusty lips.

Everything that happened next happened very quickly. All I know is one moment the corpse was prone in her coffin, barely breathing, and in the next she had shot up and let out an ear-piercing shriek. I hit the ground right away. De Lafontaine staggered back from the coffin, gripping Carmilla's wrist as she pulled her away, but Carmilla didn't move fast enough. She found herself directly in the line of fire, and when the creature lashed out with a clawed hand, it was Carmilla's lovely white neck that was slashed open.

The sound that came out of me was ungodly.

"No," De Lafontaine said, her voice rising in pitch and intensity, approaching something like fury. "No, no!"

Carmilla made a horrible garbled sound, one shaking hand coming up to press against the blood spurting from her throat. The creature clambered out of her coffin, trailing tattered fabric behind her, and crouched over the blood pooling on the ground like the dogs who devoured Jezebel. It lapped up the blood with a swollen gray tongue.

Carmilla's knees gave out and De Lafontaine caught her. By this point, I had shaken off some of my stunned terror and was crawling on my hands and knees around the coffin, towards my fallen rival.

"Laura, help me," De Lafontaine begged. She quickly unwrapped the scarf from her neck and tried to use it to staunch Carmilla's wound, but the fabric was soon soaked through.

The cut was deep and merciless. She was losing a nauseating amount of blood, and fast.

The creature shuffled closer on crouched legs, following the scent of blood towards Carmilla's convulsing body, and my anger was stronger than my fear.

"Get away!" I shrieked, waving my arms around like I was spooking a bear. "Get away from her, beast!"

The creature that De Lafontaine called Isis shrank back a few paces, then turned and scrambled down the corridor into the dark, leaving De Lafontaine and I alone with the dying Carmilla.

"Oh God," I said, my breaths coming hard. I had never seen so much blood in one place. It was seeping into the knees of my dress as I knelt at Carmilla's side, staining the white fabric red.

In an instant, every cruel word and cutting glance I

had ever exchanged with Carmilla flashed through my mind. It all seemed foolish now, inconsequential. Watching her lying there, gasping for breath like a fish on a hook, was utterly wrenching. I felt like I was bleeding out alongside her, like something in me would expire for good if I had to watch her die.

De Lafontaine cradled Carmilla's ashen face, her thumb smudging blood across Carmilla's cheek.

"No, no, no," she moaned. "Carmilla, darling, don't do this to me. I will not accept this. Laura, open her mouth."

What could I do, besides what I was told? Delicately, I used my thumb to part Carmilla's lips.

"Now hold the scarf tight against her neck, as tight as you can manage."

I pressed the makeshift dressing to Carmilla's throat, and my fingers were soon sticky with her blood. It was cooling so fast in the damp air of the catacombs, going from hot and full of life to tacky in an instant.

De Lafontaine shoved up the cuff of her sleeve and bit down into her own wrist. Twin bubbles of blood sprang to the surface of her skin when she withdrew her teeth, and she tilted her wrist and dribbled the blood into Carmilla's mouth. It reminded me of the way I had spoon-fed a very sick kitten when I was a girl, hoping desperately that it would live. The kitten had died, but I prayed that somehow, some way, Carmilla would survive this.

I wasn't entirely sure what was happening, but I had read a Gothic novel or two in my day. If the legends were true, the only thing that could turn a living human into one of the restless dead was the blood of a vampire.

"Come on," De Lafontaine said through gritted teeth. I pressed harder against the scarf, hoping against hope that somehow, the wound would stop bleeding.

De Lafontaine shook Carmilla by the shoulders.

"Live, damn you! Come back to me!"

For four long heartbeats, there was nothing. "Come back to me, Carmilla," De Lafontaine murmured. She pressed her forehead to Carmilla's, heaving a deep breath. "Come back, darling."

A cough bubbled up from Carmilla's throat, and her eyes skittered behind her blue-veined eyelids.

"Carmilla," I breathed, hope filling my chest to bursting.

Her eyes flickered open, amber so dark they looked black in the dim of the chapel. Her fingers closed around my wrist, squeezing hard enough to make me ache. Had she always been so strong?

"What happened?" she moaned.

"You died," I whispered. Something about the stone embrace of the catacomb, so like a chapel, compelled me to confess. "I watched."

De Lafontaine tipped Carmilla's chin up with two fingers, looking into her face.

"How do you feel?" she asked.

S. T. Gibson

Carmilla swallowed, then ran her tongue over her dry lips.

"Hungry," she rasped.

CHAPTER SIXTEEN

Carmilla

———

he thirst hit me like a freight train. One moment I was sated and the next I was gripped with a ferocious emptiness, opening up inside me like a sinkhole. I had never felt a need like this ever in my life; it went beyond lust or envy or hunger and was yet all of those emotions at once, tangled together like a Gordian knot.

Pure desire, distilled down into a heady elixir.

It was to be, I realized with a creeping sense of dread, the rest of my life.

This was to say nothing of the fever, of the pain. Sweat clung to my hairline and gathered at the nape of my neck and in between my breasts, and my heart beat so rapidly in my chest I thought I might go into cardiac arrest. My skin was tender to the touch, crying out under the gentle prodding of Laura and De Lafontaine's fingers, and every bone in my body felt bruised. My gums burned like I had rubbed them with acetone. There was a pounding pressure behind my canine teeth, building slowly into something agonizing.

"Christ," I swore, pushing up onto my side. I coughed a few times, then vomited up bile onto the dirt floor.

Empty. I was so goddamn empty.

Laura retrieved a handkerchief from somewhere within her stained dress and scrubbed up the bile, a gesture that struck me as almost insanely polite. She was panicking, I realized. I could see it in her flushed cheeks, in the way her pulse pounded in her jugular. I could taste it in the air, her fear and shame.

God. I could *smell* her. The scent of nervous sweat and pressed powder and the fragrant flesh beneath, all perfumed with a heady bouquet of iron wafting off her skin.

Blood. I could smell her blood.

De Lafontaine rubbed a circle in-between my shoulder blades. She smelled like jasmine and musk and beneath that, she smelled the way fresh snow smells, or clean metal, or clear water. Which was to say like absolutely nothing at all.

I wondered if all vampires smelled that way, or if there was some deficiency of character in De Lafontaine that made her unappetizing to me.

"What's happening to me?" I moaned.

"You're changing," De Lafontaine said, with so much gentleness in her voice. It was how I always wished she would talk to me, with loving kindness. There wasn't a trace of censure or judgment in her voice. "You need to feed. You need your strength. Can you feel it?" She pressed her hand to my belly, which roiled underneath her touch. "That hunger?"

"I'm so hungry I could die," I said, and for once, I wasn't exaggerating for dramatics' sake. I really was worried that if I didn't fill the gnawing void inside me, I would simply cease to exist.

"Drink," De Lafontaine said, thrusting her wrist out to me. I opened my mouth, poised to bite, hurting teeth be damned, but I recoiled at the final moment. I couldn't get past her off-putting scent and I was afraid of angering her by taking a bite out of her.

"You're right," she murmured, tugging the sleeve of her sweater back down again. "I can't offer you any real sustenance. My blood is thin with age and weak from our condition. You need lifeblood, from a living, breathing human."

Her eyes fell on Laura, still scrubbing at the floor with shaking hands. Laura glanced up, her eyes bluer than I had ever seen them. Were they always that shocking shade of cornflower, or was I just now noticing? That awful desire coiled like a snake in my stomach stirred, and I wanted desperately for her to push me down onto the steps of the coffin and finish what she had started outside the dormitory.

"Me?" Laura asked breathlessly.

"There was never going to be anyone else," De Lafontaine said.

Naturally, I rebelled against this fatalism.

"There's a whole campus full of girls out there. I don't need Sheridan to—"

"You won't make it out of this tunnel if you don't feed, Carmilla," my professor said. "You're too weak to hunt for yourself, and I'm not confident I could lure a student back here in time. It's imperative you feed as soon as possible, or your body will start shutting down. There isn't another option."

"Laura," I said, and I thought I was gearing up to lay out all the reasons why it wouldn't work, why it couldn't be her. But my body betrayed me, and her name left my lips sounding like a plea.

She looked, understandably, trepidatious.

"She could kill me."

"I won't let her," De Lafontaine swore. "I'm here to facilitate. She'll only take as much as she needs to make it to the next sunset, and then I'll teach her how to feed properly."

"Laura," I said again, stronger this time. "I'm awfully sorry about this. But I need you to agree. If you don't agree, I'll crawl out of this tunnel, on my hands and knees if I have to, and find someone else. I won't do something you don't want."

It seemed strange to me, to suddenly be so protective of the rights of refusal of a girl I was dying to sink my teeth into, a girl who would probably love to see me crawl and beg and suffer. But I decided on the spot that if I was going to be a monster, I was going to be an elegant one, like my beloved De Lafontaine. There was no sense descending into an animalistic frenzy without the full agreement of my blood donor; there was no art in it, no beauty. And I would die before I sacrificed art and beauty. Life simply wasn't worth living if it wasn't by those principles.

"You'll only take a little bit?" Laura breathed, her handkerchief abandoned. She crept closer to me.

"Only enough to live," I swore, even though I didn't know how much that was, or how on earth I was supposed to stop once I started. Already, my mouth was watering.

"Go on," De Lafontaine said, smoothing back Laura's hair like she had done to me so many times before.

Laura crept a little closer, kneeling at my side. Her curls looked like burnished brass in the light of De Lafontaine's flickering match, her full cheeks illuminated by the glow. She looked, I realized a little breathlessly, like a holy icon cast in gold.

I wanted to fall at her feet and worship her. I wanted to desecrate her in every filthy manner I could imagine. I wanted all of her, in every way, all at once.

"God, Sheridan," I said, my voice a little choked.

"No, don't try to speak," she said, pressing her forefinger to my lips. I wanted to hurt her. I wanted to taste her. I wanted to make her writhe and provoke her into punishing me in return.

"Let me," I begged, pushing up onto my elbows. I was beyond pride, beyond caring that I was making a scene there on the floor. "Please will you let me?"

In response, Laura tied her hair up into a fluffy bun with a hair tie from around her wrist and leaned down so close to me, close enough that her breath ghosted across my collarbones.

"Take what you need," she said, with such a generosity that treacherous tears stung at my eyes. I would not cry over Laura Sheridan, and I would not refuse the gift she was giving me. I would drink until I was satisfied without remorse or apology.

"Come here," I said, my voice rough with want.

I threaded my fingers into her hair and pulled her close, slotting my mouth over the sweet pulse pounding away in her throat. The taste of her skin tickled my soft palate.

"God," I moaned, and then bit down.

Something must have happened to me in the short time between Isis attacking me and my coming back to shuddering life, because my teeth pierced Laura's delicate skin without my having to rend and tear. Her blood, hot and so, so satisfying, spurted into my mouth like the fountain of youth. It trickled down my throat and coated my tongue with sweet thickness. My eyes rolled back as every muscle in my body seized and then relaxed into the sensation.

This. *This* was living. Coaxing the death out of another

person, bringing them right up to the brink, but refusing to push them over the edge.

I sank my fingers into the supple flesh of Laura's waist and thighs, pulling her tighter into me. I could lose myself for an eternity in the taste of her, the way she felt coursing down my throat. But De Lafontaine covered my shoulder with her iron grip, dragging me back.

"That's all she can take," she said firmly. "Release her, Carmilla."

In the end, De Lafontaine had to wrench me off a whimpering Laura, who pressed a trembling hand to her skin as soon as my teeth were out of her neck. My head spun with delicious delirium as her blood flooded my system.

I heaved in a breath of air. My heart galloped in my chest, pumping vitality through me with renewed vigor.

"Are you all right?" De Lafontaine asked, touching the wound in Laura's neck. I had made a mess of her, and blood was smeared across her peachy skin. My own neck, searing with pain only minutes before, now felt unmarred beneath the blood and gore.

"I-I think so," Laura stammered, staring at me with the strangest expression. It was like she was watching a priest lift the cloth from a cup of communion wine, like I was brimming with all of creation's darkest secrets.

"Good. We should go."

With that, De Lafontaine hooked her hands under my arms and hauled me gently to my feet. The world tilted on its axis, threatening to dissolve all around me. The pain of my transformation had been dulled by the heady intoxication of Laura's blood, but I was still sensitive to the touch. I swayed a little, leaning heavily on De Lafontaine for support. It was so relieving to have an excuse to cling to her.

"Laura, help me," our professor said, and Laura slung one of my arms over her shoulders. She jostled close to me, supporting me with her warm, solid body.

Between the two of them, they were able to lead me out of the tunnels and onto the quad. Every step felt like putting my weight on broken glass, and I winced, biting my lip to keep from crying out. I wanted to be brave for De Lafontaine, and I didn't want Laura to see me cry. It was strange, to suddenly care at all what my rival thought of me, but she had seen me so vulnerable, so naked with need, that I wanted to preserve whatever little bit of dignity I had left.

De Lafontaine's apartment wasn't far, and somehow, we made our trek across the grass and gravel paths without incident. By the time we got to the front door, I was so lightheaded it was hard to see straight.

"That will be all, Laura," De Lafontaine said, shouldering open the door while keeping a firm grasp on my arm. "I can handle things from here."

Laura stood in the doorway, staring at De Lafontaine with a gobsmacked expression. I knew what she must be thinking: after all we had shared together, after all she had witnessed and been party to, shouldn't De Lafontaine invite her inside?

"Ms. D," I began, attempting to plead Laura's case. Maybe it was some sort of animal connection brought on by feeding from her, but I wanted Laura close, at least for a little while more. My smudged lipstick mingled with the dried, flaking blood on her neck. An irrepressible urge to lick it off her welled up inside me, but somehow I restrained myself.

"Hush, Carmilla," De Lafontaine said, already ushering me towards the stairs. "Your transformation is underway, and you need someone with the right experience to watch over you."

"But Laura—"

"Can walk herself back to her dorm, where she'll go straight to bed and not tell a soul what has happened. Isn't that right, Laura?"

"That creature, Isis, she's still out there," Laura said. "Shouldn't we call someone? Shouldn't we do something? Shouldn't—"

"That will be *all*, Laura."

Real fury passed across Laura's face, like a parcel of clouds blocking out the sun, and for a moment she was Athena incarnate. This was the ferocious creature I had encountered in the shadows outside the party, the goddess that lived within the girl. This was the woman who would unapologetically torment a lover for the sake of her own satisfaction, who would demand nothing less than total submission.

But then the moment passed, and Laura swallowed hard, taking a step back.

"Yes, Ms. De Lafontaine," she murmured.

"Good. I'll see you at the private cohort meeting on Friday. Until then, don't call on us. Carmilla will need her privacy, and her rest."

And then, with a soft click, she shut the door. Laura's face disappeared and the whole room was plunged into darkness.

"Let's go upstairs," De Lafontaine said, her voice low and warm in my ear.

Once upstairs, I was ushered into a place I had hitherto never been allowed: De Lafontaine's bedroom. Her rumpled sheets were soft to the touch from use and many washes, and they smelled faintly of lavender soap. She sat me down on the edge of the bed and knelt in front of me, unlacing my boots.

"No, it's all right," I said weakly. "I can—"

"Hush," she said, and kept her eyes downcast as she removed one shoe and then the other. There was something almost profane about seeing my idol on her knees, servicing me in such a mundane way. De Lafontaine was not made for service, I staunchly believed. She was made for traveling the world and creating great art and inspiring young minds, not undressing a skinny girl with aspirations too big for her.

It wasn't, of course, that I hadn't imagined being undressed by De Lafontaine before. But there was no passion in her touch, no lover's curiosity. It was professional, clinical even, like she was a doctor taking stock of my condition.

"Take off your stockings," she said.

I did as I was told, shimmying out of my tights underneath my dress and discarding them on the floor. De Lafontaine disappeared for a moment, leaving me bereft of any guidance whatsoever with anxiety tapping at my ribs, and then she reappeared with a glass of water in her hands.

"Drink," she said. "Eventually, you'll be able to stomach nothing but fresh blood, but I've been told water helps, in the beginning."

I dutifully swallowed down the water, which tasted inoffensive enough, and I wondered who had taught her how to take care of someone during their transformation. Had it been her own sire? Had that writhing creature underneath the school really been a beautiful young woman once, cultured enough to catch De Lafontaine's eye?

"Lie back," she murmured, and it was so easy to do what she said, to surrender to her gentle command. She tugged my dress off over my head, exposing the flimsy lace-trimmed camisole underneath. Bare-legged and bare-armed, I snuggled down into her blankets, already feeling drowsy.

De Lafontaine slipped off her oxford shoes, removed her golden watch, and eased down on to the bed. She lay beside me, wrapping her body around mine like the choking ivy that wrapped around her apartment building. I nestled into her arms, letting her embrace me in the way

I imagined the grave embraced dead bodies. I had always heard vampires slept in coffins, slumbering in a panto-mime of death, but the reality was much less dramatic.

She heaved a shuddering sigh, and it occurred to me for the first time that this whole experience might be as emotional for her as it was for me.

"Ms. D?" I asked softly, not daring to turn my face to look at her. That would be too intimate, too close to the carnal embrace of equals.

"I've taken everything from you," she said after a long pause. "All because I couldn't bear to be alone."

"That's not true. You've given me a gift. You've given me the whole world."

She huffed out a bitter laugh, pulling me in tighter. I felt like a little mouse being held gently in the jaws of a snake. I felt that something might snap at any moment, and that I would be the collateral damage.

"You'll understand, in time. The way we suffer. The way the undying life tears everything good and beautiful from us, sequestering us to a solitary existence of a thou-sand sleepless nights."

Even exhausted and teetering on some sort of emotional brink I couldn't quite understand, she was still a poet. I volleyed back beautiful words at her, relaxing into the familiarity of the exchange.

"I'll face death bravely then, and greet her as a lover. I never liked the sun anyway."

Another laugh, a little more genuine this time.

"I never tire of the optimism of youth. Maybe that's why I chose the line of work I'm in. To stay close to you young people and all your promise. I will never leave you, Carmilla," De Lafontaine swore. "Not in a hundred years."

I could feel the ties that bound us tugging taut, like an embroidery thread knotted to her ribs and mine. All I had wanted for so long was to be possessed by her, to be completely enmeshed in her world until I had no memory of the ugly mundanities of girlhood. But now, a small pit of dread opened up inside of me. It was suddenly hard to breathe, like all the air had been sucked out of the room. I wanted desperately to open a window and let in the night breeze, but De Lafontaine just pulled me closer, squeezing the last of the breath from my lungs.

"Say you'll stay," she whispered. "Say you'll let me teach you."

"Of course, Ms. D," I murmured.

"Say it, Carmilla."

"I'll stay with you," I said, shifting my body so I could look her in the face. When I spoke again, it was soft and pleading. "Will you kiss me now?"

De Lafontaine merely smiled at me.

"No, I'm not going to kiss you. All your appetites are heightened because of the change; you aren't thinking straight."

"Will it pass?" I asked, irritated by the raging thirst on my tongue, the empty yearning in my stomach, the persistent throb between my legs.

S. T. Gibson

De Lafontaine released me, crossing to the window and pulling the curtains tightly shut.

"Would you rather I tell you the truth or tell you a comforting lie?" she asked, her voice soft in the dark.

"The truth. Always."

"Then no, it's not going to pass. But you will learn to live with it."

She eased back down onto the bed next to me.

"What about Laura?" I asked, without thinking.

I felt De Lafontaine stiffen next to me.

Wrong. I had said something wrong.

"What *about* Laura?"

"She saw everything."

"Precisely. She saw what I wanted her to see, and if she's smart, she'll realize that you are leagues above her, and that you have more recourse with me than with her."

"But she was there, she . . . fed me."

"You can't grow attached to every person you feed from, Carmilla, it's not sustainable."

"I'm not attached," I blustered, even though a quiet part of me knew exactly how preoccupied I had become with the blonde Southerner. My rapidly beating heart quickened at the memory of her hands on my body.

"You'll learn how to hunt and you'll forget all about her," De Lafontaine said. I wondered if she was trying to convince me or convince herself. "She's a passing infatuation, and your interest in her will fade with time. She's a mortal, my darling, incapable of holding our interest for long. Now hush. The sun will be up soon and you need your rest."

There was so much more I wanted to say, more I wanted to ask, but I was fading fast, lulled by the rise and fall of De Lafontaine's breathing. It was as though the events of the evening had finally caught up with me, and my body had realized just how much it had been put through.

I was unconscious in moments.

CHAPTER SEVENTEEN

Laura

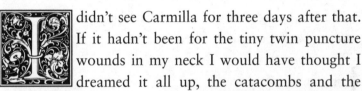

I didn't see Carmilla for three days after that. If it hadn't been for the tiny twin puncture wounds in my neck I would have thought I dreamed it all up, the catacombs and the blood and the bite of Carmilla's teeth in my skin. The monster that had skittered off into the belly of the school.

I waited for as long as I could stand it, pacing the tiny cage of my dorm room like a captured tiger, until finally, on the third night, I broke. I yanked on my milk-white cardigan and made the chilly trek to De Lafontaine's apartment, where I felt sure Carmilla was still holed up. If De Lafontaine had released her, she would have called on me, wouldn't she? We had gone through something together, something that bound us, even though I was confident I had only been allowed to bear witness to it all because it suited De Lafontaine's ends somehow. I tried to be bold, to be brave enough to knock on my professor's door and demand to see my . . . my what? My rival? My friend? No term seemed expansive enough to capture what Carmilla was to me

When I arrived at the apartment complex, I suddenly became too frightened to use the front door. So, I plucked up a small, smooth stone from the ground and hurled it up at De Lafontaine's window. Three stones and a minute later, Carmilla appeared at the glass.

My breath caught in my throat as she shimmied open the window and stuck her head out into the night. Starlight fell in silver rivulets over her dark hair, crimped in a funny way from being slept on, and her amber eyes burned like torches with pure, unbridled delight.

To see me.

She was happy to see me.

"Sheridan," she hissed down in a stage whisper. "What are you doing here?"

"Rescuing you from your convalescence," I whispered back, cupping my hands around my mouth to help the sound carry. My skin was prickling with nerves and the anticipation of something I couldn't quite name. A misdeed, perhaps. An adventure. "Is De Lafontaine there?"

"No, she went out."

"Then come down," I said, extending a spread-fingered hand out to her.

"She'll be cross," Carmilla said, but she was already pulling on a coat, and there was an irrepressible smile on her face. Within moments, she was down the stairs, out the door, and mere inches away from me, smelling like sleep and De Lafontaine's perfume.

Jealousy welled up in me like a poison spring, but it abated when Carmilla reached out and squeezed my hand.

"De Lafontaine told you not to tell a single person about what happened to me," she said, sounding admiring. "Did you really keep my secret?"

"Of course I did." The words came out of me in a rush. "I'll always keep your secrets." I realized how desperate that sounded and immediately wanted to eat my words, so I changed the subject. "Do you feel sick? Are you hungry?"

"I could eat," she said, trying to sound blasé, but I saw the desperation in her eyes. My jugular throbbed beneath the spot where she had bitten me, and I wondered if she would bite me again. If I would have to offer or if she would have to ask. My cheeks flushed hot at the thought. "I've been cooped up for days and I'm so pent up I could explode. I just want to be out of doors."

"Then lead the way," I said.

Carmilla gave me a smile as she brushed past me and began striding into the night.

Her canine teeth, I noticed, were slightly pointed.

———

We walked side by side like little soldiers all the way to the border of the campus and then beyond it, falling into single file on a well-trodden footpath leading from Saint Perpetua's into the woods. After twenty or so minutes of navigating mostly by feel in the dark (although I suppose Carmilla had an easier go of things) we reached a clearing, illuminated by nothing more than the moon and stars. In the middle of the glen was a small lake, or rather a glorified pond, rimmed with cattails. There were few signs of habitation out here except for a rickety dock that barely looked like it would support one of our weights, much less both of us.

The moment Carmilla shucked off her coat, I knew what she had in mind.

"Oh no," I said, holding up my hands. "It's far too cold."

"It's *bracing*," Carmilla corrected me. "Cold water clears the mind, quickens the blood. It's basically medicinal."

I clamped my arms around myself, suddenly embarrassed by my body, by my reticence. I wanted to be the kind of girl who shimmied out of her dress without a second thought, tossing her stockings over her shoulder and stepping into the water like a modern Aphrodite. But I was no Venus. I was a doughy overgrown girl who was too shy to even change in front of anyone else and suddenly, I was ashamed to even exist.

"I'm not getting in the water," I said, digging my heels into the grass figuratively and literally. "I'll just . . . stand watch."

"That's too bad," Carmilla said, letting down her hair

from its pale blue ribbon in a cascade of jet. "I used to come out here all the time with De Lafontaine."

That did it. Something inside me caught fire at our professor's name, and the resulting blaze was enough to keep me warm as I yanked off my sweater and bent down to unlace my Mary Janes. It was so dark out here it was unlikely anyone could see me anyway, I reasoned with myself, even as my fingers shook a little around the laces. The night would hide my many imperfections.

I did my best not to stare as Carmilla let her dress drop around her ankles and tugged off her socks by the toes. There were two dark flecks on her stomach, twin birth-marks mere inches above her navel. She wore a matching set of luxe-looking cream silk underwear, which struck me as characteristic somehow. Of course she was the kind of girl who made sure her bra and panties matched before she left the house.

It made me want to die, a little bit.

I tugged my underwear off under my slip. I would concede to getting into the water, but there was no way I was taking off the short dress.

Carmilla was struggling with her bra, her eyebrows creased together. She huffed in irritation, fumbling with the hooks behind her back. I took a tentative step forward.

"I think the latch is caught on the lace," I said. "Do you want me to . . .?"

"Fine," she said. Not exactly enthusiastic, but enough of an affirmative for me to proceed.

I stood behind her in the dark and slid my fingers between the silky band and her cool skin. It took a little wiggling, but I was able to free the hook without tearing the delicate lace trim. Suddenly the bra was open and the unblemished expanse of her back was right there in front of me, bare and inviting.

I trailed my fingers a few inches down her spine as I withdrew my hand.

"All better," I said, my voice barely above a whisper.

Carmilla cradled her bustier against her chest as she turned to face me, one eyebrow raised.

"Brave enough to take a dip with me after all, Sheridan?" she asked. "Wouldn't want you to ruin those curls."

My mouth was suddenly dry. I didn't know where to look.

"I changed my mind."

"Good," she said simply, and then let her bra drop to the ground. With one deft motion, her underwear followed, and for a glorious, agonizing instant, she was naked in front of me. Completely unbound, adorned in nothing but starlight and the grass curling over her toes.

"You're going to ruin that slip," she said, her eyes bright and curious. "It's real silk, isn't it?"

"It's just something I bought secondhand," I muttered.

"Still," she said quietly. "We must treat beautiful things with care."

Then she hooked her fingers under the hem of my dress, pulling it up over my thighs.

"Let me," she said. It could have so easily come across

as a command, especially from her imperious lips, but something about her downcast eyes, the softness of her voice, turned it into a request. Like she was offering me some sort of service.

"Go ahead," I said, trying to sound like I knew what I was doing.

She gently lifted the silk from my body until I was as naked as she was, the night air coiling over my skin and making goosebumps rise on my arms. Her eyes flickered over me only once, taking in my taut nipples, the curve of my waist, the thickness of my thighs, and then she turned from me, so quickly that it was impossible to tell if she was blushing. She delicately folded up my slip, placed it on the ground, and then dipped her foot into the water.

Was this all it was ever going to be? Tearing into each other at one moment and exchanging furtive heat in another? My head swam from all the mixed signals, but I followed Carmilla into the water all the same.

The lake was God-forsakenly cold, so cold it stole the breath from my lungs. My teeth chattered as I waded in up to my knees, then to my waist. There was no going back now. All I could do was pray that my internal temperature adjusted to the water quickly.

Carmilla sucked in a brave breath and then ducked her head beneath the lake, submerging herself whole for a few seconds before emerging gleaming and red-cheeked.

"There's no doing it in half-measures," she said. "You've got to take the plunge."

Not wanting to be bested, I waded up to my shoulders in the water, the silt squelching between my toes, and then dove all the way in.

My lungs strained against the cold weight and my heart fluttered in my chest. I let the water caress me until my lungs started to burn. I thought of how I was someone different only weeks ago, a shrinking violet who never missed a bedtime or spoke up in class. I was becoming something new, just the way Carmilla was, though with considerably less bloodshed.

A hand closed around my wrist, hauling me back to the surface of the water. I broke back up with a gasp, and realized it was Carmilla who was gripping me tight. Her hair was slicked back from her face, and the water lapped against her collarbones like the neckline of a couture dress.

"You were down there for a minute at least," she said. "I thought you drowned."

"That would make things easier on you," I said, disentangling our hands. "Then there'd be no one to compete with you for De Lafontaine's attention."

I didn't mean to say it, but now that it was out, I heard how upset I was. A dark look crossed her face.

"You don't know what you're talking about. I was trying to be nice to you."

"You're only ever nice to me when you forget that I'm a threat," I said, swimming a slow circle around her.

"Do you really think I'm threatened by you?"

"I think you know I'm competition. How much can we actually trust each other, when the professor is pitting us against each other?"

"Is that all you can think about, De Lafontaine?"

"That's the only person you ever seem to think about."

Carmilla hummed disapprovingly in her throat but said nothing.

My veins flooded with envy and I sank further into the water like a sullen frog. I would never have De Lafontaine's self-possessed ease, her sexual confidence. The bruising kiss outside the party was as far as I had ever gotten with a girl, and my hands had been shaking the entire time. Why would Carmilla spare me so much as a thought when De Lafontaine was there?

"Come on, don't sulk, Sheridan," she said, stretching her hands out to me underneath the water. The tips of her fingers grazed my bare hip, my shoulder. My body bloomed like a spring crocus underneath her touch with shameful swiftness.

"What do you care?" I demanded, not moving away from her. Maybe I was becoming more like her the longer I hung around her, more cruel, more quick to anger.

She curled those grasping fingers around my hip and pulled me closer. I gasped despite myself, a flush crawling across my skin in defiance of the chill water.

"Don't you understand yet that I care about what you do?" she demanded, her eyes flickering down to my lips, still slick with lake water. "Whether or not you infuriate me is beside the point. You're always on my mind, Laura, playing over and over again like a record."

My hand drifted up to rest on her wet shoulder. Positioned like this and drifting freely in the water, it was almost like we were dancing.

"I admit you're often on mine," I said softly, searching her face for some trace of irony, some indication that this was all an unkind joke. To my terror, I saw nothing but earnest desire.

"Let me taste you again," she said, her breath warm on my collarbone as she leaned in closer. "Just a little bit."

So that was her play. She was desperate for blood, and I was her chosen victim for the night. Why else would she have brought me out to this secluded location and taunted me into undressing with her? I didn't know whether to be flattered or insulted. I didn't know enough about vampires to know if her interest in me was purely culinary, or if it spoke to some deeper fixation.

"If I tell you no," I said, rearing back slightly but keeping my eyes fixed on her face, "will you drag me underneath the waves and take what you want from me? Pin me down and sink your teeth into my neck?"

"If I had my way it would be you pinning me down, not the other way around," she breathed, her thirst making her honest. She pulled me tighter still, her fingers almost bruising my hips. She was stronger than she knew, I gathered.

"Gently, gently," I said, pressing back against her. If it

was a tug-of-war she wanted, I would give it to her. Especially now that I knew we shared such complementary proclivities for games. "Don't get overeager or I'm likely to deny you."

"Tell me what to do, then. Anything, Laura. Just tell me."

"Say my name again," I said, partly because that was the first thing that came to mind, and partly because I was half drunk on the sound already. I was new to giving orders to a partner, but I had always been a quick study.

"Laura," she sighed, letting her forehead fall forward to rest against mine. "Laura, Laura, Laura."

It sounded like I was touching her already, urging her towards the peak of pleasure. My skin pulled taut at the sound.

"Tell me this is real," I said, my voice thick. "Even if it's a lie, I want to hear you say it."

"I don't know what this is. But it's real. At least it feels real. I want it to be real."

"Then take what you need."

My breath caught in my throat as she leaned in, tracing her lips along the curve of my exposed neck. I tried not to tense up, knowing that doing so would probably make it hurt more. Strangely, I couldn't remember if being bitten by her in the catacombs had actually hurt. It was a sensation unlike any I had ever experienced, white-hot and overwhelming, but calling it pain wasn't quite right. Maybe I had just been high on adrenaline and terror.

S. T. Gibson

Carmilla floated closer to me in the water, so close her breasts pressed against mine as her arm encircled my shoulder. She laved my neck with her tongue, just once, but it was enough to set my every nerve ending ablaze.

"Carmilla," I breathed.

She bit down.

There was pain this time, a sharp sting that quickly melted into a warm, heady sensation that spread all through my body. Despite the dull ache at the wounded spot where she lapped and sucked, it was more than tolerable. I clung to her tightly beneath the water, and then her knee slid between my thighs in a mirror image of what I had done to her outside the party.

I dragged in a shuddering breath, and my eyes slid shut.

Then the crystalline silence of the dark night was broken by a shattering scream. A young woman's scream, high and ragged with terror.

Carmilla withdrew with a huff, her mouth smeared with my blood.

"What was that?" she asked.

"I don't know," I said, untangling our bodies beneath the water. "But we should go."

Carmilla nodded and we both paddled towards the shore. Despite our intimacy mere moments ago, she dressed with her back turned to me. Was she suddenly shy, I wondered, or was she uninterested in me now that she had gotten her belly full of blood?

The scream sounded again, spooking a nightingale in

the branches above my head, and now real dread settled into my chest.

Something was terribly wrong.

I shimmied into my slip and tugged on my clothes as quickly as I could, then followed Carmilla silently down the narrow footpath that led from the lake to campus.

I wasn't sure where we were going, but I felt sure that we were both possessed by a morbid curiosity that would not be slaked until we found the person who had been screaming.

As it happened, we found the body first.

CHAPTER EIGHTEEN

Carmilla

t was one of the upperclassman girls, a French exchange student who had tried to befriend me during my first week at Saint Perpetua's on account of both of us being foreigners. I had ignored her, rapt as I was with De Lafontaine, and she had never quite forgiven me. Yvette, I think her name was, or Yvonne.

She lay at an unnatural angle on the quad, bathed in the sickly yellow glow of one of the lampposts. Her impressively red hair was spread out around her head like a halo, but as I drew closer, I realized that all that red was actually a corona of quickly drying blood. From one side, she looked perfectly serene, a porcelain doll with her eyes painted open. From the other, I could see that her skull had been bashed in and her throat ripped apart.

"Jesus, Joseph and Mary," Laura said, crossing herself quickly.

The wind changed, and the sweet, acrid scent of blood wafted towards me on the air. My body responded immediately, my mouth watering, my new canine teeth sliding further from my tender gums. In my mind's eye, I saw myself descending like a vulture on the poor girl's body.

I fumbled for a handkerchief and clapped it over my nose and mouth, hoping to keep the beast within at bay.

"Are you all right?" Laura asked.

I nodded rapidly, taking one more determined step forward, then another. I would not be afraid. I would greet death like a friend, just like I had told De Lafontaine.

I crept as close as I dared to the body, crouching down to peer at the carnage. Taking her pulse seemed beyond the point, but Laura did it anyway.

"Dead," she pronounced, her voice thin.

I estimated we had only a few minutes before the entire campus swarmed the scene.

"That wound isn't clean," I said, fixing Laura with a heavy look. "Something tore through the skin."

"Almost like teeth," she agreed.

"Isis. Do you think . . .?"

"It has to be. De Lafontaine would never. And you were with me the whole time."

We had avoided talking about our excursion in the tunnels beneath Saint Perpetua's, in part because we were too stunned to make sense of any of it, and in part because the experience had been so traumatic, for both of us. Dying was no easy feat, no matter what the poets said, and Laura had watched the life slip from my eyes. I'm sure we would both like to forget what had happened entirely, but here was the terrible proof of what we had witnessed together.

Before we could say anything else, a light flicked on in one of the dorm rooms, and then another, and another. The distant chatter of girls floated towards us on the night air.

"We should go," Laura said, wrapping her coat tighter around her. She looked even paler than usual.

"You're right," I said, standing and brushing off the knees of my tights.

"*Carmilla*," someone hissed behind me. I barely had time to turn around and witness De Lafontaine stalking towards me across the grass before she had seized me by the collar of my dress, like a mother cat picking up her kitten by the scruff of their neck.

"You're hurting me!" I exclaimed as she dragged me out of the glow of the lamplight and into the shadow of a nearby tree. My feet scrambled against the wet grass, trying to find purchase.

"Wait! I can explain!" Laura said, wringing her hands together.

"Hush, both of you," De Lafontaine said, with as much ferocity in her voice as she could manage without raising it. "Get out of the light, Laura."

Laura scurried after us, so quickly she tripped and skinned her knees before sheltering herself under the branches of the tree. De Lafontaine pressed me up against the trunk, her grip on my collar merciless.

"I told you to stay inside! I told you not to go anywhere without my supervision, to avoid exactly this scenario! You couldn't wait one night more for me to take you out hunting, could you? You had to gorge yourself on the first pretty girl that crossed your path."

"Ms. D," I gasped, wrapping my fingers around her hands. "I didn't do this! It wasn't me!"

"You *stink* of blood."

"Let her go!" Laura cried, doing her best to wedge her body between De Lafontaine and me. I was surprised by her bravery; I would never face down our teacher like that. "She didn't kill that girl!"

"What do you know about it?" De Lafontaine spit.

"Because it was me she drank from. She asked, and I let her."

"We'll finish this conversation indoors," De Lafontaine said, looking warily over her shoulder. Already, a small troop of girls was making their way from the nearest dorm with blankets tossed over their shoulders and flashlights in hand. Lights were starting to come on in the faculty apartment building as well. "Come with me, quickly."

I wasn't one to argue with De Lafontaine on a good day, much less during a crisis.

I laced my fingers securely through Laura's and started

the trek back towards De Lafontaine's apartment. De Lafontaine looked back at us only once, her eyes falling onto our clasped hands and her eyebrows furrowing in consternation.

We took the fire escape to avoid being seen by the faculty members who were now streaming out of the building to witness the carnage. Thankfully, we weren't spotted. Once we were back in De Lafontaine's apartment, she banged around in the kitchen for a moment before putting the kettle on for tea. Then she pointed at the sofa.

"Sit," she ordered.

Laura and I did as we were told, settling down shoulder-to-shoulder. I didn't let go of her hand. She was cold to the touch, and there was a slight tremor in her fingers. Her hair was still dripping with lake water, running in little crystal droplets down her temple.

"It appears," De Lafontaine said, setting down two teacups of bracing oolong brew in front of us, "that you have been conspiring behind my back."

"Nobody is conspiring—" I began.

De Lafontaine held up a hand.

"Let me finish, Carmilla. I expressly told you not to go outside without my accompaniment. And then I turn my back for a moment and I find you gallivanting around with Laura, soaking wet and blood-drunk and standing over a dead body?"

I felt myself start to shrink in her presence, to shrivel

like a flower cut from the stalk, but then Laura spoke up, brave and clear.

"She was hungry, so I fed her. We had nothing to do with the body."

"Ms. D," I said, keeping my voice low and respectful even as I pressed towards the truth. "That girl, she was . . . brutalized. Something tore her throat out. And if it wasn't me, and if it wasn't you—"

"I know, I know," De Lafontaine groaned, pressing her fingertips to her forehead as though she had a migraine coming on. "I know what I've done. What I've unleashed. You don't have to remind me."

"I don't know, actually," Laura said primly. "And I would very much like to be let in on the story. With all due respect, Professor De Lafontaine, I have been shut out of all of this. You drag me underground and you show me a monster and you make me watch—" Her voice broke, and I squeezed her chilly fingertips. "Explain this to me, please. What's going on in this school?"

De Lafontaine pressed her thin lips together in thought for a long moment, then she produced a cigarette and lit it with her lighter, silver to complement my gold. She took a long, shaky drag, then fixed us with her gaze.

"You really want the whole bloody truth, do you?"

"Yes," I piped up. "We do. We won't tell anyone, Ms. D. We swear it."

"I know you won't," our professor murmured. "You're

loyal unto death, Carmilla. Laura, I admit I know you less intimately. Can I trust you?"

Laura nodded, her wet curls swinging around her face.

"I won't breathe a word. I just want to understand."

De Lafontaine crossed to the window, leaning against the sill and gazing outside. In the quad beyond her apartment, the police had started to swarm the scene, and were restraining crying girls and sending them back to their dorm rooms. She spoke without turning to face us.

"I was in love once, with a woman. It ended. I was left distraught. I chased her across countries, crawled on my hands and knees after her for centuries, seeking absolution. But she would never answer my letters or take my calls."

"Isis," Laura breathed.

"She made her way to America, but she found the rapid industrialization of the country too brutal to bear. She ached for a simpler time, and so she decided to sleep the sleep of the dead and wake into what she hoped was a kinder age. She began her slumber forty-three years ago, when her thrall, the architect who built this school, secreted away a resting place for her under this institution. I traced her to the school, then called in every favor I could to secure a position here. I've spent the last five years searching for her, unlocking every door, walking down every dead end. The architect didn't make those tunnels easy to find."

"Why take us, though?" I asked, swept up by the story.

It was intoxicating, to be brought into De Lafontaine's confidence once again. "You didn't need us to wake her."

"Actually, I did," De Lafontaine said, glancing over at us. She almost looked guilty. "I needed living blood to call her back. It's all that will bring a vampire out of a death-sleep."

"Why choose me, then? You could have gotten anybody to bleed for you."

"You trusted me," De Lafontaine said, ashing her cigarette. "That was enough."

Something about her pragmatism stung me. I had hoped that she would tell me I was special in some way, that my blood was unique somehow. But in the end, I was just the resource that was most easily available to her.

I fell silent, mulling over this harsh truth for a moment, and then Laura spoke up.

"Why bring her back, though? If she isn't ready to wake up and she hasn't been answering your letters, what makes you think she'd be happy to see you?"

The words were cutting, perhaps unintentionally so, but De Lafontaine didn't snap at her. Instead, she just smiled sadly.

"What won't we do, Miss Sheridan, when love compels us?"

"With all due respect, Professor, love seems to have very little to do with the way Isis is acting. She very nearly killed Carmilla, and for all we know she did kill that poor exchange student tonight. I've seen enough blood for a lifetime. I want this to stop."

"Keep Carmilla's and my company and you're likely to see buckets of blood yet," De Lafontaine said flatly. "As far as Isis's conduct goes, I won't apologize for her, but she's been asleep since 1925. She's scared, and she's alone, and she's starving. She's liable to gorge herself."

Laura blinked back fat tears.

"But people will die," she said.

"Death is our bedfellow. If you want to be a vampire's companion, you'll have to learn to sleep alongside it."

"People will start asking questions. There'll be an investigation."

"You're right about that," De Lafontaine murmured, pulling back the curtains and peering out the window again. "I've managed to go many years without detection, and I would like to maintain that equilibrium. The safest way forward is for me to find Isis and confront her. She's angry and she's lashing out, but I've seen her at her worst. I'm not afraid of her."

"I am," Laura said hoarsely.

"I'll only need a little bit of help from you and Carmilla to bring her under control. You do want to fix this, don't you?"

I seethed, staring at the patterns on the rug. Mere days ago I had opened a vein for her, laid down my life on the altar of her lost love, and now she wanted more. Not just from me, but from Laura, too.

"What are you going to do?" I asked, my voice like ice. "Use Laura as bait while you and I hold Isis down and stake her through the heart?"

De Lafontaine walked over to me then, tilting my face towards hers. I knew I was scowling, but I couldn't wipe the expression from my face.

"Don't hate me for the part you played in it, darling. I did what I had to."

I said nothing, just blinked back stinging tears.

De Lafontaine tucked a wet strand of my hair behind my ear.

"You're freezing. You both need a hot bath and then you'll feel more like yourself, I promise. We'll talk more then. There are fresh towels in the bathroom cupboard, and bubbles and bath salts under the sink. Help yourself."

With that, she swanned away to her bedroom, effectively putting a pin in the conversation.

"This is madness," Laura huffed.

"Maybe so," I said, suddenly feeling weary beyond my years. "But there's no sense starting a fight while stinking of lake. Come on, let's get clean."

⸻ ◆ ⸻

Ten minutes later, I was soaking in a hot brew of white rose bath salts and bubbles. Laura sat on the edge of the tub, picking bits of gravel out of her skinned knees with tweezers. I lounged naked in the water but she had elected to wrap herself somewhat more modestly in a towel, and the fabric barely covered her full breasts, her plump thighs. Her injured knees smelled faintly of blood, the scent wafting in the air and making my mouth water. I fought the urge to stare at her and instead looked down at my feet, bare and wrinkled beneath the water.

"There are easier ways to reach out to a lover," she muttered, half to herself as she worked, "than resurrection and murder."

"I've learned not to question her, at this point," I said, soaking a washcloth in the scented water before draping it across my forehead.

"But why?" Laura snapped, her eyes cutting over to me. She seemed suddenly embarrassed by her outburst, and went back to her work, her voice softer than before. "She isn't faultless, Carmilla. I wish you could see that."

"Laura," I sighed, discarding the washcloth and pushing up in the bathtub. I wrapped my arms around her middle, not caring that I was getting her towel wet. She didn't turn to me but she didn't pull away either, just let me hold her.

"Is this another play for my affections?" she asked quietly.

"When will you understand that none of this is a game to me?" I asked, my voice raw with emotion. "Come here, Laura. Look at me."

She sullenly arched her neck to face me, but that wasn't enough. I guided her body all the way around, so her feet dipped to soak in the water as she sat looking at me. I knelt before her in the soapy water, my elbows braced on either side of my hips.

I took the tweezers out of her hand and delicately began removing the gravel from her raw knees. The sensation must have been excruciating, for all the way she squirmed and winced. I tsked at her.

"You've got to be more careful," I murmured, dropping little bits of rock into the small bathroom trash can with a tink. "You're only human, Laura. You're delicate."

She huffed out a laugh.

"You were human once, too, and I didn't see you treating yourself with kid gloves."

"Yes, well, I rectified my humanity as soon as I could."

I kept my tone light, but there was a slight tremor in my hands as I set the tweezers down and began to daub at Laura's skin with a clean washcloth.

"The blood," she said, suddenly understanding. "It must be driving you crazy."

"I'm fine," I said, but my voice was thick. I wrung out the washcloth into the bowl at Laura's side until the water ran pink. "I can control myself."

"I don't want you to have to control yourself. Not around me."

I looked up at her with wild desperation, then hooked my fingers behind her knees. My thumbs dug into the soft flesh there, seeking her pulse, and Laura gave a little gasp as I tugged her forward on the edge of the bathtub.

She looked so perfect, from this vantage point. It was exactly how I had imagined her a thousand guilty times before, down to the rapid rise and fall of her chest, the flush in her cheeks.

I wanted to capture the moment in amber, to make it last for ever.

"Go ahead," she said softly.

I pressed my open mouth to the wound on her knee. Laura clapped her hand over her mouth to stifle a cry. Whether of pleasure or of pain, it was hard to say.

I circled her wounds with my tongue, a shiver passing through me at the tang in my mouth. My body flared to life, pumping blood faster towards my fingertips, to the secret spot between my legs.

Laura tilted her head back and closed her eyes. I lapped at her until both her knees were clean and slick from my mouth, then I rocked back on my heels and wiped my lips with the back of my hand.

"You can't understand how good you taste," I said hoarsely. "Like heaven."

"Heaven is far from where we are," Laura said, still a little breathless.

We never got a chance to follow this conversation to its natural consummation, because De Lafontaine rapped primly on the door.

"Get dressed, girls," she said. "The sun is coming up, and Carmilla and I need our sleep. Laura, you'll be missed if you don't make it to your classes on time."

"Let me have a quick soak," Laura said. I dutifully climbed out of the tub, wrapping myself in a towel and stepping aside. Laura dropped her towel and settled into the still-hot waters I had been steeping in moments before, and as I watched, she squeezed her eyes shut and slid beneath the water. She stayed like that for a long time, bubbles gathering in her eyelashes, her hair spreading around her face, and for a moment, I saw her as though in death. Death, that great leering chaperone who had separated us in a way so profound I don't think either of us truly grasped it, death which lingered in the air between us like a sour perfume.

"Please don't leave me," I whispered, while she was still under the water. My voice was so soft even I barely heard it. "Don't leave me alone with her."

Another strident rap at the door.

"The sun's nearly up, girls. I won't ask again."

CHAPTER NINETEEN

Laura

 armilla and I didn't speak for a few days after that, which drove me near to the brink of insanity. I had held her life in my hands, I had been her sustenance when that awful thirst gripped her, I had sprung the locks on that gilded box De Lafontaine insisted on keeping her in and I had given her back her freedom. If I had been infatuated with her before, our growing intimacy only worsened my condition. I couldn't stop thinking about her, about the dark and glittering world De Lafontaine had inducted her into, about how I was party to it all and yet an outsider at the same time.

One night a few days after the girl's body was found, I was stirred from sleep by an impatient rapping at my door. I tossed back the sheets and tugged my flimsy nightdress down over my thighs, then opened the door to find Carmilla standing in the hallway, resplendent in an inky jumpsuit and a black beret. She grinned at me, all teeth and mischief.

"Get dressed and meet me on the quad," was all she said. "Wear something black."

With that, she was gone, striding down the hallway towards the stairs. Feeling foggy and as though I might still be in some sort of waking dream, I wiggled into a pair of dark jeans and tugged on a black sweater bearing the stitched logo of my home parish. She hadn't specified what sort of shoes to wear, but I opted for my dingiest trainers, not knowing if we were going to be traversing treacherous territory. Ten minutes later I was out on the quad, my hair still bushy from sleep, not a drop of makeup on my face.

Carmilla wasn't alone on the grass. She was standing in a tight circle of three other senior girls, who were passing a glowing cigarette between them. When I approached, Carmilla held it out to me and I took a puff to steady my nerves. My nostrils were filled with the sharp scent of tobacco, laced with the earthy sweetness of marijuana underneath. Feeling daring, I pulled the smoke into my lungs and held it there, allowing the concoction to wear down the edges of my anxiety.

"What are we doing?" I asked, keeping my voice low in case a wandering security guard might overhear and shoo us all back into bed. It was nearly two in the morning, after all, and Saint Perpetua's observed a de facto 11 p.m.

curfew, plus quiet hours after nine. That had never stopped any of the girls from stumbling back from townie bars in the wee hours, though, and it certainly hadn't deterred Carmilla and me from causing a ruckus in De Lafontaine's apartment well after dark. But since the death of that poor exchange student, campus security had been on the prowl after dark, mostly to keep parents from yanking their daughters out of this "unsafe institution".

"Observing tradition," Carmilla said.

"You're sure she won't squeal?" one of the older girls asked, a blonde with an upturned nose that gave her a snooty air. I recognized her from De Lafontaine's seminar and knew she came from factory farming wealth, but I couldn't remember her name. As a matter of fact, I recognized most of the girls in the small gang, simply because they were among the lesser stars that orbited Carmilla's captivating center of gravity. The hangers-on that Maisy had so little respect for. I had memorized most of their faces during the early days of my obsession with Carmilla, when I had scanned for her visage in every crowded room.

"She's good for it," Carmilla assured her contemporary, taking one final drag of the spliff before crushing it under her heel.

"If you say so," the blonde sniffed.

I shifted from foot to foot. I had no idea why I was here, what had gotten into Carmilla to convince her to bring me along on this misadventure. Was this some sort of hazing ritual?

Another one of the girls, Miranda, the daughter of a Mexican diplomat, glanced at her watch. We had astronomy together and she was quiet in class, sometimes even napping through lectures, but now her eyes glittered with excitement.

"We should hurry," Miranda said. "Is everyone ready?"

There were murmurs of approval through the group, and then Carmilla began leading us all towards the upper-classmen dorm, affectionately nicknamed Ol' Louise by the girls who lived there. I had been inside plenty of times to visit Elenore, but there was something illicit-feeling about sneaking in under the cover of darkness.

"We've got to keep quiet," Carmilla whispered over her shoulder to us all. "Can't wake anybody."

We tiptoed through the front door, closing it as quietly as we could behind ourselves, and climbed single file up the stairs to the uppermost floor. Carmilla walked briskly and silently down the hallway, throwing glances over her shoulder to make sure there was no one awake to spot us, then ducked into the ladies' room. To my surprise, all the other girls followed her. I hesitated only a moment before shouldering open the door into the bathroom, wondering what we were getting up to. Some of the black and white starburst tiles on the floor were cracked, and the porcelain sinks were stained from countless girls' spilled hair dye, but the communal space still had a cozy, lived-in feel to it. It was markedly larger and better maintained than the freshman dorm.

"According to the graduate I talked to, the entrance should be just here," Carmilla said, pulling back the curtain to the single bathtub. We crowded around the tub, which was tucked behind a modest half-wall in one corner of the bathroom, and looked up at the ceiling panels. One panel, I saw, was slightly loose.

"Seems high," Miranda said doubtfully.

"Don't be a scaredy-cat," another girl put in, an incredibly wispy classically trained ballerina who spent her early mornings pirouetting in the exercise studio before class. She often wore her hair in a tight bun all day long, as though to remind us all of her true vocation. School, I knew, was simply a formality for her. "You go first then, Edith," Miranda shot back.

"Fine," Edith said, pulling her flimsy black cardigan tighter around her white arms. "I will."

"I'll give you a boost," Carmilla said, squatting down and latticing her fingers together into a makeshift stirrup.

Edith looked a little wary, but she placed her foot firmly in Carmilla's grasp and let the other girl hoist her up towards the ceiling. With a dainty grunt of exertion, Edith popped open the ceiling tile, revealing a dark hole that must have connected to some sort of attic space. Ol' Louise was the first building constructed on campus, and it featured an ancient bell tower that had once been used to wake the students and send them scurrying to class. I had never heard the bell ring the entire time I was at Saint Perpetua's. I assumed it was broken, or inaccessible.

Apparently, I was wrong.

"Up you go," Carmilla said, and gave one final shove to help Edith up through the opening. In seconds, the tiny girl had disappeared into the dark. For a long moment, there was no sound, and we all stared up at the hole as though it had eaten our classmate. Then a skinny arm was thrust out of the ceiling, and Edith appeared at the edge of the opening, ready to help up the next girl.

"It's wild up here!" she exclaimed, a silly smile on her face. "You have got to see this."

"Laura, you're next," Carmilla said, offering me her makeshift step. Immediately, my face got hot. Edith was a slip of a girl compared to me, and I was suddenly self-conscious about my wide hips, my soft tummy. I was heavier than Carmilla, which meant I was definitely heavier than Edith.

"You all go," I whispered back. "I'll stand watch."

"Don't be stupid," Carmilla replied. "Get over here."

Letting out a sigh, I delicately placed my trainer-clad foot in her hands. I expected her to crumble under me, but when I put my weight down, I was catapulted towards the ceiling instead. Surprised by the sudden movement, I let out a squeak and grabbed for Edith's hand. She clasped her fingers around my wrist and tugged hard, and with a little undignified wiggling, I was pulled up into the attic space. For a long moment there was nothing but darkness, the scent of dust and damp, and the sound of Edith breathing beside me. But then Miranda was propelled through the opening, and she had the foresight to bring a flashlight.

When she clicked it on, I saw that we were in a long, low space, with ancient floorboards beneath our knees and the exposed beams of the roof above us. The ground was littered with paraphernalia of girls past: abandoned hair ties, candy wrappers, crumpled newspapers bearing dates as far back as the twenties, empty glass flasks of cheap alcohol. Miranda swept the flashlight down the long corridor of the attic space, illuminating a rickety wooden staircase at the far end of the room, leading up towards the bell tower.

"Give me a hand," someone said from below, and I leaned over the hole in the ceiling to help the snooty blonde girl up. Between Miranda and me, we were able to haul Carmilla up through the opening last. Once we were all safely inside the attic and the ceiling tile had been replaced, effectively disguising our crime, we grinned breathlessly at each other in the dark, high on adrenaline and a shared secret. I felt at once part of something bigger than myself, as though I had been inducted into a secret society of blithe girls fueled by nothing more than poetry and jazz cigarettes.

We carefully traveled across the creaking floorboards, and I prayed that they wouldn't give way beneath us. But the floor held fast as we approached the staircase, with Miranda and her flashlight leading the way.

We climbed single file up the old staircase, which led

up into the bell tower itself. There wasn't much room to stand, except for on a thin walkway that circled the grand old bell, which was chipped and covered in ancient dust. I marveled at the bell, wondering when the last time it had been rung was. As I got closer, inching along the walkway and pressing up against Edith to make room for Carmilla, I could see that countless classes of seniors had carved their names into the bell, along with their graduation year. It was completely covered in the loving scrawl of the girls who had come before us.

Carmilla produced a small knife from her pocket, grinning widely.

"Who wants to go first?"

They all took turns tattooing their names onto the bell with the pocketknife. It was difficult work, especially at the awkward angle that came from having to lean precariously far over the walkway to reach it, but everyone managed. Finally, it was my turn. Carmilla blew the metal shavings off the tip of her blade and held it out to me.

"You're up, Sheridan."

"I'm not a senior," I said, my cheeks warming. I was here only because of Carmilla's magnanimity, and I didn't want to overstep my place in front of the other girls.

"Maybe not now, but you will be someday. Somebody has got to keep the tradition going with the rising class. That's your job now."

Her dark eyes shone with a strange fervor in the glare of the flashlight, and I took the knife from her with steady fingers. Leaning as far as I could over the walkway without toppling down into the belly of the tower below, I painstakingly carved my initials into the bell. I left off my graduation year, promising myself that I would return as a senior with a whole new crop of girls, the friends I was determined to make, and leave my triumphant mark then.

When I had finished, Carmilla swung an arm over my shoulders, and Edith gave a cheerleader whoop of delight.

"Now what?" I asked, wondering if we should make ourselves scarce before someone discovered us.

"Now," Miranda said with a smirk, dropping the small backpack she carried onto the ground and unzipping it to reveal flavored nips, metal flasks that sloshed temptingly, and a handheld radio, "we party."

The rest of the night passed in a dreamlike haze. I can only remember it in snatches, putting away half a flask of strawberry schnapps, dancing with Miranda to The Yardbirds while Carmilla dealt out cards for a quick and dirty game of blackjack, laughing until I gasped at Edith's spot-on impersonations of some of our more eccentric professors.

We stayed ensconced in that private world for hours and hours, until the first blush of dawn started to creep across the sky. Carmilla threw open one of the windows of the bell tower and swung her leg over the sill, determined to crawl out onto the roof. I tried to pull her back inside, but that devolved into a fit of giggles and her pulling me out after her onto the shingles.

My stomach flip-flopped when I looked down at the trees five stories below, so I fixed my eyes on the sky, watching new light blossom across the horizon.

"You should get back inside," I said quietly, careful not to let the other girls hear us. "The sun is coming up."

"It should always be like this," Carmilla said, her voice a little hoarse from cigarettes and sleeplessness.

"Like what?" I asked. Our shoulders and knees were touching as we sat cross-legged side by side.

"It should always be senior year," she said with a conviction that surprised me. "I should always be twenty-one, with nothing but life ahead of me. It should always be sunrise, at the start of a new day."

"It will be," I replied. "You've stopped time, Carmilla, stopped yourself aging and dying. It will always be just like this."

"But it won't, will it? The other girls will graduate, and you'll go on to do whatever it is your heart desires. You'll have babies or get married or fly an airplane or write the next great American novel, but I'll be just like this, for ever."

"I thought that's what you wanted."

"I thought so too," she muttered, glancing at me from underneath her lashes. She blinked a few times, banishing the water gathering in her tear ducts. "But then I got what I wanted, and now I don't know what to want. I've always known what I wanted, Laura, I'm positively made of wanting. It's strange, to be sure of so little."

I leaned against her a little more, angling my body towards her. The sounds of the party winding down echoed behind us, but we could have been the only two people in the world for all I cared.

"Is there anything you are sure you want?" I asked softly.

Carmilla looked up at me then, a single tear trickling down her cheek. Then she cupped my face in her hands and pressed her lips to mine.

The kiss was gentle, as far as the kisses we had shared went. There were no teeth or blood or cutting words. There was only agonizing tenderness, so freely given that it made my heart ache.

I slid an arm around her shoulder and kissed her back, kissed her like this would be the last time. We melted into each other as the sun slithered up over the horizon.

"Does this mean we're . . . an item?" I hazarded.

Carmilla chuckled, rubbing her nose against mine.

"You and I are two sides of the same coin, Sheridan. I'm not sure how we were ever going to end up anywhere but here. Yes, we're an item."

Then she pulled away, shadowing her squinting eyes from the glare.

"So bright," she croaked.

I gingerly helped her to her feet.

"Come on," I said, brushing off her skirt. "Let's get you to bed."

CHAPTER TWENTY

Carmilla

———❖———

e Lafontaine summoned Laura and me to her apartment the next day with two vague letters in our school mailboxes, and when we arrived, we found her curled up on the couch, smoking a cigarette in a long holder while she graded poems. I tried to spy over her shoulder, but De Lafontaine swatted me away.

"Patience, darling. You'll get your grade on Monday just like the rest of the class."

Laura shifted from foot to foot, looking like an intruder into the scene.

"Laura, sweetness, come here," De Lafontaine said, cajoling. I sat in my usual spot at her side on the arm of the sofa. Laura wandered over, and De Lafontaine took her hand and pressed a jovial kiss to her wrist. "Good news, girls. I've decided to take you out into society."

"Society?" Laura echoed.

"Vampire society, of course."

An electric thrill ran through me. De Lafontaine was so mysterious about her own condition, the condition that we now shared, that I almost believed she was the only vampire within a hundred-mile radius. But to find out there were more of us, enough for an entire society? Well, it was beyond exciting.

"You're kidding, Ms. D."

"I most certainly am not. There's a gathering of, shall we say, like-minded people scattered across New England, and a small quorum will be meeting for an informal affair next Saturday in Boston. I'm friends with the hostess and can secure you both an invitation, if you wish it."

"I wish it!" I exclaimed.

Laura was more reticent.

"What does a room full of vampires want with me?" she asked.

De Lafontaine ashed her cigarette.

"It won't be just vampires in attendance, there will be companions and thralls as well."

"What are those?"

"Both indicate a human who willingly surrenders their blood for the nourishment of a vampire. A companion has an informal sentimental attachment to their vampire, while a thrall indicates a more established relationship and a long-term commitment. There's also usually some exchange of power with thralls, but I won't bore you with specifics."

"Are companions . . . romantic attachments?" Laura said, blanching a little bit.

"They don't have to be. Some attachments are a meeting of minds, some are purely sexual, other are true romances. Carmilla was my companion, weren't you, darling? A real mentor–mentee bond of the highest order. But I suspect there might be more than just friendly affection between the two of you, is that right?'

Laura opened her mouth and then closed it again, looking paler than a winter moon. I flushed hot, and snagged De Lafontaine's cigarette and took a long drag to cover up my embarrassment. She wrinkled her brow at my rudeness but didn't chide, used as she was to my childish antics.

"I'll take that as my answer, then," De Lafontaine said. "You must understand, girls, you can have anything you want in this life, anyone you want, as long as you respect the hierarchy of nature. Of predator and prey. Of elder and fledgling. Do you understand what I'm telling you?"

"Yes, Professor," Laura and I chorused, although I wasn't entirely sure I did. De Lafontaine nodded, then plucked the cigarette from me and put it out in a crystal dish before continuing.

"Grand. Then mark next weekend on your calendars, and dress sharply."

"I want you both on your best behavior," De Lafontaine said sternly as she slipped from the driver's side of the car. She was dressed in tails and a silk blouse and tiny white lace gloves that showcased the blue veins in her wrists. I had opted for a blood-red dress with a low neckline – a little on the nose, perhaps, for a vampiric debut – and Laura was wearing her family tartan skirt, a cashmere sweater, and shined black shoes.

"Laura, you're here as Carmilla's guest," De Lafontaine went on as she led us up the dimly lit street. Sleepy brownstone houses with neatly manicured postage-stamp yards lined the road. We had ridden much of the two hours from Saint Perpetua's to Boston in silence, Laura dozing against my shoulder in the backseat, as it was well past her bedtime. "So don't stray from her side. Unsavory things happen to unattended humans at these parties."

"Yes, Ms. De Lafontaine," Laura said with a little shudder. I laced my fingers through hers and gave a reassuring squeeze.

We walked until we came to a townhouse that, from the outside, seemed soundly asleep. It took closer inspection for me to notice that the windows were not indeed dark but were rather hung with heavy curtains, and that the faint sound of tinkling glass and laughter could be heard through the front door.

"Chin up, Carmilla," De Lafontaine said, pressing a flat palm between my shoulder blades to straighten my spine. "You carry yourself with dignity here."

And with that, she was knocking on the door.

The door cracked open, revealing an athletically built man with slicked-down black hair and an impressive mustache. He wore a widely cut pinstriped suit and smoked a cigar while he surveyed us.

"Evelyn," he said in an Italian accent, puffing on his cigar. "We weren't expecting you."

De Lafontaine smiled at him in a way that showed her teeth, resting one hand protectively on my shoulder.

"I hope my invitation still stands."

"Always. And who's this?" He nodded down at Laura, giving a little smile that didn't quite reach his eyes. They were dark as night and rimmed in kohl, like a cabaret master of ceremonies.

"My name is—" she began, her Southern manners not failing her for an instant.

"Laura Sheridan," De Lafontaine said primly, patting Laura's curls like she was a well-trained Pomeranian. "She's my protégée's companion. This is Carmilla Karnstein, of the Austrian Karnsteins. This is to be her debut."

I gave a boyish little bow at the waist, but the guard at the door didn't seem impressed.

"You chose quite the crowd of sharks to introduce someone newly sired to," he said with a laugh. "But I won't turn anyone of Evelyn's away. You're a favorite guest of our host, you must know that. And it's been so long since anyone's seen you."

"The trials and travails of academia are engrossing."

"Well, you're all very welcome. Please, come in."

"Thank you, Fabrizio," De Lafontaine said. "Shall we?"

Fabrizio stepped aside and ushered us into the house, which was soporifically warm and smelled strongly of orchid perfume, cherry wine, marijuana, and a strange tang of metal underneath. The walls were hung with velvet tapestries and oil paintings that seemed ancient to my untrained eye, swirling landscapes and unsmiling portraits. My ears pricked up at the sound of conversation and, if I wasn't mistaken, moans of pleasure coming from deeper inside the house.

We followed obediently as De Lafontaine led us through a door strung with beads and into the front room, which was outfitted with lavish furniture. Floral upholstery and carved mahogany fixtures added a touch of old-world elegance to the otherwise modern environs. A rock and roll record was spinning on the turntable, filling the room with driving guitars, rattling tambourines, and the eerie vocals of Jefferson Airplane.

There were half a dozen people in evening dress gathered around a round table, playing an animated game of cards with a heap of foreign cash and jewelry in the middle of the table. A pair of women sat on a chaise longue in front of a smoking blue glass hookah, the blonde's teeth buried deep in the brunette's neck while the brunette's head lolled back as though in ecstasy. Near a divan in a shadowy corner, a young man and a young woman knelt between the spread legs of an older man, alternately kissing each other and . . . *Oh*.

Laura swallowed hard and averted her eyes when she realized what they were doing.

Virgin, I thought affectionately.

De Lafontaine headed for the merrily crackling fireplace at the head of the parlor, in front of which a beautiful woman with brown skin, bright black eyes, and raven curls sat in a wingback chair. Unlike her guests, who wore clothes on the cutting edge of modernity, she was wearing an impeccably maintained Edwardian evening gown trimmed in petal-pink lace. Fabrizio was standing at her side, leaning down to whisper something in her ear.

"Evelyn's here?" she said in a crisp soprano, then turned to face us.

"It's a pleasure to see you again, Magdalena," De Lafontaine said, stepping forward to take our host's offered hand and drop a kiss to the knuckles. Magdalena gave a sly smile, availing herself of a paper fan that wafted the scent of cardamom and mandarin over to me.

"The pleasure is all mine," she said. "We'd thought you'd given up society. Who have you brought with you tonight?"

"This is Carmilla Karnstein, one of my star pupils, and her companion, Laura Sheridan. Laura is a talented poet in her own right."

Magdalena's eyes glittered with interest.

"You've got the scent of the freshly reborn on you,"

she said, holding out a hand to me. "Come here so I can have a closer look at you."

I obeyed, stepping forward into the glow of the fireplace. Magdalena lightly held my face and turned it this way and that, taking me in from every angle. Her touch was gentle and clinical, like the kindest nurse.

"An extraordinary beauty," she pronounced. "And an extraordinary mind, I'm sure, if our Evelyn has taken an interest in your education."

"Thank you, ma'am."

"Oh, please call me Magdalena. Now you listen to me, dear Carmilla. This house and everything in it is your Elysium. The laws of men and God do not apply here, so long as you abide by our simple mantra: respect the privacy and pleasure of your contemporaries. Can you do that for me?"

"I think I can, Magdalena."

"Beautiful. Now, let's have a look at that companion of yours."

Laura stepped forward as bidden, and even dropped into a little curtsy in the presence of this regal woman. Magdalena was so clearly out of another era, perfectly at home in her silk and chiffon. She took Laura's hand between her own, turning her wrist up so she could admire the latticework of veins beneath the skin.

"A strong pulse," she said with such admiration that Laura blushed. "And such a beautiful Rubenesque figure. Men of my age would have been lining up to paint you,

Laura. You're welcome to sample all this house has to offer, so long as you abide by our rules for guests. You mustn't breathe a word of what you see here to anyone else, and you must ask Carmilla's permission before letting anyone else drink from you."

"Oh, I wouldn't let anyone else drink from me," Laura said quickly.

A little smile touched Magdalena's rouged lips. "We'll see how you feel by the end of the night. Please, have a refreshment. The younger set still have a taste for spirits, but we're not in the habit of keeping food out, I'm afraid; it doesn't agree with us by and large. If you get hungry, just let Fabrizio know and he'll conjure something. We wouldn't want you fainting away, would we?"

Magdalena gestured towards the room's bar cart, which sported a modest collection of liquor.

"Enjoy the party, duckies!" Magdalena said, clapping her dainty hands together as though we had made her night simply by arriving. De Lafontaine lingered at her side a little longer, leaning down to speak in low tones near her ear, but Laura and I were turned loose to enjoy the rest of the party.

CHAPTER TWENTY-ONE

Laura

———◆◆◆———

armilla and I were left entirely unsupervised, which was a rare treat after months of living under the watchful eye of De Lafontaine.

We wandered from room to room, the lovely and ferocious faces of the guests blurring together as my champagne flute sweated in my hand.

Carmilla absolutely glowed under the curious attention of Magdalena's guests. She beamed, her cheeks pink as a rose, and introduced me proudly to everyone who made our acquaintance.

"This is the magnificent Miss Laura Sheridan," she would say, sweeping her arm towards me gallantly as she showed me off to various vampires and their human companions and thralls. The humans tittered over me and petted my hair, and the vampires were all courteous to me, some kissing my hand in an antiquated style or offering me a firm handshake, but I warmed under the hungry curiosity in their eyes nonetheless. I had never been so sure that a roomful of people wanted to devour me, perhaps in more ways than one.

In the parlor, a dark-skinned human girl no older than me giggled as a middle-aged vampire woman knelt before her, lapping up the blood trickling from twin punctures on her wrist. In the den, a lithe young person in a velvet turban and a silk kimono did a sinuous dance to the delight of a small band of vampire men sitting on velvet cushions. And in the dining room, a vampire meticulously hand-fed slivers of strawberry and shavings of chocolate to both his thralls, a pair of women who sat bound and blindfolded with smiles on their faces. My skin tightened at the sight.

This was, perhaps, a den of iniquity, unbefitting of a good Episcopalian girl like me, but it was also a place where I could be myself, letting all my affections and predilections roam freely, and that thrilled me.

The gathered members of this strange society conducted themselves without shame, carrying on their dalliances in the warm light of red-shaded lamps right in the middle of the room. There were all sorts of tender indecencies going on in the house, and after stomaching my initial embarrassment at the flagrant display of carnality, I slowly grew accustomed to it. The champagne helped, warming my belly and evaporating the shock in my brain until all I felt was soft-edged curiosity. And Carmilla's presence put me at ease. I was steadied by the warm, heavy weight of her palm against the small of my back as she steered me from room to room, and her occasional murmured observations in my ear made me giggle. I may even admit that the proceedings piqued my appetite so much that I began to wonder if Carmilla would be amenable to being pulled into a coat closet and ravished until she saw stars.

Carmilla must have noticed me pouting and throwing my eyes around the room, because she tugged me away from a conversation with someone who introduced himself as the Count of Saint Germain and guided me back towards the parlor where it had all begun.

"Shall I find you a quiet bedroom to entertain yourself in?" she teased, pinching my hip.

I tried to bare my teeth at her, but couldn't help laughing.

"Oh fearsome, fearsome," she said, smoothing my hair away from my face. "I shall call you my little lioness."

"You're a flatterer," I said, lacing my fingers through hers.

"The very best, to be sure. I've flattered my way into plenty of hearts, and a few strange beds in my time."

"And will you find yourself in a strange bed tonight, do you think?"

"If I'm lucky, for sure, or maybe even a familiar one."

Before I had a chance to volley back another innuendo, we were spilling back into the parlor, almost colliding with two men who were dancing with each other to the mournful electric guitar on the record player.

De Lafontaine had pulled up a chair next to Magdalena and was speaking in hushed, urgent tones. Magdalena's pretty mouth was tight, and there were twin furrows between her brows. She didn't seem to notice us as we drifted closer, as she was staring into the fire.

"All I'm asking for is the assurance of your assistance should the need arise," De Lafontaine was saying.

"You know very well I've come to your assistance multiple times before in this . . . pursuit," Magdalena said, spitting out the final word like it was an olive pit. "I was willing to indulge a broken heart, Evelyn, but this . . . this is beyond the pale."

"What wouldn't you do," De Lafontaine asked, teeth flashing in the firelight, "for love?"

Magdalena turned to face her then. I expected her to be angry, but her face was strangely serene, as though it had been schooled over years to not betray strong emotions.

"And what do you know," she said softly, "of the atrocities I've committed for love? Love is sacrifice, Professor. Whether it's you on the butcher's table or not, someone always bleeds."

She glanced over her shoulder at us, sending a meaningful silent look to De Lafontaine, and then her hospitable smile was back once again.

"Look at you both, flushed and smiling. Isn't youth lovely, Evelyn? Surely a commodity to be coveted. How are you enjoying the party, girls?"

"Very much, thank you," Carmilla said breathlessly, one hand gripping my own while the other grasped a crystal glass of sherry. Her second or third, I wasn't sure. I myself had put away two brim-full glasses of champagne and was enjoying the glossy film it laid over my world. I wasn't drunk, but I was loose enough to have forgotten my inhibitions.

"Your friends are so . . ." I grasped for the right word while Magdalena smiled indulgently at me. "Free."

"Someone very close to me once called this path a life without laws to chafe against. In that, at least, he was right." Her eyes fell down to our clasped hands, skimming over Carmilla's open collar, the smudge of ·lipstick she had left against my jaw. "Will you two be spending the day with us? We have plenty of open bedrooms."

"Oh no, we couldn't—" I began.

"Abuse your hospitality," De Lafontaine finished, shooting a pointed look at Carmilla. She hardly seemed to notice. Her pupils were blown, her mouth was stained red with sherry, and she was taking in the carnal proceedings with a hungry air. She wanted to swallow this night down whole, like a snake might do with a baby bird, and spit up nothing but bones.

I wanted, in that moment, to be that helpless little chick, cradled in the hot wet of her jaws.

"Oh, but you've barely tasted my garden of earthly delights," Magdalena said with a wry smile. "Stay a while longer."

De Lafontaine pressed her lips together tightly but said nothing.

And that's how Carmilla and I found ourselves sitting on cushions on the floor, observing as a large plush duvet was laid out in the middle of the room. A handsome young pair of lovers seated themselves on the red silk, a girl with corn-silk hair and a brown-skinned boy with the lascivious gleam of the undead in his eyes. I watched, my heart in my mouth, as he unbuttoned her dress to the waist and pushed the cotton off her shoulders, exposing her breasts to the warmth of the room.

"There's an artistry in our appetites," Magdalena narrated. "In the savagery of them, the tenderness. We hold life in one hand and death in the other. Look at the way he cradles her skull. He could just as easily snap her neck. And yet he waits for her acquiescence."

I looked. Really looked, refusing to deny myself the pleasure. I looked at her rouged nipples and her fluttering throat, I looked at the way the young man mapped the contours of her jaw with his fingers, tipping her chin back to expose her throat. Her hands wandered his body freely as he arranged her for the climactic bite, running across his chest before dipping lower still.

I stole a glance at Carmilla. There was a high color in her cheeks, and she was staring with amazement. There was something about the atmosphere that agreed with her, that illuminated some shadowy part of her I had yet only perceived in glimpses.

Silently, I reached over and laced our fingers together. Her skin was hot beneath my touch, her pulse thumping in her palm.

The couple on the duvet shed clothes like snakeskin. I blinked and then the boy was bare to the waist, and the girl had her dress pushed down around her hips and rucked up over her thighs.

She shuddered when he sank his teeth into her neck with such precision that it seemed almost surgical, if not for the way his grasping fingertips left divots on her creamy skin. The girl let out a little moan, unpinning her thick blonde hair and letting it spill down her freckled back.

I stole a glance at Magdalena, who was watching the proceedings with an insider's appreciation, like an equestrian admiring dressage. De Lafontaine's expression was still pinched, but she had accepted a glass of brandy from Fabrizio, which seemed to put her more at ease.

When I glanced back at the couple, they had become even more entwined. The girl had tugged the boy's trousers down over his firm ass, and he rolled his hips against her as he drank, the muscles in his back moving fluidly. The record player in the corner skipped and then fell silent, and then one of the partygoers watching the display stood up casually to flip the record.

A warm blanket of smoky vocals settled over us all as the girl on the duvet parted her knees for her partner and let him slip inside her.

The lovers moved together with unhurried languor, as though they had all the time in the world and no audience to speak of. I shifted in my seat, trying to alleviate pressure from the throbbing between my legs. I stole a glance at Carmilla, who was squirming similarly. Her nipples were firmly peaked beneath the thin fabric of her dress.

What sort of wanton creatures were we becoming?

The boy lapped blood from the girl's neck, pressing a kiss to the punctured skin the way a mother might kiss a child's skinned elbow. The girl giggled, nipping at his earlobe as he thrust deeper inside her. Then his eyes cut across the room to where we were sitting. He smiled lazily at Carmilla, who arched an interested eyebrow at him.

"I think he fancies you," Magdalena said, no different than if she were observing a schoolyard crush. "You may go to him, if you wish."

Carmilla pushed up on her knees, casting only the most cursory glance to De Lafontaine, who shook her head almost imperceptibly. Carmilla merely tossed her hair and handed me her glass, then padded over to the center of the room and sat down on the corner of the duvet. She perched so primly, with her knees pressed together and her ankles crossed, as though she were watching an instructional film, not public sex.

A tight, hot feeling coiled through my stomach. Lust, surely, chased with the heady liquor of jealousy.

The boy disentangled himself from his partner. He took Carmilla's hand and pulled her gently closer. She knelt beside him and he very softly, almost shyly, pressed his lips to the hollow of her throat. She hummed low with pleasure, and the sound dropped right into the pit of my stomach.

Carmilla, ever the bold one, wrapped her fingers around his firm length. The boy gasped and then chuckled as she stroked him. My heart beat faster and faster in my chest, threatening to burst through my sweater and get blood all over everything. I was aroused and confused and delirious with possessive greed.

I wanted to put a stop to the proceedings immediately. I never wanted them to end. We may have agreed on being an item, but Carmilla and I hadn't even come near the discussion of going steady. It would be unfair for me to hold her explorations against her, no matter how much watching them made me burn.

The boy pressed his fingers beneath Carmilla's chin and guided her face down to the girl's, easing her into a sweet, smiling kiss.

That shattered something inside me.

I stood up suddenly, accidentally toppling Carmilla's glass of sherry over onto the undoubtedly expensive rug. Fabrizio appeared with a butler's efficiency, washcloth in hand, but I barely saw him. I was walking towards the duvet, staring at Carmilla kissing someone. Kissing a girl.

Another girl.

"That's enough for now," I said, my voice quiet but leaving no room for argument. I tried to summon the same self-assuredness that had overcome me when I had pushed Carmilla up against the bricks outside the Halloween party. It glimmered just out of my reach, as though teasing me for my own shyness.

The boy gave me a slightly irritated look but dutifully removed Carmilla's hands from his body. The girl on the floor blinked, a little dazed, as Carmilla broke their kiss.

"Your name?" I asked the boy. My fingers were trembling with nerves, so I balled them up at my sides. If I stopped to think about what I was doing at all, I would surely come to my senses and crumble under the embarrassment.

"Ezra," he said, wiping his mouth with the back of his hand.

"And yours?" I asked the girl.

"Susan."

I turned to Carmilla, pushing her dark hair out of her face. She had a wild look in her eyes, like she could kiss me or bite me at any moment.

I loved it.

"You can have anything you want," I said, "but you'll have it on my terms, do you understand?"

"Yes, Laura."

"Good. Now," I took a shaky breath, trying to steady myself, "kiss Ezra. I want to see that."

As though proving her devotion to me, Carmilla moved with no hesitation. She nudged her nose against Ezra's, coaxing his mouth open with her lips. He moaned softly, then threaded his fingers through her hair and pulled her closer.

"Good," I said. Fabrizio was circling the room with a gleaming brass case of Embassy cigarettes, and I took the one he offered and lit it on the flame he extended. Smoke left my mouth in a curl as I watched the singular focus of my obsession kiss someone else right in front of me. The sight was strangely exhilarating, infuriating and liberating in the same breath.

"Take your time with him," I said, making it up as I went along. It seemed like something one of my erotica heroines would say, and it felt good, giving orders, so I continued to improvise. "And touch her while you kiss him."

Obediently, and perhaps with more enthusiasm than I had anticipated, Carmilla reached out and circled her fingers around the little pink bud between Susan's legs. Susan's head fell back with a sigh. Time slowed to a crawl. Around us, partygoers tittered and smoked and carried on private conversation, but all I could see was Carmilla. Beautiful, brutal Carmilla, with her dress open at the throat and her wet lips parted eagerly. Every atom in my body ached to reach out to touch her, but in the end, I was nothing if not a coward.

"Keep going," I said, my throat dry, my fingers still shaking as I knotted them into my skirt. I could practically feel the heat wafting off their three bodies.

Ezra's wandering hands made quick work of the tiny

velvet buttons running down the front of Carmilla's dress, and soon the entire room was treated to the sight of her pink silk brassiere. I wondered if her panties would match again, if she would let Ezra strip her bare right there in the middle of the parlor. I wondered if I could stand the sight, or if it would drive me as mad as Cassandra.

Carmilla kissed Ezra again, teasing light kisses that left him short of breath. Then she pressed two fingers inside Susan, curling those digits in a way that made the other girl arch her back off the ground.

My skin was on fire, my head buzzing as though my brain was nothing more than a hornets' nest kicked to the ground.

Carmilla's eyes cut over to me, electric in the dark. I couldn't parse the strange gleam I saw there. Was it mere lust, or reticence, or something more?

"Carmilla," I said, my voice firm. I expected another order to follow, but my voice was suddenly small and hoarse. I felt like I was treading water in honey, slowly being drowned in sweetness, and the waves were closing over my head.

I was losing control, and that terrified me.

I dragged a breath into my lungs, then another. I couldn't breathe, all of a sudden. All I could hear was Susan's little mewls of pleasure and my own heartbeat in my ears, thundering deafeningly loud.

"Laura," Carmilla said, stepping out of her role as silent

muse surrendering to my artistic vision. It was like watching a sculpture come to life. "You don't have to do this."

"I don't know what you mean," I huffed as Ezra kissed Carmilla's neck insistently. Had the room been so hot mere moments before? I wanted to strip off my sweater and socks, throw open a window and gulp down the night air.

Carmilla dropped a small, almost apologetic kiss to the golden curls between Susan's thighs. When she faced me again, her eyes were searingly clear.

"No more games. This is about us, you and me."

Ezra and Susan shared a private glance, and seemed to understand one another. They gathered up their clothes and disappeared somewhere deeper in the house to continue enjoying each other. I was left with Carmilla in all her red-cheeked glory.

She crawled slowly across the duvet to me, as though I was a mare that might startle. Then she knelt before me, her knees peeking out from beneath her askew dress.

"We're long overdue for this," she murmured. "Do you want to try and find an empty bedroom?"

I slotted my fingers into her hair, just as I had wanted to do for so long, and tugged. She stared up at me, her lips gleaming from Ezra's kiss, a high color rising across her chest.

"Why wait?" I said, surprising even myself. If I had come this far, certainly I could take things one step farther.

Carmilla raised her eyebrows, but she didn't pull out of my grasp.

"But you've never . . .? Not with anyone?"

"I don't care where we are, or who's watching." I lowered my voice to a whisper, pressing my forehead to hers. "I want it to be with you."

I released her, my heart hammering in my chest. She could have done anything at that moment. She could have stormed off, or thrown her head back and laughed at me, or gently explained that she wasn't interested. Any one of those contingencies might have desolated me. But instead, she leaned forward and kissed me.

I dissolved into her. My hands moved of their own accord, sloughing off the remains of her dress, and she made short work of the zipper on my skirt. With her help, I shimmied out of my sweater until we were pressed together, my softness against her stark angles. I was dimly aware that the room was descending into further debauchery around us, that clothes were being shed and that bodies were melding together, but I didn't care.

I felt like the burning sun at the heart of the universe, the white-hot center of gravity, and Carmilla was every orbiting star. She was the velvety expanse of space wrapping around me, the kiss of asteroid dust against my exposed skin.

Perhaps Carmilla had been right, that day in the library. Maybe I was a bit of an exhibitionist.

I helped her out of her silky panties (they did match,

God) and laid down on my stomach before her, hooking her thighs over my shoulder. And then, without a single thought to the consequences, I licked the sweet heat between her legs.

Carmilla let out a sharp whimper, as though she had been pierced. I lost myself in the sensation of her, in the scent, in the taste. She was acidic and sweet, like under-ripe fruit sprinkled with salt, and she was perfect. I trailed worshipful kisses over every inch of her, doing my best to follow the rise and fall of her breath, the growing sounds of her pleasure. I felt certain that I could perish like this, suffocated by her thighs, and die perfectly happy.

And then, sooner than I expected, Carmilla dug her fingers into my shoulders and let out a little sob of ecstasy. Her thighs trembled under my hands, but I didn't stop suckling and kissing her until she was entirely spent.

"Laura," she breathed, and then I was being pulled up towards her, wrapped in her arms. At some point, the electric lights in the room had been put out, and now we were lit only by firelight. A small mercy from our host, perhaps, to create the illusion of privacy. The illumination gave her skin an amber glow, and I couldn't believe that she was really underneath me, flushed and smiling with sweaty curls sticking to her forehead.

"Will you let me return the favor?" she asked wryly.

Before I had any chance to respond, Carmilla had

pushed me back and was tugging down my high-waisted underwear. I squirmed underneath her touch, suddenly uncomfortable. I didn't like my stomach being exposed to anyone, certainly not someone so effortlessly beautiful.

"It's all right," she said softly, kissing my nose like we were best friends, like she had known me her whole life. "I love looking at you, Laura. There's no need to be shy."

I took a deep breath and decided, against all odds, to trust her. I let her undress me until I was totally naked, and then she discarded her bra as well and lay down against me, skin to skin.

"Show me what feels good," she said, then slipped her fingers between my slick folds.

I gasped and then lost myself entirely to a warm delirium. Carmilla stroked me languidly and then with more insistence, nudging open my knees.

"Let them see you," she breathed in my ear. "You're so gorgeous like this."

I did as I was told, my stomach trembling at the thought of being watched by so many people.

I very much enjoyed being a centerpiece, I realized. A gleaming apple in the eye of a room of apex predators.

I whimpered and keened as Carmilla worked me over, chasing my pleasure mercilessly. Just when I thought the experience couldn't get any sweeter, she slipped a finger inside me, and I made a sound so wanton that embarrassment flooded through me.

"So needy," Carmilla said, pumping in and out of me. "Will you let me hear you come?"

I didn't have to be told twice. By the time I finished I was writhing and had made a mess of the duvet, but she didn't seem to care. She was just beaming down at me like I was a revelation straight from the mouth of God, like my base animal nature was a miracle.

"We should do that again as soon as possible," she whispered, and then kissed me hard on the mouth.

The rest of the evening passed in a blur. Somehow I ended up back in my underwear, and then someone, Fabrizio I think, passed me my sweater while Carmilla zipped up my skirt. I had kept my socks on but had misplaced my shoes at some point in the night, and Magdalena retrieved them from under the couch for me and even bent down in her ball gown to help me with the buckles.

I noticed that De Lafontaine's seat was conspicuously empty, and I wondered when she had left the room.

I helped Carmilla dress in turn, and then she let out a big yawn.

"We should find your chaperone," Magdalena said sweetly. She smoothed Carmilla's hair and then gave my hand an encouraging squeeze. She looked like a a graveyard angel in the candlelight, I thought, half-drunk on the taste of Carmilla. "No doubt she's at the gaming tables."

True to Magdalena's word, De Lafontaine was in the

kitchen, deep into a game of blackjack with three male vampires. One of them had a pretty young man balanced on his lap who kept pressing little kisses to his cards, as though for luck.

"Are you two quite done?" De Lafontaine asked frostily, gathering up her winnings and tossing down her cards. "The sun's almost up."

"Yes, Ms. De Lafontaine," Carmilla and I chorused, sharing an abashed look.

Magdalena was kind enough to walk us to the door, her hand hovering over the small of my back.

"You certainly came into your own tonight, little one." She leaned in closer, lowering her voice. "I think we have an affinity with each other. I also enjoy doling out pain and punishment, the thrill of control."

My eyes widened as she stepped back, but Magdalena merely smiled at me, as though we had come to some sort of understanding.

"Evelyn," she said, turning to De Lafontaine, "I wish you all the best with your star pupils. As far as your personal problem goes, I only wish that I could be of more assistance."

"I understand your position," the professor said curtly. She settled a hand on Carmilla and my shoulders. "Thank you for your hospitality."

"Always. Rest well, and good luck on the road ahead."

I had the distinct feeling they were talking around some larger issue, but I was too drowsy to interrogate the matter further. So, I said goodnight to Magdalena and followed De Lafontaine back out to the car, where I slid into the backseat and slumped against Carmilla.

A tense silence settled over the sedan as we raced the dawn back to Saint Perpetua's. De Lafontaine took the corners tightly and played fast and loose with the accelerator, her fingers tight around the steering wheel. She was still wearing that disapproving expression from the party, and her look only soured when she glanced back in the rear-view mirror and found Carmilla asleep on my shoulder.

I tangled my fingers together in my lap, digging my nails into my palms. The shame was creeping in like an ocean tide, rising up around me and threatening to swallow me whole.

What had I been thinking?

There had been people *watching*.

De Lafontaine had seen *everything*.

De Lafontaine threw the brake into place as we parked in the gravel lot behind her apartment. She looked over her shoulder at us.

"Carmilla, with me. Laura, I think it's time for you to go home. If you're quick you can get a few hours of sleep before your classes."

I looked over to Carmilla, who seemed so helpless in her exhaustion.

"I'm really not that tired, Professor," I said timidly. "Maybe I could help you get her upstairs and then—"

"Go home, Laura," De Lafontaine said, her voice deathly quiet.

I bit my lip to keep it from wobbling, then unbuckled my seatbelt, slid out from underneath Carmilla, and popped open the door.

"Laura?" Carmilla said, her voice slurred with sleep.

De Lafontaine merely shook her head at me.

So, I started my long, cold walk back to my dormitory, my eyes watering from the sting of the wind and the shame of what I had done.

CHAPTER TWENTY-TWO

Laura

———◆◆◆◆———

armilla didn't call on me for two days after that, and I was too racked with embarrassment to be the one to reach out. De Lafontaine canceled the seminar the final week before fall break to "give the class more time to write", which ensured that I didn't see my beloved even in passing. I seethed when I found out about the cancellation, and had to walk three laps around the track field just to calm down. De Lafontaine was icing me out, punishing me for my indiscretion at the party. Carmilla was always going to be her favorite pupil, her shooting star, and I had somehow tarnished her shine.

They were probably just fine without me, I thought miserably as I kicked rocks down the track. They were probably joking about my crude mannerisms in French while they shared cigarettes and planned hunting trips into Boston without me. I would only slow them down, after all; at the end of the day, I was only human. I had hoped to spend the break with Carmilla, leafing through poetry books while lounging together in bed or hiking the grounds beyond campus hand in hand, but now I saw that those dreams were delusions, so I fell back on earlier plans.

I was sweaty and windblown from my angry walking when I knocked on Elenore's door. She answered the door wearing silk, in a set of mulberry pajamas that matched the turban protecting her hair. Never mind that it was well past noon; she was the image of luxurious repose.

"Laura!" she exclaimed. "Golly, it's been ages since I saw you around. Girls were starting to whisper that you'd transferred to Smith. Is everything all right?"

I had told myself I was going to keep things cool and casual, but my earnest nature outwitted my best efforts once again.

"Not particularly. I'm sorry I've been such a rotten friend. I've just been so busy with schoolwork and life and—"

"Carmilla?" she prompted, not unkindly.

"Yes," I said, my shoulders sagging in relief. It was good to be understood by someone else, even for my faults.

"Well, come inside. I've got a pot of peony tea brewing. It will calm your nerves. Don't mind my saying, but you look a mess. Do you want a hairbrush or something?"

"Please."

I sat on the edge of Elenore's bed, brushing out my tangles with one of her wide-toothed combs as she poured me a drink. I was soothed by the sounds of tea splashing against china and a tiny spoon tinkling against the cup's rim. She waited until my hair had been fixed and my cup was half drained before posing her question.

"So what's up, buttercup? The rumor mill has all sorts of ideas about what you've been up to, but I'd rather hear it straight from the horse's mouth."

I stared down at the tea swirling in my cup. I had to proceed carefully, to protect Carmilla's secrets, and mine. My hand trembled slightly as I raised the cup to my lips and affected an unbothered air.

"Carmilla and I hooked up."

"Maisy owes me money, then. How was it? No, don't answer that, it's rude of me to ask. Let me try again: how do you feel about things?"

"In over my head, to be honest."

"Are you two going steady?"

"I thought we were, but now I see that I was wrong. There are other . . . factors in her life complicating things. I threw myself all in with her and I got . . . bruised. I feel so stupid for not being more careful."

"Careful doesn't really come into play when the heart's involved," she said, settling down at her vanity. It had once been a desk, but she had transformed it into a beautification station with various crystal dishes of powders and creams and a large mirror in the shape of the heart. "You don't love her, do you?"

I opened my mouth and closed it again. Elenore looked at me sympathetically through her mirror as she reached for a pot of moisturizer.

"Oh, you do, don't you? Poor thing. Love is the pits sometimes."

"I was ready to give her everything," I said, the dam of emotion breaking. "I wanted to spend all my time with her, I wanted to disappear together, I wanted . . . I wanted too much."

"You two need a little break, is what I think," Elenore said, smoothing the cream over her clear brown skin. It was strangely soothing to watch her work. It reminded me of sitting with my mother when I had been a very young girl and watching her make herself up, before she passed away. "Get out of your head, go somewhere new, kiss a stranger. Then, after the break, if you still want to work things out with Carmilla, you can give it your best shot."

"That's good advice," I muttered, knowing very well that I had nowhere new to go.

Elenore began plucking her brows, moving with mercenary precision.

"My offer still stands, you know. It's so boring in the San Francisco apartment alone by myself during the day, and going out at night is always more fun when you have a friend." She shrugged one shoulder, the picture of effortless cool. "You'd be doing me a favor, really."

Warmth bloomed in my chest and spread all the way to the tips of my fingers.

"I think you're one of the most decent people I've ever met, Elenore Robinson."

"Now don't let anybody hear you say that, I've got a reputation to protect."

We both giggled, slipping right back into the easy rapport of friendship.

———◆———

The flight to San Francisco was hot and cramped, but I was so nervous that I barely noticed. I drank soda water like it was going out of style and did crossword puzzles until we landed, and then stepped out into the balmy California weather. Seventy degrees in November; what a revelation.

My father had been more than understanding about my not coming to Mississippi for Thanksgiving, especially since I swore up and down that I would be home for Christmas. Privately, I thought he was relieved that I was finally making friends, and that I had made a good enough impression on Elenore to be welcomed by her family. He paid for my plane ticket and even mailed me a little spending money.

Elenore, who had arrived before me, picked me up at the airport in a stylish baby-blue Lincoln about the size of a speedboat. Her father's car, no doubt, since he owned a detailing garage.

She honked and squealed when she saw me on the curb, as though we hadn't seen each other mere days prior. I gave her a big hug when I slid into the passenger seat. Maybe, I hoped privately, everything was going to be all right after all.

Elenore was keen to hit the town, so as soon as I had dropped my bags off at her parents' apartment and dabbed a little powder on my nose, we headed to Haight-Ashbury. The district was crawling with young people. They spilled out of record stores, head shops, and music venues, and clogged up the crosswalks in groups of three and five. These California kids were so much less buttoned-up than my New England classmates. Everyone wore their hair long, even the boys, and the girls out here were fond of chunky sandals and prayer-bead necklaces and flowing tunics with out-of-this-world patterns. There were buskers playing mandolins on the corners, transients lounging in the shade of trees with their dogs at their sides, and protestors carrying painted signs boldly proclaiming birth control, voting rights, and psychedelics for all. A faction of students strode past us, arguing loudly amongst themselves about what sort of civil disobedience would be most effective in putting a stop to the war in Vietnam.

"Isn't it groovy?" Elenore asked, linking her arm through mine as we scurried across an intersection. She was wearing her trademark graphic eyeliner, along with a bright yellow micro dress with eccentric sleeves. I was both too hot and laughably demure in a knit cardigan over a pink skirt. "You can be whoever you want here, and nobody bats an eye. Come on, let's get some records."

Fresh off last year's Summer of Love, the atmosphere in the air was one of optimism and anticipation of something just out of reach, some grasped-for utopian moment that would transform culture from the inside out. It reminded me a bit of Magdalena's party; a world out of time where everything was permitted and nothing was taboo.

Time melted away as Elenore and I hit the shops. She turned me on to The Velvet Underground and I insisted she try out a Simon & Garfunkel record, then she picked up a stack of Temptations for her parents and a Monkees EP for her little sister, who had a big crush on Davy Jones. The Latino boy behind the counter had feathers hanging from his ears and flirted shamelessly with Elenore as he bagged up her purchases. She practically glowed under the attention.

I was struck, all of a sudden, by the normalcy of it all. Two friends walking arm in arm down the street, frequenting shops, gossiping together. It was almost enough to make me forget the strange, dark world of blood and fealty that De Lafontaine and Carmilla had drawn me into.

We went shopping for clothes next, and Elenore convinced me to pick up an itty-bitty skirt made of blue velvet. I insisted I had no idea where I would ever wear it, and she made me wear it right out of the store. I was grateful for her boldness, for her refusal to shrink from controversy or attention. She was the opposite of me in so many ways, and I adored her for it.

After we had burned all our spending money on ice cream and incense and clothes I could never wear home to visit my father in, we headed back to her parents' place. Will Robinson and his wife Amari welcomed me heartily, as did Elenore's little sister Eden, who interrogated me about my taste in TV shows before proclaiming that I was "nifty". Will was a man of few words but he smiled widely and hugged his daughters without reservation, which endeared me to him immediately. Amari was more loquacious. She told me about her work as a secretary for the chamber of commerce as well as a volunteer for the local Black Panther Party as we peeled potatoes and sliced carrots for dinner. We ended up discussing women's lib, a topic I was reluctant to talk about unless I felt totally sure that I wasn't going to be laughed out of the room for it, and she gave me some thoughts to chew on about strategies for centering the needs of low-income women in the cause.

We ate in true American style, on TV trays in front of a rerun of *I Dream of Jeannie*, and it reminded me so much of Sunday nights at home that I teared up a little bit. Eden, insightful beyond her years, passed me a tissue and a glass of juice to cheer me up. I could hardly believe I had gotten so lucky, to be welcomed into a family clearly full of love and mutual support. It made me miss my father terribly, and my absent mother more. But even more than the missing, it filled me with genuine, uncomplicated joy.

After the plates had been cleared and the channel had been changed to *The Andy Griffith Show*, Elenore poked her head into the living room with the phone in her hand, an almost apologetic look on her face.

"Laura, it's for you."

"For me?" I asked, a bit dumbfounded. No one knew I was in California except my father, and I didn't even think he had Elenore's address.

Elenore merely nodded, holding out the receiver. I stepped into the kitchen, lit only by the light over the stove, and Elenore left me to my conversation.

"Hello?" I asked, pressing the phone tight to my ear.

"You left," Carmilla said, and every ounce of my devotion came rushing back. My knees jellified, and I very nearly had to sit down.

"Carmilla?"

"You left and you didn't say where you were going." Her voice was high and strangely tight. I realized, with a pit in my stomach, that she was trying not to cry. "I had to ask half a dozen girls where you were and then a half a dozen more to get Elenore's home number. I thought . . . I thought you might have told me."

"I'm sorry," I said, lowering my voice. "It's just, I didn't think you wanted much to do with me after the party."

"What about how I acted at that party makes you think I'm anything less than devoted to you?"

I did sit down at that. I slid down the wall of Elenore's parents' kitchen and sat right on the tile, my knees pulled up to my chin. The curly plastic wire of the landline pulled taut.

"I don't understand," I said, because I didn't, because this was all too much, because this vacation had been about getting Carmilla out of my head and now here she was crawling back around my mind.

"Laura," she said again. She was talking quickly and quietly, as though afraid of being overheard. "I meant what I said on that roof. I want it to be you and me. I want a fair shot with you. So, if I've done anything wrong, I apologize, and I—"

"You've done nothing of the sort," I said, with a ferocity that surprised me. "You're a marvel, Carmilla, and I want a fair shot with you too."

"Then don't let me go. I need you to hold tight to me, do you understand? I'm afraid of losing myself."

"What do you mean? Has something happened?"

"I can't, not over the phone."

"Carmilla, you have to tell me if you're in any sort of trouble."

"It's not like that, it's just that she—"

"Who are you talking to?" De Lafontaine asked in the background, and my blood turned to ice.

"The student affairs office," Carmilla replied.

The line went dead.

Somehow, I managed to pull myself up off the floor

and hang up the phone. I turned to find Elenore leaning against the kitchen doorway, watching me keenly.

"Trouble in paradise?" she asked.

In response, I walked over and folded her into a tight hug.

"Someday," I said into the crook of her neck, "I'll tell you the whole of it. But right now, I have to protect Carmilla's privacy."

"Just be careful you don't put yourself in harm's way in the process," she said, rubbing a small circle into my back. "She's a tricky girl, that Karnstein. All lovely smoke and mirrors."

"I promise."

"We should get back in there. Just tell my parents it was your dad checking up on you, yeah? No need to make them worry."

I vowed in that moment never to forget Elenore's kindness, or her willingness to steward my secrets.

CHAPTER TWENTY-THREE

Carmilla

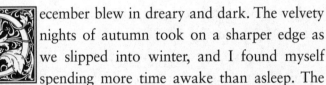

ecember blew in dreary and dark. The velvety nights of autumn took on a sharper edge as we slipped into winter, and I found myself spending more time awake than asleep. The dormitories emptied out during autumn break so I spent much of my time in De Lafontaine's apartment, curled up under a heap of blankets on her couch while catching up on my reading and drinking weak black tea. The drink didn't exactly agree with me, and it certainly didn't satisfy the gnawing hunger in the pit of my stomach, but it warmed me and reminded me of my girlhood in Austria, especially when served with a tipple of De Lafontaine's brandy.

De Lafontaine took my vampiric education just as seriously as she took my academic enrichment. She would draw the curtains, settle into her armchair, and lecture for an hour or two at a time. I, ever the eager student, took notes.

I learned that oral records of vampirism had existed since before the time of Christ, and that despite many old wives' tales about the first vampire, no one knew how we had come into existence. I learned how we grew more powerful with age despite growing more vulnerable to the sun and more intolerant of food and drink, and I learned that vampires could find no nourishment by drinking from other creatures of the night or from animals, hence our reliance on human prey.

De Lafontaine seemed to think vampirism was a natural aberration, a transmittable condition not unlike hereditary diseases. I thought this perspective stripped away some of the romance from this way of life I had so pined after, but I didn't argue.

"How many of us are there in the world?" I asked one night as I lit the taper candles stuck into empty wine bottles.

"I couldn't say," she mused, swirling her hair up into one of those effortlessly elaborate buns of hers. "Some vampires prefer to form small family systems and hunt together, but most of us keep to ourselves. I've met fewer than fifty other nightwalkers during my long life, mostly at dedicated gatherings."

"Like Magdalena's party," I supplied carefully. We had avoided discussing that fateful night altogether, mostly because irritation flashed in De Lafontaine's eyes whenever we came close to having that conversation.

"Yes, Magdalena is strangely social for a vampire, and she's the type to maintain a little household of thralls to keep herself company. She enjoys her pop-up salons, although I think she mostly does it to gather gossip and keep tabs on major players she wants to ingratiate herself with. She is, at her core, a politician. Did you know she helped put John Paul VI on the papal seat? Although to hear her tell it, she privately supported a much more progressive candidate."

"Did you ever keep a household like her?"

"No," De Lafontaine said, smiling at me across the room. The firelight danced on her face, making her prominent cheekbones even more gaunt. "When it was just Isis and me, I felt like she was all I needed . . . But then I met you, and I started to imagine building a family for myself, with you as a cornerstone. I've spent my life searching for a worthy protégée, and isn't it strange? In the end it was you who came knocking on my door. Like fate made flesh."

I smiled back at her, but the room felt suddenly hot and stuffy. I looked down at my notes so she wouldn't see how my smile faltered, and I underlined my last sentence so hard the lead of my pencil snapped.

"That's enough history for now," De Lafontaine said, yawning languidly. She tucked her feet up underneath her on her chair and retrieved a slim volume of Rimbaud from the bookshelf. "Will you recite for me, darling?"

I swallowed hard, then flipped open the book and began, with as much of a level voice as possible, to read "Ce qu'on dit au poète à propos de fleurs".

De Lafontaine closed her eyes and let the words wash over her.

I shaped the French vowels mechanically, but privately, my mind turned.

I was De Lafontaine's singular object of focus, her pet obsession, her clear favorite. I spent every hour breathing in her air, following in her rarefied footsteps. I napped in her bed, availed myself of her library, drank out of her china cups, dabbed on her perfume. Before Laura, it would have been the culmination of everything I had ever wanted. But now that my life had been pierced by the golden arrow of Laura's presence, I was rapt as St Teresa by her loveliness and light. I tossed and turned during the day, accosted by visions of her cornflower eyes and golden curls, imagining her laughing or tugging on my ponytail or spreading her milky thighs for me. My stomach twisted during the wakeful night, reminding me of the way I had been so careless with her heart at the party, how I had pushed us both beyond the boundaries of convention and decency.

I was miserably vexed by her presence, but I was just plain miserable without her.

It didn't help that I was hungry.

De Lafontaine took me hunting only once, and coached me through plying a townie boy with beer at the local dive, and then hurrying him out into the back alley for an illicit bite. I was stiff and awkward as we necked, and I did my best to dodge his sloppy kisses as well as his wandering hands. The bite itself was anticlimactic, but I was careful to hide the pinprick marks of my teeth beneath a hastily applied hickey. When De Lafontaine tried to congratulate me on my first successful hunt, I brooded in silence. He tasted awful, like cigarette ash and cooking grease, and I craved the sustenance that flowed through Laura's veins.

"What happens when we get found out?" I asked abruptly on the drive home. "You used to feed from me and I used to feed from Laura, and that was a closed circle. What happens when locals start realizing they're being drained?"

"We leave, of course," she said, as though it were the simplest thing in the world. "You and I, under the cover of night. Won't that be fun? We can pretend to be spies."

It did not, in fact, sound fun. Especially since it entailed leaving behind my books and my closet of couture clothes and my Laura.

"Oh," I said.

I didn't speak to De Lafontaine for the rest of the drive.

—◦—

I didn't expect to see Laura until the poetry seminar reconvened, but on the last night of fall break, as I was drowsing in De Lafontaine's bed, there was a knock at the door.

I smelled her before I saw her. All pressed powder and well-worn wool and strawberry-wine blood. I threw open the door and she threw herself into my arms, squeezing me tightly.

"Carmilla," she breathed, her sweet breath stirring my hair. "God, I missed you."

"I'm sorry I called," I babbled. "I just got so lonely here and I thought you didn't want anything to do with me, and I panicked, and—"

Laura silenced me with a kiss. One of our kind of kisses, firm and demanding. I parted my lips for her and let her devour me right there in the doorframe.

"Where's De Lafontaine?" she asked, barely breaking the kiss long enough to speak.

"She walked into town for cigarettes. She won't be back for an hour."

Laura kissed me again, and I melted into the perfect bliss of the moment.

Somehow we ended up in De Lafontaine's room, with Laura pushing me down onto the edge of the rumpled bed. I gazed up at her, all adoration and delight, as she looked down at me with an imperious air. She was so beautiful like this, like a queen out of a storybook.

"Undress for me," she said, in that tone of voice I could never resist.

This probably wasn't a good idea. De Lafontaine could walk through the door at any moment. But somehow, that only made it more exciting.

I started with my knee-high stockings, tugging them down over my calves and bare feet. Then I unfastened the pale blue ribbon from my hair and draped it over the bed frame. Laura's eyes followed the gesture, suddenly hungry.

An Education in Malice

"What are you thinking?" I asked, taking my time unfastening the buttons of my blouse. It was a billowing chiffon thing, cut for a taller woman than me, and I had filched it from De Lafontaine's dresser.

"Just something I've always wanted to try," Laura said, running her tongue over her bottom lip as though to taste the smudge of lipstick I had left behind. "Do you want to play a game with me?"

"I'm game for anything if it's with you," I said, letting the blouse slip from my shoulders. Laura stepped out of her Mary Janes, and the simple gesture sent a shudder up my spine.

"Lie on your back," she said, and I did as I was told. The familiar scent of lavender soap and well-worn cotton enveloped me. Laura kneeled over me, her knees digging into either side of my hips, and she looped the ribbon around my wrists.

"Too tight?" she asked, cinching the ribbon. The pressure was delicious, enough to make me aware of my own heartbeat and breath without pinching too much.

"Not at all," I said.

"Keep your hands there for me, sweetheart," Laura murmured, and then dipped her head and kissed me. I was so lost in the heady sensation that my hands drifted up of their own accord to caress her cheeks.

Laura broke the kiss and pressed my wrists up over my head with surprising force. I was dimly aware that I held very real power in this situation, that I could pin

267

her down without so much as breaking a sweat, but there was something so sweet about surrendering to her.

"Hands up, or everything stops," she said, a wicked grin on her face. She was an effigy on fire, everything I had ever only dared to dream of.

"I think I love you," I blurted.

Laura's expression softened, and she leaned down to kiss me on the forehead. Her touch was light, almost shy, in sharp contrast to her merciless grip around my wrists.

"I think I love you too," she whispered, then that mischievous expression was back. "But we'll see how you feel once I'm done with you."

I let my head fall back against the pillows, my eyes fluttering shut. Relief at being loved and the anticipation of being handled as though I was anything but pooled warmly in my stomach.

"Do your worst," I said.

—◆—

Forty-five minutes later, I was a trembling, sweating mess. Laura staunchly refused to let me touch her or myself, and I had maintained my valiant effort to keep my hands above my head. I had been kissed, bitten, and licked to the point of near delirium, but Laura snatched my climax back the moment it came into my reach.

"Please," I groaned as she dragged her fingers through the wetness between my thighs. "You *sadist*."

"I consider myself more of a disciplinarian," she said, circling my clitoris with her thumb.

"Did you pick that word up from one of your books?"

Laura's cheeks turned pink at being caught out, and she cut me off by pinching my thigh.

"What could I have possibly done to deserve this?" I said, barely able to string words together. The room was spinning, and I was fairly sure I could taste colors.

"All your little backhanded compliments and snide remarks those first months we knew each other? Don't think I've forgotten them."

"I didn't *mean* it, not really."

"Yes, you did," she said with a chuckle.

"Fine," I gritted out. "I meant it all."

Laura pressed an exploratory finger inside me, stroking my inner walls gently. I tossed my head, biting my lips. I needed more pressure, more force, *more*.

"Laura," I pleaded, "have mercy."

"The great Carmilla Karnstein, reduced to begging."

"Yes, damn you, I'll beg. I'll do anything, Laura, just let me—"

I never got to finish my sentence, because Laura started pumping in and out of me. I cried out, holding on to the bed frame for dear life, but I never lowered my hands below my head.

I came so hard I saw stars. A solitary tear trickled down my cheek, and Laura kissed it away.

"You're magnificent," she said. "All that rage and beauty . . . it's the stuff they write poems about."

"Can I put my arms down now?"

"Yes."

Letting out a big sigh, I hooked my bound hands behind Laura's head, pulling her into my embrace. I tangled our legs together and breathed in her scent, my mouth watering as my lips sought the pulse in her throat.

"May I?" I breathed. I was so overstimulated I could barely think straight, but there was still a needy ache deep inside me, to taste her, to devour.

In response, Laura delicately removed her Oxford shirt, which had somehow remained unrumpled for the duration of our game. I took a moment to marvel at her, the creamy skin, the generous curves, the pillowy décolletage peeking out from a balconette bra, and then I slotted my mouth over her jugular.

Bone-deep relief washed over me as her blood spurted into my mouth. I trembled in her arms as she tensed and then relaxed against the pain, offering up her life for mine.

How had I ever been able to survive without her?

I drank from her greedily, but I was careful not to take too much. I fed until my stomach stopped gnawing at itself, and then I released her. She looked down at me, her eyes slightly glassy with tears, or with love.

"Did you drink from anyone else?" she asked softly. "While I was away?"

I pulled her closer to me.

"I had to," I said, my voice barely louder than a whisper. "I was so hungry. I didn't know if you were going to come back to me. Are you cross?"

"No," she said, sounding pensive. "I don't think I mind if you feed from other people, so long as you always come back to me in the end."

"I would want you even if you weren't my blood donor, you must understand that. I don't want to think—"

"I don't. And I rather like being your companion, madam vampire."

I giggled, rubbing my nose against hers, and then I stiffened as a sound wafted in through the open bedroom window.

Slingbacks on gravel, the telltale sign of De Lafontaine returning. I watched Laura turn white as we both heard the jingle of keys in the main door lock.

"Get dressed," she whispered, as though De Lafontaine was already just a room away. I scrambled out of bed and started tugging on my clothes while Laura shimmied back into her shirt and then dashed into the en suite bathroom to wash her hands and fix her hair. We left the bedroom door ajar when we left the room, just as we had found it, and then draped ourselves with as much louche boredom as we could across the living-room furniture.

De Lafontaine walked in moments later, her dark hair windblown. She sloughed off her coat and raised an eyebrow at Laura, as though she were a naughty cat who had toppled over a vase while De Lafontaine was gone.

"Laura, you're back. I assume Carmilla let you in?"

"Couldn't let her freeze out there," I said, carefully blasé.

De Lafontaine nodded as she hung up her coat and tugged off her leather gloves.

"Hospitable of you. I'm afraid I'm fighting a migraine, girls, so if you wouldn't mind entertaining yourselves quietly while I lie down in the next room, that would be very much appreciated."

She breezed into the bedroom and Laura, who had been pretending to scribble in her daybook, looked up at me with wide eyes. Perhaps we had gotten away with something after all.

I stole a glance into De Lafontaine's bedroom from my vantage point in the armchair, and I watched as she kicked off her shoes and unpinned the studs from her ears and turned down the blankets.

Then, she paused.

Her fingers grasped the edge of a sheet, bringing the cloth up closer to her face. In the dim light of the bedroom, I spied two tiny droplets of blood on the white fabric, as stark as roses in winter.

De Lafontaine locked eyes with me, her gaze burning.

Then she shut the door, severing the connection between us.

CHAPTER TWENTY-FOUR

Laura

———◆◆◆———

lasses resumed. It felt strange to be going about such mundane tasks like homework and assigned reading when my entire world had been turned inside out mere weeks before, but I did my best to apply myself. The sentiment on campus was wary, edging towards paranoia, as the exchange student's death hadn't been neatly resolved by a quiet investigation administration no doubt hoped would be wrapped by the time break was over. Campus security took to prowling the grounds at all hours of the day, and a strict 9 p.m. curfew was enforced across the board, even for the professors that lived on campus. Girls caught out of the dorms after dark were corralled towards their bedrooms by well-meaning faculty and staff, and students took to walking to class in lockstep groups of threes or fours, as though numbers were any defense against a supernatural killer.

It was impossible not to notice that Carmilla had stopped showing up for her daytime classes, but De Lafontaine planted a rumor in the teachers' lounge that Miss Karnstein had fallen into a dissolute lifestyle of partying and late nights. She was taking the girl under her wing, the professor assured her colleagues, and would be personally responsible for her rehabilitation. The two were near inseparable after that, and could often be seen striding side by side across the quad after dark. Privately, I envied them, their synchronicity, their mutual understanding, but the jealousy was soothed every time Carmilla held my hand or pressed a kiss to the corner of my mouth. We had to be careful about how affectionate we were in public, but Carmilla was bold, and she often linked her arm through mine as we strolled to class, or sat so close to me in De Lafontaine's seminar that our knees touched.

Meanwhile, our secret meetings in our professor's apartment continued.

"Poetry is an outlet for the passions," De Lafontaine said during one of these private sessions. She had been reading to us from John Berryman's *The Dream Songs*, and I had been moved to tears by the melancholy in his words. "It reminds us of our humanity by allowing us to express all those feelings that polite society would deem inappropriate, monstrous even."

Carmilla retrieved a handkerchief from her breast pocket and dabbed at my eyes, then gave me a sweet kiss on the cheek. De Lafontaine stared at us as though we had committed some atrocity, as though tenderness was anathema to her.

Our professor snapped her book shut.

"That's enough lecturing for one day, I think," she said, turning from us and snatching up her coat. "I need to eat. I'm going hunting at the bars. I don't know when I'll be back, so lock the door behind me."

"But there's still an hour left of our time together," Carmilla said. She looked offended at being robbed of her precious time with De Lafontaine. I, for one, was relieved. I could only subsist for so long under De Lafontaine's exacting gaze, and she made me second-guess everything I did and said. It was easier to breathe when she wasn't in the room.

"And I'm hungry, Carmilla," De Lafontaine said, sounding suddenly tired. "You know very well I can't feed from you anymore, so I'll ask you not to begrudge me this. I'm sure you two can find a way to pass the time without me."

And with that, she was gone, the door swinging shut behind her.

"She's such a prickly pear sometimes," Carmilla grumbled, tossing her long legs over my lap. I ran my hand idly along her calf, watching De Lafontaine stride across the grass in the direction of campus from the living-room window.

"Well, I'm not going to sit around and wait for her," Carmilla said, standing suddenly. "Are you coming, or not?"

"Where are we going?" I said, already standing and reaching for my coat. Where wouldn't I go, if she asked me?

"Aren't you the littlest bit curious about what's going on down there?" she said, jerking her head in the direction of Seward Hall. "I haven't been able to stop thinking about it since . . . since that night."

"How much of it do you remember?" I asked quietly. I had largely avoided discussing Carmilla's death with her, as it seemed impolite.

"It's blurry, but I remember a coffin, and De Lafontaine standing over me, and a lot of blood."

"That was the general gist, yes."

"I've waited long enough for De Lafontaine to loop me in on what's going on. I want to find out for myself. Are you in?"

I took Carmilla's face between my hands and kissed her.

"So long as we're quiet and quick. And you must promise me to be careful. I almost lost you once. I couldn't live through it again."

"I swear it. And you must swear to me that you'll take care of yourself, too."

"Of course."

We crept out down the fire escape and then ran hand in hand across the rain-wet grass, our cheeks bitten red by the cold.

Seward Hall was locked up at this time of night, but

Carmilla managed to spring the front locks with one of my bobby pins, and we were careful to close the door behind us. Retracing our footsteps from Halloween night, we traveled down the staircase to the basement level and managed to locate the trapdoor after some grasping around in the dark.

The catacombs beneath the school were just as cold and damp as I remembered, but Carmilla's presence emboldened me. We maneuvered our way by the light of a small flashlight Carmilla had filched from De Lafontaine's closet. The sweeping yellow beam made the atmosphere even eerier, since everything outside its purview was pitch black.

"Which way was it?" I whispered, glancing behind me. I was starting to feel unsure about my ability to find my way back, and that frightened me.

"Straight ahead, I think."

"You're sure it wasn't to the left?"

"I died that night, Laura; my memory isn't the best."

I didn't say anything else as we crept forward, seeking that strange stone coffin. We hadn't discussed our ultimate aim, but I felt sure that if we could find our way back there, we would find answers to all our burning questions. What sort of creature had been entombed beneath Saint Perpetua's? What did De Lafontaine want with her? And was she really responsible for that grisly murder on the quad?

The corridors seemed to stretch on for ever, and I could

S. T. Gibson

hear scrabbling and squeaking, a sure sign of rats ahead. Just as I was about to firmly suggest that we turn back, Carmilla froze and grabbed my wrist.

"Listen," she hissed.

I listened. There, beyond the persistent drip of rainwater and the hammering of my heart, was the unmistakable low lull of voices.

I shot Carmilla a glance and she doused the flashlight. Together, we pressed on ahead, walking on tiptoe and feeling our way along the wall. We followed the voices around a corner, and then another, and then we were rewarded with the flickering of firelight in the distance.

We stopped at the mouth of the corridor, peeking as far as we dared into the room beyond. There, standing ramrod straight with her hands folded genteelly in front of her, was the monster who had attacked Carmilla all those nights ago. Only she looked much less monstrous now. Her face was still gaunt, her skin papery and sallow, but her hair was thicker than before, and her dark eyes were clear. She wore the shabby black dress she had been buried in, but she looked, for all the world, like a very sick young woman, not one who had been recently dead.

"You didn't do as I asked," she said. Her voice was low and resonant, like the ringing of a church bell.

"How could I?" a second voice said. "After all this time, you still ask too much of me."

The blood froze in my veins.

That voice. I knew that voice.

278

De Lafontaine stepped into the light of a taper candle melting into the floor, her hands stuffed deep into her jacket pockets. She seemed smaller, from this vantage point, less stately.

"How many girls have you delivered to me before?" Isis said. "I don't see why this one is any different."

"You know why she's different," De Lafontaine replied. Her expression was one of abject misery.

"Do as I ask, and I will forgive you. Do this one thing and we can be together again."

I was overwhelmed by the sensation that I shouldn't be here, shouldn't be witnessing this, but I was transfixed by the sight. Carmilla clutched my hand, her chest rising and falling with quick, shallow breaths.

De Lafontaine took one step towards Isis and then faltered, staying rooted to the spot. She clenched and unclenched her fists at her sides.

"You were the one who left," she said, her voice deathly quiet. "Not me. Why am I being punished for your decision?"

"Oh, my love," Isis sighed, closing the space between them. She reached out a thin hand and cupped De Lafontaine's face. De Lafontaine didn't pull away. "It isn't a punishment. It's proof."

Her lips hovered over De Lafontaine's, but De Lafontaine broke away at the last moment.

"We can't keep meeting like this," she said brusquely. "And you can't go on leaving corpses in broad daylight."

S. T. Gibson

"Has the thought of murder become so distasteful to you? I hadn't realized the ivory tower had softened you so much."

"This isn't about me, it's about you, and it always has been. It's a small school, Isis. People will put the pieces together eventually."

"And what then, Evelyn? Will you let them come for me?"

I never got to hear what was said next. Carmilla leaned too far around the catacomb wall, and she slipped against the mossy brick. Isis's face wrenched towards our hiding spot, and I yanked Carmilla back into the darkness with all my strength.

"Time's up," I whispered into her ear, and then started moving as fast as I could back the way we came, my fingers laced tightly through hers. We scrambled across the uneven ground like two little mice, dodging puddles and debris alike. I was dimly aware that there were sounds behind us, the unmistakable slap of shoes against the stone underfoot.

"Faster," Carmilla breathed. We turned a corner and broke into an all-out sprint, not caring what sort of noise we made. My lungs ached and my heart pounded, and my head was spinning with delirious fear. I had no idea what would happen to us if we were caught, but I was sure it wouldn't be pleasant.

"There," Carmilla gasped, pointing ahead. If I squinted I could make out the outline of the open trapdoor, and the narrow ladder that led back up into Seward Hall. The footsteps behind us had gotten quieter, and I prayed the darkness of the catacombs had obscured our identities and discombobulated our pursuer.

I shoved Carmilla up the ladder ahead of me, then hauled myself out of the underground and into the basement of Seward Hall. Working together, we pulled the trapdoor closed and then continued our mad dash out through the lock-picked door and across the quad.

I slipped on the wet grass and Carmilla hauled me up, her slender arms preternaturally strong, and all but carried me through the door of De Lafontaine's apartment building. If De Lafontaine came back and found us missing, that would undoubtedly raise suspicion. The moment we were up the stairs and through the apartment door, breathless words burst out of me.

"What on earth was that about?"

"I don't know," Carmilla said, doubled over with her hands on her knees. She was taking in great gulps of air. "But I do know that De Lafontaine hasn't been honest with me. With us."

"That seems like the least of our problems," I said. I strode into the kitchen and poured myself a finger of bourbon, straight. I usually wasn't a big liquor drinker, but my nerves were frayed to the breaking point. Wincing as I swallowed it down, I rinsed out the glass and put it back where I had found it. "Do you think De Lafontaine has been helping her, all this time? Just putting us off by telling us it's not our business and that she'll take care of it?"

"I don't know. I don't know anything anymore."

"We have to do something, Carmilla."

Carmilla opened her mouth to respond, but the sound of footfalls on the stairs outside shut us up. We exchanged panicked glances, then sat down at the coffee table and began to studiously pretend to play an abandoned game of Scrabble.

De Lafontaine walked through the door mere moments later. She was regal once again, but she still looked wan. I wondered when the last time she had eaten was.

"Hello, girls," she said, tugging off her gloves one finger at a time.

"How were the bars?" Carmilla asked, her voice as bright as ever. My darling liar.

"Uneventful," De Lafontaine said, pressing her lips together. "I didn't get what I wanted out of the excursion. I may have to go back tomorrow night."

Carmilla and I exchanged wary glances as De Lafontaine breezed past us into her bedroom. I sat stiffly as I listened to her undress through the door, from the click of her shoes against the hardwood to the clink of her jewelry in the little dish on her bedside table.

"Happy hunting," I said weakly.

CHAPTER TWENTY-FIVE

Carmilla

e never told De Lafontaine about that terrifying night beneath the school, but I don't think it mattered. She seemed to understand that we had been up to something illicit, just as she had seemed to understand that there was something more than malice between us in those early months of our acquaintance. She was a force we couldn't escape, like gravity, or the chill that had blown in with December.

I had spent the summer term fantasizing about a winter by De Lafontaine's side, close as the silk lining sewn into her coat. But now that I had gotten what I wanted, it was nothing like what I imagined. De Lafontaine was moody and demanding, jealous in the extreme though she would never admit it, and either totally neglectful or so saccharinely attentive that it left an unpleasant taste in my mouth. And then, there were the lies.

In the darkest, quietest part of my heart, resentment took root. How dare she lie to me after that lecture in her office about not keeping secrets from each other? How could she make excuses for that monster lurking beneath the school, knowing full well that she was responsible for a death so grisly it jeopardized all our safeties? As much as I hated the control De Lafontaine exercised over my life, I hated the power Isis seemed to have over her more. Why weren't we smoking her out from under the school, or leaving little breadcrumbs for the police that led right into her den? Why did De Lafontaine insist on pretending that the world could go on turning just as it always had?

Every time I walked across campus to class, I couldn't help but wonder if Isis was scrabbling around under my feet like a rat, enjoying free run of the catacombs below campus. She had a death grip on De Lafontaine's heart still – that much was obvious – though I had no idea why. Nostalgia for a long-dead love, I reckoned, was more potent than any intoxicant, and just as likely to lead to poor decision-making.

I only tried to discuss it with her once, with relatively disastrous consequences. We were sitting in one of the less popular bars on the outskirts of the nearest town, the ones Saint Perpetua's girls would never be caught dead in. It was too passé, too popular with the older locals, and they only played oldies and jazz standards. Naturally, that made it the perfect place for De Lafontaine to get away from the prying eyes of her students. We could sit close in the dark with our heads bowed together and carry on intimate discussions without worrying about sparking any rumors about inappropriate behavior between teacher and student. Administration was willing to tolerate a little fraternizing within the safety of the bounds of campus, but students and their professors meeting up to drink in shadowed bars was more irregular.

That night, we were sharing our second bottle of merlot as the live band plodded through a mournful rendition of "Smoke Gets in Your Eyes". We had been drinking in silence for some time, applying ourselves to getting drunk as fastidiously as PhD students at work on a thesis. Whenever I tried to catch De Lafontaine's eye, she would glance over to the band, or drop her eyes to the silver lighter she was irritably flipping open and closed in her lap.

"Did you bring me all the way out here just to give me the silent treatment?" I asked, once the quiet had become unbearable. My arms were strapped across my chest, just as much to express my displeasure as to hold myself steady as the room, gone blurry at the edges, threatened to spin.

De Lafontaine ran her hand over her mouth, shockingly colorless now that she had gnawed her lipstick away, and then finally looked up at me.

"What, exactly, would you like to talk about?"

"You're the professor; didn't you bring your lecture notes?" I muttered, downing the last of my fourth glass, or my fifth. "I'm just the student, remember? I don't get an opinion."

"I thought you liked spending time with me."

"I do. Just not when I feel like you only ask me out to keep me away from Laura."

De Lafontaine's eyes flashed in irritation, and my heart skipped a beat. Perhaps the storm that had been brewing for so many weeks would break, and we would fight, and I would finally feel some relief.

But then she sucked a breath in through her teeth, let it out through her nose, and tipped the last of the bottle into her wine glass. The stem was greasy with fingerprints and the rim was smudged with her lipstick. I felt, acutely and miserably, that I was that wine glass dangling from her fingers, covered in marks of her ownership.

"Time wears away the contours of love like a rock washed smooth by the ocean," she said, her vowels slightly slurred. "You won't even remember the color of her hair, in time."

I snorted out an unladylike laugh.

"You're one to talk. Pining after someone for forty years."

"That's entirely different."

"I don't see how."

De Lafontaine leaned closer to me across the table, lowering her voice.

"She was capable of forever, do you understand? She could have loved me for eternity, if she had just tried harder."

"Then why do I get the impression that you were the only one who was interested in trying?"

De Lafontaine opened her mouth for one of her infamous dressing-downs, but then, as though someone had cut the marionette strings suspending her in midair, she slumped back against her seat.

"You're a mean-spirited little thing," she said quietly. "But you know me better than most."

"I certainly thought I did."

"That's enough, Carmilla."

"I don't understand why you don't just run off with her, like you so obviously want to. I was only a placeholder, wasn't I? Something to entertain yourself with until she waltzed back into your life, ready to forgive and forget."

"Shut up, darling," she said, flat and final.

I sat in silence for a long while, not sure how to maneuver my way through the rest of this conversation. De Lafontaine cradled her chin in her hand and watched the band play on, and for a moment I though the subject had been dropped.

"I never even learned her given name, do you know that?" she said suddenly. "I would try to guess, make a game of it. But to me she was always Isis. Maybe I should have seen her for what she was, all along. What all goddesses are."

"What's that?" I asked. I still found De Lafontaine's flair for storytelling impossible to resist, even when I was angry with her.

De Lafontaine shook her head as she retrieved a cigarette from her case and placed it between her lips.

"Capricious."

"Professor De Lafontaine?" someone said behind me. I craned around in my seat to find a Saint Perpetua's girl standing at our table, an uncertain smile on her face.

"Elenore," De Lafontaine said, like someone had punched the wind out of her.

Elenore Robinson took a step forward, smoothing a nonexistent crease from the skirt of her mod-style dress.

"I spotted you from across the bar. Suffice to say I was surprised to see you. Hello, Carmilla."

"Hello," I said back, feeling a little lightheaded. Elenore wasn't known to be a gossip, but there was still no guarantee that the entire school wouldn't know that De Lafontaine had been out drinking with one of her students by the next morning.

"What are you doing here?" De Lafontaine asked, the wine washing away the finer points of her manners.

"Bobby's playing in the band tonight," she said, nodding towards a handsome boy with broad shoulders and slicked-back hair playing the trumpet on stage. His dark brown skin gleamed underneath the stage lights. I dimly remembered seeing his face in a heart-shaped frame on Elenore's vanity when she had invited the poetry cohort over for tea after the first week of class. I had been so wrapped up in my obsession with De Lafontaine that I had barely registered how she went out of her way to be kind to me, pouring my Earl Grey and asking me well-meaning questions about Austria. I had ducked out at the first opportunity to write in De Lafontaine's apartment, leaving behind the room of giggling girls.

Maybe, in another life, Elenore and I would have been better friends. Maybe, in a world where De Lafontaine never existed, I would actually have real friends.

"How sweet of you," De Lafontaine said, "to turn out to support him. Nice to see you out and about. Enjoy the rest of your evening."

Our professor turned back to her glass, but Elenore squared her shoulders and took another step forward.

"Actually, Professor, I'm glad I ran into you. I've been wanting to talk to you about something, but it's . . . a sort of delicate issue, and I wasn't sure how to bring it up."

"Well, you're here now," De Lafontaine said wearily. "What is it, Elenore?"

"It's Edith," Elenore said, lowering her voice and perching her hip on the edge of the table so that she could lean in a little closer to De Lafontaine. I wrinkled my nose at this gesture of familiarity, offended as always whenever anyone tried to get near my professor. I might not be very pleased with De Lafontaine at the moment, but that didn't mean I wanted to share her with anyone else. Still, I had to admire Elenore's tenacity. Most girls didn't have the guts to get within spitting distance of our teacher.

"What about Edith?" De Lafontaine asked.

"No one's seen her for three days. She isn't answering

the letters in her box, and she hasn't been coming to meals . . . I went by her room and knocked the other day, but no one answered, and the door was locked. That's the strange part. She never locks her room, because she's always losing her key. I can't help but worry."

"What, exactly, are you implying happened to her?" De Lafontaine went on. Her voice was level, but I knew her well enough to recognize the tightness around her mouth as panic.

"I'm not sure, but I hoped you might have some insight? She admires you a lot, you know. I thought maybe she had left a note or told you where she was going . . ."

"I'm afraid she didn't. But you know she's always going on trips to dance and compete; her missing school isn't too out of the ordinary. I'll join you in anticipating her safe return."

"Oh. All right," Elenore said, her expression plainly conveying that she didn't buy what De Lafontaine was selling. She turned to go, but De Lafontaine reached out and grasped her wrist. Elenore stared at the point of contact as though it might brand her for life.

"And there's no need to tell anyone that you ran into me tonight," De Lafontaine said sweetly. "Even professors are entitled to a little privacy, don't you think?"

"Sure thing," Elenore said, removing her hand from De Lafontaine's grasp and stuffing it into the pocket of her dress. "Get home safe, and all that jazz."

With that, she disappeared into the crowd.

"It's happening again," I hissed the moment she was out of earshot. "Edith, that poor girl, she's gone missing, just like the girl before her, and you know who's to blame, don't tell me that you don't—"

"I need air," De Lafontaine said, pushing her chair back so violently it squealed against the floor. With her wine glass still cradled in her hand, she tossed her coat over her shoulder and stalked towards the back exit.

I sat seething, my glass and my heart both miserably empty, until I couldn't stand it anymore. I yanked on my gloves and jacket and all but ran into the alleyway behind the bar after De Lafontaine.

She was staring up at the moon, taking in big gulps of night air. The first snow of the season had started while we were inside, and flakes were gathering in her eyelashes.

"You're the only one who can stop this," I said, my voice hoarse with desperation and barely restrained tears. I had lost my composure somewhere in the night, and I had no idea how to get it back. "But you won't, because you're a *coward*."

"You have no idea what she's like, Carmilla, how impossible she is to say no to—"

"I can't believe I spent so long fawning over you!" I said, my raised voice ringing off the brick walls of the alleyway. "Christ, I was so stupid. You never loved me. I was just a blood bag to you."

"If you knew what she was asking of me, you wouldn't dare say—"

"You don't care about me at all, do you?"

De Lafontaine hurled her wine glass against the bricks. It shattered into a thousand glittering pieces, littering the ground like fallen stars.

I nearly jumped out of my skin. Some of the glass shards skittered across the pavement towards my high-heeled shoes, and I just stared at them, dumbfounded. De Lafontaine had always been mercurial, and her mood swings could feel violent at times, but she had never actually demonstrated material *violence* in front of me.

"Y-you," I stammered, every muscle in my body tight and poised to sprint. "You just—"

"Oh God, darling, I'm so sorry," De Lafontaine said, rushing towards me like waves desperate to kiss the shore. All at once, the tempestuous expression evaporated from her face. The naked vulnerability that appeared in its place was breathtaking in its tenderness. "I lost my temper; I shouldn't have done that."

"No," I said, my voice small. "You shouldn't have."

"Are you all right? Watch your step, dearest. Come here, please."

Taking my shoulders in her hands, she gently guided me through the broken glass, onto a clear patch of asphalt, and into her arms. She folded herself around me, and I buried my face into her jacket, breathing in her perfume as I clutched at her back. I've always had the strangest instinct to run towards whatever is hurting me, to bare my neck to any predator that caught my scent, and that instinct was even stronger in times of crisis.

I squeezed my eyes shut and took big breaths, willing my skittering heart to slow. De Lafontaine pressed her cheek to mine, rubbing a soothing circle into my back.

"You must understand," she said, "I cannot lose you, Carmilla. The idea of an existence without you at my side . . . it's abhorrent to me. I've corrupted you, and whatever god there may be knows I'll have to answer for that one day, but I cannot be without you. I'm not strong enough."

"I'm not going anywhere," I mumbled into the wool of her coat. De Lafontaine just held me tighter, as if she didn't believe me.

"You're in the full flower of love," she said, her voice a little thicker than before. "It would be wicked of me to deny you that joy. I just . . . I get so frightened sometimes that you won't need me anymore, now that you have Laura."

"No one could ever replace you, Ms. D," I said, letting her rock me back and forth. Despite the rend in the fabric of our relationship, I still clung to her closeness, the affection she offered. Sweetness from her could be fleeting, but I had been weaned on it like mother's milk, and I still craved it every day. "You're extraordinary."

De Lafontaine pulled back and looked me square in the face, giving me a watery smile. The snow gathered in her dark hair like a coronet. All at once, I was struck by her alien beauty, how singularly lovely she was. For the thousandth time, I ached to be like her, to carry myself through the world with such grandeur.

"I want to try harder," she said, nodding as though to convince herself. "I'll be kinder to you. To Laura, too. It's shameful of me to sulk around like a woman jilted when young love is something to be celebrated. It's what all the great poets wrote about, isn't it?"

"I suppose so," I said with a sniff. The cold and my barely restrained tears were pressing up against my sinuses.

"Let me show you how kind I can be. You deserve that, at least. And let's not talk anymore about Isis tonight. She doesn't matter right now. Only you and I matter. Do you understand?"

"Yes, Ms. D."

She kissed my forehead, then rubbed up and down my arms, trying to will some warmth back into my limbs.

"Come back inside with me and have a little water. Then I'll drive you back to my apartment and I'll read to you. You can sleep with me in the big bed and tomorrow I'll tell your chorale teacher you have a sore throat so you can skip class. Doesn't that sound nice?"

"It does," I admitted, letting her thread her arm through mine and lead me back into the bar.

But of course, that was only a half truth.

The nicest thing, by far, would have been to spend the rest of my night with Laura.

CHAPTER TWENTY-SIX

Laura

he atmosphere on campus deteriorated further as the tension of finals ratcheted up. Saint Perpetua's during exam season could be cutthroat even under the best circumstances, but it became downright poisonous now that a girl's throat had actually been cut – and right on the quad, for God's sake. Girls coped with the trauma by undermining each other at every opportunity, spreading rumors in the cafeteria about who was taking amphetamines to give themselves an edge, or who was quietly bribing straight-A students to ghostwrite their essays. Some even went so far as to rip out essential equations and diagrams from library books so their academic rivals couldn't study them.

Students were spotted napping on library couches because they had stayed up all night reviewing their notes, or chain-smoking outside Seward Hall in order to summon the courage it took to face down the professors at their most demanding. De Lafontaine was in draconic form, stalking around the room as her students recited line upon line of verse and ordering them to start the whole poem over again if they so much as flubbed one word. She routinely reduced girls to tears by tearing into their compositions with a ferocity better reserved for the coliseum.

The cohort gossiped that she must be so grouchy because of all the grading she had ahead of her, but Carmilla and I knew better. She was a woman sick with love and assailed by anxiety, and there would be no peace for any of us until something released De Lafontaine from an emotional crucible of her own making.

Edith's death didn't help matters.

Miranda was the one who found her, a full week to the day after she went missing. She marched into the dean's office and demanded that campus security do a wellness check, and when the officer forced open Edith's locked door, Miranda was the first to enter the room.

She found her friend draped inelegantly in the en suite bathtub, the one Edith had insisted her father pay for since she needed private space to take ice baths in. Her body was bloodless and bruised in strange places, especially around the neck, which was bracketed by a necklace of black and blue. She wore nothing more than a lace-trimmed slip, although it appeared whoever killed her had taken the perverse time and care to paint her toenails bubblegum pink. Practical Edith would never waste lacquer on toes that were so routinely abused in the dance studio.

Miranda didn't say a word to anyone for two days after that, and then, the next weekend, she was simply gone. Maisy somberly explained to me that she had withdrawn from all her courses and returned home to her family's mansion in Mexico. She was receiving psychiatric care, we were told by the RA on her floor, although from the sound of the letters she sent Elenore, she was spending most of her days crying in bed.

I took the shock on the chin to the best of my ability. I hadn't known Edith well, but my natural proclivity towards guilt had my stomach sour for days over the ways I had envied her. What sort of person was I, to carry around bitterness for a girl I barely knew, who from all accounts might have been a very fine person indeed? Carmilla threw herself into her schoolwork, insisting she didn't have time to stop and grieve, but I knew that this, in her way, was its own type of grief.

Carmilla and I grew even more entangled, like flowers who, denied sufficient sunlight, entwine their leaves around each other and grow up strangled with love. We were rarely apart, except for those nights when De Lafontaine would insist Carmilla spend an hour or two alone with her, walking the grounds or taking lecture notes or simply reading in companionable silence. But even these outbursts of possessiveness lulled in the wake of Edith's death. Despite how ferocious she was in the classroom, in private, De Lafontaine was softer with me. With Carmilla, she was downright sentimental. It was almost as if she had witnessed some terrible vision of her life without either of us in it, and, when faced with that reality, she was willing to make accommodations to keep us close.

One bitterly cold day, when I had spent all my daylight hours and some of the nighttime ones in the library poring over astronomy textbooks, I looked up to find De Lafontaine standing in front of me.

"Professor," I said in surprise. We didn't often socialize outside of class or our private sessions in her apartment; mostly, I thought, because she didn't want to stoke the simmering jealousy some of her students had in regard to her playing obvious favorites. But here she was, smiling wryly at me like the Pied Piper in a silk shirt and loafers.

"Walk with me," was all she said, and then she started towards the door.

I scrambled to stuff my notebooks and my large carafe of coffee into my bag, then scurried after her and out into the frigid night. It hadn't snowed in some time, but there was ice on the fallen leaves underfoot, and the opaque, starless sky told me a storm was on its way.

De Lafontaine walked close to me as we strolled through the quad, so close that our shoulders almost touched. I couldn't help but steal little glances at her despite my best efforts to keep my eyes forward. I took in her regal nose, her perfect mouth. She reminded me of the black-and-white photos of Greek statues I had seen in history books as a child, as though she had stepped to life right off the page.

"How are you keeping?" she asked, as though we were any other professor and student discussing finals. "Getting enough sleep, I hope."

"I am," I lied.

"I'm happy to hear that."

We walked in silence for a few minutes more, ambling around the quad with no clear destination, and then De Lafontaine spoke again.

"And Edith's death? How are you handling that?"

It was strange to hear her speak so calmly on a subject most of the cohort couldn't approach without breaking down into tears.

"I'm . . . managing. What about you? She was your student. You must have known her well."

"Death is a part of life. But it never loses its sting, not entirely."

I nodded solemnly, uncertain how to proceed. Any discussion of Isis was usually met with a frosty reception, but her presence loomed large over the conversation.

"Do you think it was . . .?"

"I know it was."

"I see."

"I want you to know that I'm going to handle this. I

S. T. Gibson

just haven't decided how to . . . put an end to things yet. But I don't want you to take this on, Laura. You're a sweet girl, and a smart one, and I was the one who brought you in to all this. Isis is my monster to manage, not yours."

"Thank you," I said quietly. I doubted her words would help me feel any less complicit, but I appreciated them all the same.

"Give me until after Christmas," she said, slowing and turning to face me. "Will you spend part of your holiday with Carmilla and me? We can take refuge in each other, try to recover some joy in these awful circumstances. I know I haven't been very fair to you. I've let my own petty jealousies cloud my better judgment. I've been no better than my maker. But I remain dedicated to your education and your wellbeing above all. Say you'll come, Laura."

I stared up at her, dazzled despite my best efforts by her graciousness. I was reminded of the way she had enchanted me in the early days of our acquaintance, and there was a heady satisfaction in being lauded as valuable by her once more. After embarrassing myself at Magdalena's party, I never wanted to run afoul of De Lafontaine's disapproval again.

"Do you ever miss the sun?" I blurted. I had been curious about that ever since discovering her true nature.

"Would you believe me if I said no?"

"I would."

I couldn't even imagine De Lafontaine as a daylight creature, as a smiling girl my age with ribbons in her hair and color in her cheeks. She seemed supremely suited to the shadows, to every mysterious bit of her second life.

"So," she said, taking a deep breath, as though she were the one that was nervous instead of me, "will you come?"

"I will. Of course I will."

"I'm so glad."

De Lafontaine glanced over both her shoulders, ensuring that we weren't being watched, and then she leaned down and dropped a chaste kiss to my cheek. The kiss was so swift, barely a brush of her lips, that I could have almost missed it, but my skin tinged in response. I felt color heat my cheeks.

"Thank you," I said quietly, wringing my hands together in front of me. "For seeing I'm no threat to you. We both want what's best for Carmilla."

"I know," she said, a strange sadness in her voice. We resumed our walk, strolling beneath the bare trees that lined the quad. "And I hope, in time, you'll realize I want what's best for you, too."

CHAPTER TWENTY-SEVEN

Carmilla

aura went away for four days before Christmas to visit her father, no doubt regaling him with sanitized tales about her university exploits, and I languished in De Lafontaine's apartment, playing solitaire and making little castles out of the cards while I waited for Laura's return. When she finally stepped back through the door, all rosy cheeks and windswept hair, I kissed her so soundly I think I bruised her lips. She was to spend the rest of the holiday with De Lafontaine and me, and as nervous as I was about living all together in close quarters, I was overjoyed to have more time with my beloved.

I've always found Christmas to be one of the loneliest times of the year. All the glittering lights and brightly wrapped presents can't make up for the oppressive darkness, the dolorous sermons, the constant reminders that one's mother is fled and one's father is a drunk. There's a wistfulness to Christmas that I was finely attuned to, even as a child, and I expected it to sweep over me as the calendar crept closer and closer to the 24th. But then, the miraculous happened. Joy broke in.

Laura's presence lit up my world like the solstice sun on a crystal-clear day. She returned from Mississippi with arms full of packages tied up with gleaming red ribbon, not to mention a tin of home-baked sugar-spice cookies that were so delicious I kept nibbling on them, even when they soured my stomach. To De Lafontaine she gifted a wickedly sharp fountain pen and a pink puff with a tin of imported French setting powder. I received a first-edition book of Sylvia Plath with a silk ribbon, and a golden necklace with a tiny ruby for a pendant so very much like a droplet of blood that it took my breath away.

"I'll never take it off," I said, when she clasped it around my throat. It hung nestled in the hollow between my collarbones, a subtle symbol to the whole world that I was cherished. Delighted in.

Owned, a quiet, needy part of me hoped.

On Christmas Eve, De Lafontaine disappeared without a word and came back an hour later with her arms full of brown-paper bags filled with eggnog, honey ham, whipped potatoes from the grocery deli, and a hot dish of green beans in mushroom sauce for Laura. For me, she produced a box of Earl Grey and a bottle of Scottish gin.

"Shall we have a little party, then?" she said with a smile. "Laura, if you would be so kind as to put a record on?"

As it happened, De Lafontaine owned a record of classic Christmas piano, and Laura and I busied ourselves in the kitchen brewing drinks and dishing out food as De Lafontaine lit the candles she had stuck into empty wine bottles. She dimmed the lights so that the room was illuminated only by firelight and the glow of the tiny artificial Christmas tree she had erected in the window.

We sat on cushions on the ground enjoying our respective meals while De Lafontaine cleared empty glasses and the ashtray from the coffee table so we could play a round of inexpert poker. I won, to my great triumph, and De Lafontaine was honest enough to gift me the costume earrings she had wagered as my prize.

De Lafontaine chuckled from the couch as Laura and I slow-danced to a mournful rendition of "The Carol of the Bells", our arms entwined. We grinned at each other as we did our little two-step across the carpet, our stockinged feet bumping together.

Maybe, I hoped privately, it could always be like this. Maybe Laura and I would nurture our fledgling relationship, and maybe De Lafontaine would forget her jealousy. Maybe we could craft some shaky semblance of stability, and maybe the spirit of Christmas would last long through the year.

Maybe we could be a family.

Laura and I slept in late on Christmas Day, and rose to the smell of piping-hot Assam tea and cinnamon rolls rising in the oven. We wrapped ourselves up in our dressing gowns and eagerly tore into our presents from De Lafontaine while she watched us with those sharp green eyes. Laura was gifted with a new daybook, bound in real leather, and I received a tiny pocket knife inlaid with mother-of-pearl.

"Little tokens of affection for my two favorite pupils," De Lafontaine said magnanimously. She was trying so hard, I realized, to make up for how cold and demanding she had been in the past. I fervently hoped we were truly turning a corner together, all of us.

At noon, the downstairs doorbell rang. Laura volunteered to go answer it, and returned moments later with an unmarked white envelope in her hands.

"It's for you, Ms. De Lafontaine."

"That's strange," De Lafontaine said. "There's no mail service on Christmas. Let me see that."

She ripped open the envelope and read the note inside, once over and then again. Then she pinched the bridge of her nose, took a deep breath, and snagged the bottle of gin from the kitchen.

"I'll be in my room," she said, and swung the door shut behind her without another word.

Laura and I exchanged looks that bordered on panic, then crept over to where De Lafontaine had tossed the note down. We each grasped an edge of it and read in silence.

It won't stop happening until you come home to me.
  -I

My heart sank into my shoes.

The rosy bubble we had been living in over the holiday had been unceremoniously popped, and De Lafontaine's dark mood had returned. It meant that she would be cracking down on us all over again, and that my dreams of roaming the campus freely had been dashed.

Moreover, it meant that none of us were safe.

CHAPTER TWENTY-EIGHT

Laura

hey found the third body on New Year's Day, once the snow had finally started to thaw. She had been dumped in the little riverbed that ran behind the Curie building, half covered up with sticks and leaves. Gossip traveled like wildfire through the school, and one of the literature professors rang De Lafontaine to ask if she had heard about "that poor Barlow girl" only forty-five minutes after her body had been discovered.

De Lafontaine stalked through the apartment, slamming cupboards and yanking open drawers as she retrieved her coat, scarf, and gloves.

"Field trip," she said gravely, and Carmilla and I understood that we were to stop laying on the couch reading magazines and get our shoes on.

The ground was marshy beneath the thin crust of ice

clinging to the grass like a confectioner's glaze. We crowded up against the perimeter the police had erected behind the science building, peering down onto the riverbank where the body had been draped with a gray blanket, probably for the sake of decency. The bare foot sticking out from the corner of the blanket was pale and streaked with mud, perfectly painted coral-red toes peeking through the grime. Half a dozen girls and a few professors were staring at the crime scene from just beyond the perimeter, seized by puerile curiosity, but I supposed we were no different.

What is a vampire but a vulture and her companion but an accomplice, after all?

De Lafontaine stood statuesque in the January chill, steam and cigarette smoke pluming from her mouth. Carmilla was bundled up in one of De Lafontaine's old fur jackets, a cropped thing that looked like it had been lifted from a theater's costume department, or maybe directly from the 1920s.

"Ladies, back if you please," a police officer with an impressive mustache said, herding us like ducklings further from the murder scene. We stepped back only as far as was strictly necessary, sticking around even when a few of the less determined hangers-on turned around and headed home.

"Do you think it was her?" Carmilla asked quietly, sliding her arm around my shoulder. We were safer out here, with fewer people to witness our affection, and who could besmirch two friends huddling together in the cold?

"I know it was," De Lafontaine said gravely.

"What are we going to do about it?" I asked, quieter still.

De Lafontaine just scowled, crushing her cigarette butt beneath her heel.

"You two aren't going to do anything. You're going to leave this to me, understand?"

Carmilla and I exchanged skeptical glances, so subtle and private even De Lafontaine's keen eyes passed them over. De Lafontaine hadn't done anything about Isis yet, and we weren't inclined to believe she was going to suddenly take drastic measures, even as the violence escalated.

She was in love, and that was dangerous.

After all, what horror wouldn't I tolerate, if it was meted out by the hand of my beloved?

———✦———

Campus became downright hysterical after that. One death might be considered a tragedy, two an ill omen, but three seemed far too deliberate for even the strongest suspension of disbelief.

Of course, as far as I was aware, only three souls on campus knew that the murderer was indeed a creature of the night, and I was one of them. The burden weighed on me, hanging from my neck like an albatross on a rope. If I told someone what I knew, another adult maybe, would they be able to stop the next act of brutality before it happened?

In the end, I was too much of a coward to confide in anyone but Carmilla or De Lafontaine, especially because I didn't fancy being sent to a sanatorium to wait out the rest of my freshman year. The world was more enchanted than I had ever dreamed, but it was also more terrible and strange. I didn't want to share the private arcadia De Lafontaine and Carmilla and I had built with a stranger. How could anyone else possibly understand how rare and precious it truly was?

To assuage my guilt, I did what I had been brought up to do. I went to confession.

Saint Perpetua's chapel was laid out in classic cathedral style, with a long nave and two transepts jutting out from the sides that, when viewed as a whole from above, formed the image of the cross. It was built from the same rain-washed gray stone as the rest of the campus, and boasted delicate stained-glass windows depicting scenes from the Bible.

Confession was held every Thursday just after sunset, and the schedule had been maintained despite the rash of violence on campus. The first afternoon I wasn't otherwise occupied, I decided unburdening my heart would do me some good.

I shouldered open the heavy carved wooden doors that led into the narthex, put immediately at ease by the scent of warm candle wax and smoldering frankincense resin. Dust motes spun in the air, captured in the dusk light streaming in through the windows. Above my head, Isaac lay bound on the altar, his father's knife hovering over his chest.

I slipped into the sanctuary and walked down the central aisle, my kitten heels clicking on the flagstones, and took my seat in the pew closest to the confessional booth. Having a whole booth just for confessionals seemed lavish to me, bordering on Catholic, but Saint Perpetua's had spared no expense in the construction of the chapel. Today, there were only two other girls waiting with their heads bowed for their turn in the confessional, which wasn't uncommon. I was one of a few people on campus who seemed to have any interest in the sacrament. Religion was passé after all, for squares and their parents. But I didn't mind being considered old fashioned or even prudish for my interest in the institution. I didn't follow blindly, wasn't hurting anyone with my beliefs, and cherished the deep well of academic and spiritual tradition the Church offered me. If communion was the most carnal of the sacraments, confession was the most cathartic. I often worked myself up into a cleansing cry in the booth, and always left feeling so much lighter. It helped that the priest, Father Frise, was a patient man with a good head on his shoulders.

I waited patiently as the two girls ahead of me took their turns in the booth, trying to run through a brief set of prayers. But whenever I attempted to clear my mind and say my Our Father, that fire crept back under my skin. I squirmed in my seat, trying to get comfortable on the hard pew. Nothing helped.

S. T. Gibson

Finally, it was my turn. I slipped into the cool embrace of the confessional and took a seat, lacing my fingers together. In the chamber next to me, the priest shuffled and cleared his throat. According to the campus gossip, last year's priest had been a stunningly beautiful Welsh man who had drawn record crowds to his sermons. The diocese had replaced him because apparently an attractive unmarried priest in a school full of girls was a recipe for scandal. I privately resented the diocese for their decision. I would have been impervious to the charms of any man, priest or no, and a younger spiritual leader could have helped me greatly in my own formation. Father Frise had a good heart, and he knew his church history, but it was quietly understood that he didn't approve of the movement to ordain women that had been passed in the Church just the year before.

Still, I wasn't exactly in a position to be picky. The little room smelled faintly of the previous girl's lilac perfume, and of the leather oil on the priest's shoes just beyond the honeycomb screen that separated penitent from confessor.

"Bless me, Father, for I have sinned."

On the other side of the screen, Father Frise cleared his throat, then spoke in his lulling baritone.

"The Lord be in your heart and upon your lips that you may truly and humbly confess your sins: In the name of the Father, and of the Son, and of the Holy Spirit."

"Amen," I murmured.

Gradually, the world began to fall away. In this little booth, there were no exams or school holidays, no gossiping friends, not even any Carmilla or De Lafontaine. There was just me, my heavy-burdened heart, the disembodied voice of my priest, and the presence of God, clinging to my skin like muggy Mississippi heat.

I began to run through my litany of garden-variety sins: envy of other girls' grades and hair and friend groups, short-temperedness with students who cut in front of me in the lunch line, taking of the Lord's name in vain when I laughed and swore with Maisy and Elenore during our late-night study sessions, and a handful of other banal sins that might have afflicted any other young person my age. I all but sped through them, eager to reach the climax. The priest, familiar with my unflinching style of confession, made the occasional sympathetic humming noise but didn't interrupt me.

"And," I said, lacing my fingers together tight in my lap, "I've lusted after another person. Well, I'm not sure about that, actually."

"You're not sure?" the priest prompted gently.

I sucked in a deep breath, squeezing my fingers together so tight my knuckles went white. I wasn't in the habit of confessing my sapphic proclivities as a sin, since I didn't consider them to be one, but my idolatry of Carmilla definitely counted as something worth confessing.

"Is it still lust, if the other person feels the same way?"

"Are we speaking about fornication now?"

"I suppose we are," I said, picking at a fraying thread on my sweater. "In a sense."

"My child, if you mean to confess you must speak plainly."

I breathed in deeply through my nose and then let it out through my mouth.

"Perhaps it was fornication," I mused. "But there was love in it, too."

I sat, dutifully quiet, as the priest treated me to a gentle but unflinching sermon about the sins of the flesh, and prescribed a dozen decades of the rosary as penance. I fingered the beads of my red glass rosary as I exited the confessional, eager to get right down to apologizing to God, but then I spotted a familiar face in the near-empty chapel.

De Lafontaine was seated in one of the front pews, her face half-obscured by an out-of-fashion cloche hat. Her chin was tipped upward, as though she were meditating, or admiring the stained glass.

"I didn't realize you were religious," I said, sliding into the pew next to her. I don't think I had ever seen De Lafontaine darken the door of the chapel, not the entire semester.

"Oh, I'm not. I'm merely an admirer of art, which the Church hoards in abundance."

I folded my hands in my lap and studied the austere lines of her face in the dim light of the chapel.

"I should have never woken her up," she said quietly, as though half to herself. "I had forgotten her self-interest, and her cruelty."

I didn't dare to say anything. It was so unlike De Lafontaine to show weakness around me, much less to express regret.

"I thought, perhaps," she went on, "that in her gratitude for being brought back to life, she might . . . soften towards me. I was wrong. Some things are better left dead." She turned to face me, arching a thin eyebrow. "I know you two saw me, that night in the catacombs."

All the blood drained from my face.

"I'm sorry, Ms. De Lafontaine. We were just—"

"Curious, I know. And you have every right to be. I've drawn you both into a brutal passion play hurtling towards an uncertain end. This is my fault, Laura. The deaths, Carmilla's condition, it all comes back to me."

"I like to think you've done the best you could," I said.

She smiled wryly. "You're too good natured, Laura. Someone will take advantage of you someday."

I slipped my hands beneath me, rocking back and forth. I should probably have left the conversation there, but I couldn't help the questions that bubbled up inside me.

"What did Isis want from you? You were refusing her something, I overhead that much."

"She wants proof that I'm still devoted to her above all else. An offering, if you will. She thinks to test my loyalty by asking me to surrender what is most dear to me."

"Carmilla," I said, understanding crashing over me like a cold wave. "She wants you to let her kill Carmilla."

"I always said you were a quick study, Laura."

"But you *can't*."

"And I won't. Perhaps when I was younger and hungrier for her approval, but not now. Carmilla is the closest thing I have to a daughter, and I feel responsible for her wellbeing. Especially now that she's transformed."

"Does Carmilla know?" I asked, lowering my voice even more.

De Lafontaine shook her head, her bobbed curls swaying.

"No, but she must suspect. You can keep a secret, can't you?"

I pressed my lips together. I felt like I was living in a tower of secrets that might collapse around me at any moment, and I didn't like the idea of lying to Carmilla.

"Yes, Ms. De Lafontaine."

"We're running out of time. Isis will drain half the student body and jeopardize all of our safeties if it means getting her way, and she's growing tired of waiting for me to make up my mind. She's getting bolder, more indiscriminate in her killing. She won't leave the school without me, but she won't release me either. I've designed my own torture, it seems."

"The tunnels beneath the schools are a labyrinth, and she knows them better than you do. If there was a way to draw her out and onto neutral territory, perhaps she could be reasoned with."

De Lafontaine let out a little laugh.

"There's no reasoning with her once she sets her mind

to bloodshed, I know that much. But you might be right about enticing her above ground . . . I just don't know how to go about it."

I cleared my throat, hoping she wouldn't notice that I was sweating through my blouse. I had of course walked a dozen possible solutions to our monstrous problem in my guilty late-night hours, but only one option now seemed viable. It was brazen, and it was dangerous, but that might be what we needed.

"If you don't mind, Ms. De Lafontaine, I think that I might."

She slid an arm around my shoulder and pulled me closer, bending down so that I could whisper in her ear.

"Tell me everything," she ordered.

CHAPTER TWENTY-NINE

Carmilla

he plan was simple, in theory. All I had to do was stand in front of the greenhouse and look distressed. That shouldn't be difficult considering how fast my heart was beating in my chest.

De Lafontaine squeezed my shoulder, holding me in place. She stood behind me, looming like a specter.

"Almost time now, darling. Deep breaths."

I did my best to haul air into my lungs, even though they felt like they were being crushed between two textbooks. I don't think I had ever been so scared, and I was shivering, despite the heavy fur coat I wore. De Lafontaine had draped me in it as she described exactly what would be happening, outlining my role step by step as she buttoned up the coat and ran a brush through my hair.

Now we stood on the grass, the greenhouse glass

gleaming in the moonlight. Dawn would be upon us soon, and there were tendrils of early-morning mist curling around my ankles.

"What if something happened?" I breathed. "What if Isis hurts her? What if—"

"Chin up, Carmilla. Don't lose your nerve now. It's you Isis wants. And I've never known her to pass up the opportunity to leverage human collateral."

Before I could fret any more, the sound of sticks snapping and leaves crunching underfoot cut me off. Two people were approaching, navigating their way through the narrow footpath that led from the campus to De Lafontaine's garden.

I saw Laura first, and relief flooded my veins. Her cheeks were bitten pink by the January cold and there was animal roundness to her eyes. She was just as frightened as I was, then.

Isis stepped through the trees behind her, turning her face up towards the moonlight. Besides bruised circles under her eyes, she looked almost alive again. Her lips were rosy, her eyes were bright, and her hair, impossibly long and dark and so very like my own, was piled up on top of her head. She was still wearing her funeral dress, despite the fact that the tattered fabric left her collarbones and arms exposed.

I wondered if she even felt the cold.

"Evelyn," she said, stopping a stone's throw from us.

For a long moment, there was silence, broken only by

the chirping of morning birds and the distant trickle of the stream behind the greenhouse. The two women gazed at each other, the all-consuming gaze of an enemy, or a lover, as they breathed in the icy air.

"Isis," Evelyn said, and I heard it, that treacherous tenderness in her voice. I stiffened, suddenly aware that De Lafontaine's love for her sire was an unkillable thing, one that existed beyond the scope of reason or ethics. In her apartment earlier that night she had kissed my eyelids and told me that she wouldn't let a single hair on my head be harmed, but now I felt her protective grip on my shoulder slacken.

"I got your note," the woman who had killed me once before said, holding up a slip of paper between her fingers. "Delivered so politely by your messenger girl. I found her scrambling around the catacombs like a frightened little rat. Draw her a map next time."

Laura took an uncertain step forward, trying to move closer to me, but Isis closed her fingers around her wrist and pulled her back.

"Not so quick, little one. I think I'll keep you, for the time being."

Laura let out a little squeak as Isis looped an arm around her waist and pulled her in tight. The hair on the back of my neck stood up, and I wished ferociously that I was an older and stronger vampire, that I might be able to wrestle Laura out of her grasp.

"Let the human girl go," De Lafontaine said. "She isn't

S. T. Gibson

the one you want; we both know that. There's no need
for dramatics tonight."

"Maybe not. But she's dear to your protégée, and I'm
inclined to think keeping her close at hand will encourage
good behavior from all parties."

I glanced behind me to find De Lafontaine glowering
at her great love, her eyebrows drawn together as though
in some sort of agony.

"Ms. D?" I asked.

The grip on my shoulder tightened again, almost painfully, and she walked me forward a few paces. This close,
I could smell the turned-earth and rainwater-rot scent
clinging to Isis's clothes and hair, and I could taste the
fear wafting off Laura like a perfume.

"Is this what you want?" De Lafontaine demanded, her
voice deathly quiet. "An orgy of blood to satisfy your
appetites? I was never enough for you, not even when I
was delivering a dozen girls a month to your hunger.
There's no pleasing you, Isis, no satiating that pit inside
you. It's true what they say: some of us come back wrong,
and there's something deeply wrong with you."

I thought such a scathing assessment might wound Isis,
or provoke her into anger, but instead, she just tossed her
head back and laughed. There was a wild light in her
eyes, a feral delight that spooked me viscerally.

"God, I missed this. Missed you, with all your cutting,
sharp edges. I could spend a lifetime fighting with you,
Evelyn. You're the only thing that makes me feel alive. I

don't intend to repeat the mistake I made when I left you behind the first time."

De Lafontaine swayed slightly behind me, as though stepping onto shaky ground.

"Don't pretend to care. Not now, years later, when it doesn't matter anymore."

Isis petted Laura's hair idly as she thought, the way one might pet a cat. Her fingernails, I noticed, were long and cracked. Laura squeezed her eyes shut, swallowing hard.

"We're not done, you and I. We never will be. My blood flows through your veins, Evelyn. I taught you to hunt, taught you to carry yourself in society, taught you the meaning of pleasure and pain. I was always going to come back for you. You must believe that."

"I don't," De Lafontaine said thickly. I had never once seen her cry, but I worried that I might see that now. I tried to turn and look at her, but De Lafontaine held me in place with a bruising grip.

Isis stepped forward a few more paces, until she was close enough to reach out and touch me. Laura squirmed in her grasp, and we shared a panicked glance. I threw my eyes towards the treeline, urging her with every fiber of my being to run, save herself at the soonest opportunity, but Isis held her fast.

"I want to summer in the Alps with you," Isis said, suddenly wistful. Her eyes softened like chocolate. "I want to wake up beside you in Paris. I want to hunt with you in Argentina and watch the moonrise with you over the Pyramids. You've spent so long searching for me, my love, and you've sacrificed so much. You don't have to live this pantomime of professorship anymore. You can be who you were always meant to be, with me."

"Ms. D," I whispered, suddenly desperate. I tried to wrench out of her grasp but another hand came up to grip my other shoulder, rooting me to the spot. I felt, with a sudden awful awareness, that I was a rat in a trap.

"Forty-three years," De Lafontaine said, her voice hoarse. "Forty-three years I searched for you while you slept. Forty-three years alone."

"Let me mend what I broke. We can be as we once were. All I ask is that you do as I ask, just like you've done so many times before, and let me wipe the slate clean on the pitiful little existence you've had to scrape out here. Give me the girl, Evelyn. Just like all the other girls before her. I'll even kill her quickly. Let me put an end to this."

De Lafontaine didn't say anything for a very long time. Tears stung at my eyes, and one trickled treacherously down my cheek. I had never been much for religion, but my lips formed the shape of the Lord's Prayer all the same.

This was my end. I was going to be sacrificed on the altar of someone else's love just as my own love story was beginning.

"Let Sheridan go," De Lafontaine said eventually. She spoke confidently, like she had made up her mind about something. "This doesn't concern her. I don't need another witness, and you don't need another body to bury."

"Fair enough," Isis said. Then she released Laura, who, god bless her, sprinted as fast as her legs would carry her back into the trees.

"You can't do this," I said, twisting and turning in De Lafontaine's grasp. She just yanked me closer, pressing our bodies together. "Ms. D, please don't do this. I love you, Ms. D, I'll do anything. Just don't let her take me, please just stop—"

Isis pressed two fingers, as cool as stone, to my lips, and my tears trickled down over her fingers.

"Be good and hold her still for me," she cooed, as though she were undressing De Lafontaine, not guiding her through a murder. I thrashed outright then, biting at Isis's fingers and trying to kick backwards at De Lafontaine, but her grip was tight as a vice.

"Let me do it," De Lafontaine said. "Let me show you how much I love you. Let there never be any doubt again."

I screamed then, a blood-curdling cry of terror and betrayal. After giving every inch of myself to De Lafontaine, after surrendering my youth and my faith and my very lifeblood, I was nothing more to her than a sacrificial lamb. Her awful, misshapen love for Isis was always going to be stronger than whatever bond we shared, and she was always going to pick her sire over me, even when my life was on the line.

"Quiet, Carmilla," De Lafontaine muttered. She dragged

me towards the greenhouse, ignoring the trails of broken grass and mud my thrashing feet left on the ground. Then she lowered her voice, pressed her lips to the hollow behind my ear, and said, so softly I almost could have been imagining it, "I'm sorry, darling."

De Lafontaine shouldered open the door to the greenhouse and hauled me inside, and I kicked over plenty of her precious plants along the way. Pots shattered underfoot as soil flew into the air. This gave me a jolt of mean satisfaction; if I was going to die, at least I would destroy her meticulously cultivated garden along the way.

Isis drifted into the greenhouse after us, her eyes wide with interest. She was the type to enjoy a show, then. Fine. I would put on a grand show for her, and ensure she never forgot what she had done to me.

"I hope you burn in hell," I spat, angling a kick her way. "Both of you."

"You always liked the fighters," Isis said fondly.

De Lafontaine picked up her silver sickle from the nearest table, and pressed the cold edge of the blade against my throat.

"One cut," she panted, wrestling me to my knees. Now I was sure she was crying. "One cut and it's over."

I tried to crawl away, but De Lafontaine slotted her fingers into my hair, yanking my head back and holding me in place. I glared at Isis, trying to burn a hole in her with my hatred.

"You'll forget she ever existed," Isis said, pressing her

bare foot against my chest and pushing me down onto the ground. "Open her for me, beloved. Show me the sweetness under her skin."

She leaned forward, offering up an undoubtedly long-awaited kiss. De Lafontaine crushed her mouth against Isis's like this was the kiss that might save her life, like it was the only thing worth living for.

"I never stopped loving you," De Lafontaine breathed against Isis's skin.

Then, with the fluid precision of someone cutting down a sheaf of wheat, she reared back, swung the blade, and slashed open Isis's throat.

Hot blood splattered across my shirtfront and splashed into my open, screaming mouth. Isis collapsed to her knees, clutching her shredded jugular while making a horrible, bubbling sound in her throat. She slumped against me, pressing me to the earth with her dead weight.

Just about the moment I thought I might die, suffocated by dead flesh and choking on someone else's blood, De Lafontaine hauled Isis off me. I blinked the blood out of my eyes, too stunned to speak or even move. De Lafontaine knelt down beside Isis and cradled her in her arms.

"It was always going to be this way," she said into Isis's hair. "One of us was always going to bleed for the other."

Then she took up her sickle once again, wedged the cutting edge of the blade into the gushing wound in Isis's neck, and severed her head with one wrenching motion.

The head rolled across the ground and came to a stop

at my feet, its expression fixed permanently into betrayal. I scrambled back from it, trying to put as much distance as possible between myself and the body in the process, and ran smack into De Lafontaine.

"Shh," she said, wrapping her arms around me. Instead of confining me, now her touch comforted and supported me. Maybe it was the shock, or force of pure habit, but I embraced her despite the fact that she had threatened my life moments before. "Shh, my darling, it's over."

She was trembling, deep tremors that racked her entire body, but still she wanted to soothe me. I crawled into her lap and clutched her blouse, sobbing freely.

The greenhouse door slammed open, shattering one of the glass window panels, and Laura dashed in, brandishing a knife. She looked out of breath, like she had run all the way to De Lafontaine's apartment and back, just to come to my defense.

"Laura," I hiccupped, holding my arms out to her.

Despite the blood and the dirt streaked across my skin, she sank down next to me and wrapped me in her arms. The knife clattered to the ground, forgotten.

Laura rocked me back and forth while De Lafontaine smoothed my hair, making low sounds of reassurance.

"Christ," I gasped. "She was going to . . . She tried—"

"It's over," De Lafontaine said, as much for her own benefit as mine. Her voice was raw, like she was the one who had been screaming, and there were tear tracks on her face. "It's over now."

CHAPTER THIRTY

Laura

t was backbreaking work, burying her. Six feet didn't seem like much until I was putting all my weight onto a shovel, doing my best to dig down far enough to prevent the body from being unearthed by animals or curious passers-by. We all took turns digging, racing against the dawn threatening to break over the horizon, and then De Lafontaine hoisted up Isis's body and settled her into the earth, arranging the severed head on the gruesome stump of a neck just so. She pressed her lips to Isis's cold, gray mouth in one final farewell. By the time it was all said and done, all three of us were soaked in mud and blood and plenty of other unmentionable substances.

De Lafontaine, who had said virtually nothing the entire time we dug the grave and then refilled it with soil, stood with her hands stuffed deep into her pockets, staring at the turned earth. She was still shaking, and every once in a while, her bottom lip would tremble dangerously.

I thought, perhaps, that she might say a few words, or ask for time alone with the body. But in the end, she just turned abruptly from the murder scene and took Carmilla and my hands in each of her own.

"Time for bed, girls," she said, sounding positively ancient.

We walked hand in hand back to De Lafontaine's apartment, a dour funeral procession in the thin morning light. Once we were safely inside, De Lafontaine poured herself three fingers of gin, not bothering with ice or with turning on any lights, and Carmilla and I showered off in the bathroom until the water ran clear. When we were done, De Lafontaine took her turn. Her skin was so pink when she emerged that I thought she must have scrubbed herself almost raw.

"Will one of you recite for me?" she said, cradling her near-empty glass to her chest and pulling her silk kimono tightly around her. Her hair was loose and wet, sticking to her neck like the tentacles of an octopus. "Please?"

Carmilla retrieved a volume from the shelf and began to read. De Lafontaine drifted into her bedroom, curling up with her knees to her chin on top of the covers, and Carmilla and I followed. We took turns reading to her, steadfastly ignoring the tears trickling from her eyes, and lowered our voices to a whisper once she finally fell asleep.

"It must be so terrible," I murmured later, after we had

left De Lafontaine to her slumber and were curled up on the couch together, Carmilla's head in my lap. "To have to kill the thing you love most."

Carmilla snuggled closer to me. I never wanted to let her out of my sight again, much less stop touching her. This was my whole world, wrapped up in one awful, wonderful girl.

"If you're the one that does the killing, you guarantee that no one else will ever take what you love from you," she said, letting her eyes slide shut.

I didn't argue with her, and I didn't press the point. I just shut the living-room blinds against the rising sun, shrouding us in forgiving darkness, and surrendered to sleep.

<hr/>

Carmilla graduated that spring by the skin of her teeth, despite not making an appearance at any of her daytime classes. De Lafontaine pleaded her case to the professors, who grudgingly allowed her to complete much of her coursework from her dorm room, and on her own schedule. I, for my own part, drifted through my coursework as though in a dream. I dozed off in daytime classes, only truly coming to life after the sun dipped low on the horizon. Ever the straight-A student, I eked out a measly B minus in astronomy and church history alike. Poetry was my refuge, the one safe place I could process what I had borne witness to, and my metaphors took on a bloody tinge. Life only felt truly real, truly worth living, in the confines of De Lafontaine's poetry seminar.

De Lafontaine called off our Friday-night meetings for the rest of the semester, insisting that she needed time to herself. Carmilla and I took to spending Fridays together, visiting the local bar a few miles from campus or tangled up in bedsheets. I wondered privately if De Lafontaine was all right, if she would ever truly recover from what she had done, but it didn't seem like my place to ask. I knew that De Lafontaine occasionally called on Carmilla in the middle of the night, inviting her on long meandering walks in the moonlight, and I wondered what they talked about between themselves, but I knew that wasn't mine to know, either. It seemed to me that De Lafontaine was trying to recalibrate the nature of her relationship with Carmilla, to implement healthy boundaries of some kind. But they had already transgressed the boundaries of professor and student together; they had plunged headfirst into the darkness and the darkness had nearly swallowed them up.

I wasn't sure if there was any coming back from that.

One spring evening, when the petals on the flowering trees were just starting to unfurl, we visited De Lafontaine's apartments to find her carrying a set of matching suitcases out to her car. There was a small charity van parked in front of the apartments, and two muscular townie boys were hauling De Lafontaine's velvet sofa and pink-shaded lamps out of the building. Carmilla stared in confusion for a moment, then fury passed over her face. She stormed across the gravel, tugging me behind her by the hand.

"You're leaving," she said to De Lafontaine. An accusation, not a question.

"I was never awarded tenure," De Lafontaine said breezily, as though her decision had anything to do with academia. "I decided my skills were better put to use elsewhere. There's an opening at a finishing school in Nice; they said I could start immediately."

Carmilla reared back and attempted to slap De Lafontaine, but the professor caught her wrist before the blow could land.

"Save your rage, darling. You'll need it, in this life."

I thought that Carmilla might lay into De Lafontaine, or try to hit her again, but instead she just broke down in tears. De Lafontaine pulled her into a tight embrace and Carmilla sobbed and sobbed, getting mascara stains all over De Lafontaine's seafoam blouse.

"But you aren't really leaving?" I said, feeling stunned.

In response, De Lafontaine just held out her hand to me. I stepped into her embrace and she rocked Carmilla and me back and forth.

"I am. My business here is done, and I fear that staying at this school any longer would just cause anything good left in me to rust and corrode. I need a fresh start, somewhere no one knows my name. Somewhere I can put all this misery behind me."

"Take us with you," Carmilla pleaded, looking up at

De Lafontaine with a naked worship I had never seen before or since. It reminded me of mothers with sick children who cast themselves at the feet of statues of saints. "We can leave tonight."

De Lafontaine smiled down at her, and if I wasn't mistaken, there were tears shining in her eyes too.

"You have too much life left to live for me to ask you to throw it away. When I first met you, I saw a kindred spirit, a wildfire of a girl who would never be domesticated. But I was so afraid of losing you that I tried to tame you. I learned love at the hands of a monster, and in the end, I worry I did to you what Isis did to me."

"But Ms. D—"

De Lafontaine pressed her fingertips to Carmilla's lips, keeping one arm wrapped tightly around me.

"If I don't leave you now, Carmilla, I will never let you go. It will destroy us both, this obsession. Do you understand? I've thought long and hard about this and it's one of the most difficult things I've ever had to do in my life, but it's what's right. I want to try doing what's right, for a change."

I couldn't help myself; tears spilled over my cheeks. We all held each other for a long moment, our tears mingling on each other's faces, and then De Lafontaine pulled away and produced an envelope. It was made from thick, creamy paper, and smelled faintly of mandarin.

"I asked to see you for a reason. A letter came for you last week. I thought about burning it in a fit of possessiveness, but in the end, my better nature won out."

Carmilla scrubbed her face with her sleeve, then took the letter and delicately tore it open. I crowded close to her to read over her shoulder, my eyes skimming the florid handwriting as fast as I could manage.

Carmilla,

I hope this letter finds you well. Ever since our meeting, I've been preoccupied by the thought of you. It's rare for someone so young to be inducted into our ranks, and, now that you've graduated, I worry you won't have the proper guidance you need to come into your own. The undying life can be a lonely one.

I've been in talks with Evelyn about your future, and I would like to offer you a place at my side, should you choose to accept. I'm summering in Spain and would appreciate a young woman of letters to take dictation for me and help me stay abreast of correspondence. Laura is very welcome as well, of course. I was so taken by her sweet nature and her bright mind, and I would never dream of separating you from your companion.

Think on it, and give me your reply by the twentieth of May. My household is eager to meet you, and I look forward to seeing you again.

Sincerely,

Magdalena

"The princess in shadows has taken an interest in your education, it seems," De Lafontaine said.

"You arranged this," I breathed. "For both of us?"

"Think of it as an unorthodox internship. Laura, you would be free to return to school after the summer vacation is over, or to forge your own path elsewhere. Carmilla, the world is at your feet now, darling." She cradled Carmilla's face in her hands. "Don't squander your precious second life."

Carmilla let out a little sob and threw her arms around De Lafontaine.

"I'll never forget you," she swore. "I'll live my life to the fullest. And then, when you're ready, I'll come find you."

"I very much look forward to it," De Lafontaine murmured.

Then, to my surprise, she strode over and wrapped me into a tight hug.

"Take care of my Carmilla," she whispered. De Lafontaine kissed me on the forehead, like a peace offering, then retrieved her car keys from her pocket and started walking towards the sedan.

"Excelsior, girls," she called behind her. "Onwards and upwards."

Carmilla and I clutched each other and waved as she pulled out onto the winding dirt road. Then the car turned a corner and De Lafontaine disappeared from our lives entirely.

"What are we going to do?" Carmilla asked as we stood there, the gravel poking through our shoes, the movers casting sympathetic glances our way. The sky was quickly dimming, dusk giving way to endless night.

"Well," I said, taking a deep, steadying breath, "I've never been to Spain."

———————

Three weeks later, I was penning a letter to my father on Magdalena's stationery, curled up on the divan in the parlor of the townhouse she had rented for the duration of her Boston season. Fabrizio had arranged a little plate of meats and cheeses for me to snack on for dinner, not wanting the human girl to famish, and I nibbled on some salami and sipped Earl Grey as I wrote. I was fabricating somewhat, talking up a summer exchange program with a visiting professor that would immerse me in Spanish language and culture, but I supposed even that wasn't too much of a lie. It was early morning, and the shades in the house were drawn tight against the rising sun. The entire house was asleep, except for me.

Well, almost.

I looked up at the sound of creaking floorboards and found Magdalena standing before me, resplendent in tousled hair and a men's dressing gown she had probably stolen from Fabrizio.

"You're up," I said, polishing off the tea. "But it's morning."

"I am afflicted with occasional bouts of sleeplessness," Magdalena said, sitting down next to me on the divan. "I always get this way before travel."

The entire household – Magdalena, Fabrizio, Carmilla, and me – were scheduled to depart for Europe on a red-eye flight the following night.

"I'm sorry," I said, because it seemed like the polite thing to say to a vampire insomniac.

"I'm glad I caught you. I wanted to talk to you. Alone."

I put down my pen and cradled my chin in my hands. I had a bone-deep admiration for Magdalena, but I wasn't as intimidated by her as I had been by De Lafontaine. I felt that we could speak frankly.

"What about?"

"It's a hard thing," she said, her voice soft from sleep. "Loving an immortal. It asks everything of you, and sometimes, it doesn't give much back. I know that as well as anyone."

"Is this about Carmilla?"

"In a sense. But mostly, it's about you, and your future. Fabrizio made a choice, a long time ago, to remain human. To remain open to the highs and lows of mortal life, and to accept death when it came. But others have made a different choice."

Magdalena took my empty cup and positioned it on the table in front of her. Then, with all the languor of someone lighting a cigarette, she plucked up a sharp letter opener from the nearby table and made a shallow incision in her hand. Blood sprang to the wound, dribbling down her wrist.

Magdalena held her hand over the cup, filling it with an inch of blood. Then she wrapped her palm tightly in a handkerchief, staunching the flow.

"I want to offer the choice that was once offered to me. A life in the dark or a life in the light. Regardless of what you choose, I will support you and protect you. You're my charge, now."

I picked up the china cup by the handle, my hand shaking slightly.

"And Carmilla?"

"She would have offered to change you herself, but she's too young." Magdalena gently squeezed my elbow. "One bite and one sip, and you'll be forever changed. Or, you can refuse me, and preserve your humanity. I can't tell you what choice to make, Laura. But it's a choice I think you deserve to make yourself."

Tentatively, I sniffed the blood. It smelled overwhelmingly of metal and wrongness, with a touch of violet perfume underneath. My lips hovered over the rim.

Time unspooled like a silver thread all around me. In that moment, there was nothing real in the world outside of the blood in that cup and the gleam in Magdalena's dark eyes. When she smiled at me, her pointed canine teeth caught the light.

Perhaps for the first time in my life, I wasn't afraid of death, and I wasn't afraid of what lay ahead of me in life. I was keenly aware of my own power, which had finally surfaced after so many years of trying to quash and silence it.

No more Laura the saint, I thought. No more Laura the scared little girl. I was Laura the night creature now, regardless of what path I chose to take.

I looked down at the blood one more time, running my tongue over my lips.

Outside, a new day dawned crimson and clear.

Acknowledgements

This book put up a tremendous fight when it came to getting words on the page, and I owe its completion to the people I'm blessed to have in my life.

I am indebted, as always, to Kit, who upheld me in every conceivable way throughout this process and lent me his creative powers when I needed them. Thank you to Devin, for her unflagging support, and to Chris for the honor of their friendship and encouragement. Thank you to my little coven of writers: Hannah and Lyndall and Eliza and Ellie, for every idea-bouncing session and late-night commiseration. Thank you to Elias, for always being there with a themed cocktail and a wise word.

Thank you to my Princeton Seminary friends, for having so many of the adventures with me that made their way into this book, and to my university professors, who fed me on a steady diet of poetry and always pushed me towards my best.

Thank you to Nadia, for her editorial brilliance and sanity-saving gentleness, and to Tara, for representing me tremendously while also offering all the pep talks I needed. Thank you to every member of the Orbit team who helped turn this book from a fever dream into a novel, and to everyone at Hachette who believed enough in my work to invest in me.

Thank you, finally, to my readers. The depth of love you've shown me, my worlds, and my characters is truly breathtaking. I'm grateful for each interaction I have with every one of you, and look forward to many more to come.

Excelsior.

Meet the Author

Elizabeth Unseth

S. T. GIBSON is the author of *A Dowry of Blood*. She holds a bachelor's in creative writing from the University of North Carolina Asheville and a master's in theological studies from Princeton Theological Seminary. She currently lives in New England with her partner.

Interview with the author

When did you first start writing?

I've been writing since I was six years old, when I checked out the X-Men encyclopedia from the library and lost myself in the tangled family trees and play-by-plays of universe-shaking plot points. I started out trying to write comic books, then realized pretty quickly I didn't have the talent for visual art, so I shifted into fiction! But I do think that my love for soap-opera style, character-driven plots with flashy action sequences can be traced back to my love for long-running comic series.

Can you tell us a bit about your writing process?

I always say that I start with a music video; a vibes-heavy mental reel of set piece scenes and snippets of dialogue. The characters tend to form very early on, and I build the story around them. *An Education in Malice* emerged in flashes: a blonde girl clutching her rosary in the confessional, bared teeth at a vampire house party, New England autumn foliage, whiskey out of teacups, pages of poetry rippling in the wind, and kisses on rooftops. From there, I reverse engineered the plot and hammered out the inciting action, midpoint, climax, and denouement so I had a roadmap to refer to while writing.

Where did the idea for *An Education in Malice* come from, and how did the story begin to take shape in your mind?

I knew there was more I wanted to say about love, obsession, and the undying life after writing *A Dowry of Blood*, and I have been in love with dark academia literature since I first read *The Secret History* the winter of my freshman year of college. Exploring those themes and motifs within the (very loose) framework of one of the classics of sapphic and vampiric literature felt natural.

Both Laura and Carmilla's voices are so palpably strong and lyrical, how did you tackle narrating this from their different perspectives? What was the most challenging aspect of writing their characters?

Thank you for saying so! Originally, the story was only going to be told from Laura's perspective, but I found Carmilla's perspective so compelling that I just had to include her. I rewrote the book from beginning to midpoint four separate times, trying out different approaches and points of view, until I found their individual voices. Once I cracked that code, I was able to write the rest of the book pretty smoothly while alternating between Carmilla and Laura. The most challenging aspect of this decision, and perhaps the writing of the book as a whole, was making their voices sound distinct while still being complementary for as cohesive a reading experience as possible.

If you could spend time with any of your characters, who would it be and why?

Evelyn De Lafontaine, hands down. I find her mercurial temperament, poetic prowess and countless secrets endlessly fascinating.

Do you have a favourite scene in *An Education in Malice*?

One certain debauched vampire house party. I also love the scene of Laura and Carmilla racing each other to class in the rain.

What's one thing about *An Education in Malice*, either about the world or the characters, that you loved but couldn't fit into the story?

I originally wrote a Dorian Gray character into the story but just couldn't make him fit within the world! The girls' love story and De Lafontaine's personal journey took center stage, and everything else fell away. Maybe that just means there's an open door for a Dorian book in the future.

Who are some of your favourite writers and how have they influenced your work?

There are so many! I've been heavily influenced by Donna Tartt's character work, Catherynne Valente's lyrical prose, Alan Moore's blending of esotericism and social commentary, Vladimir Nabokov's stunning command of language, Maggie Steifvater's lived-in magic, Madeline LeEngle's ferocious tenderness, and of course, Anne Rice's perfect marriage of religiosity and carnality.

When you're not writing, what do you like to do in your spare time?

I love to read tarot cards for loved ones and friends, try new restaurants, go thrifting for vintage rosaries and blazers, read romance novels and spiritual poetry, and explore my neighborhood on foot.

And finally, if you could choose to live an eternal life as a vampire, would you take that chance?

When you're an author in my position, you end up asking yourself that question a lot. I think, ultimately, I'm just too in love with the beauty and brutality and countless mundane mercies of humanity to abdicate it.

if you enjoyed
AN EDUCATION IN MALICE

look out for

A DOWRY OF BLOOD

by

S. T. Gibson

This is my last love letter to you, though some would call it a confession....

Saved from the brink of death by a mysterious stranger, Constanta is transformed from a medieval peasant into a bride fit for an undying king. But when Dracula draws a cunning aristocrat and a starving artist into his web of passion and deceit, Constanta realizes that her beloved is capable of terrible things.

Finding comfort in the arms of her rival consorts, she begins to unravel their husband's dark secrets. With the lives of everyone she loves on the line, Constanta will have to choose between her own freedom and her love for her husband. But bonds forged by blood can be broken only by death.

I never dreamed it would end like this, my lord: your blood splashing hot flecks onto my nightgown and pouring in rivulets onto our bedchamber floor. But creatures like us live a long time. There is no horror left in this world that can surprise me. Eventually, even your death becomes its own sort of inevitability.

know you loved us all, in your own way. Magdalena for her brilliance, Alexi for his loveliness. But I was your war bride, your faithful Constanta, and you loved me for my will to survive. You coaxed that tenacity out of me and broke it down in your hands, leaving me on your work table like a desiccated doll until you were ready to repair me.

You filled me with your loving guidance, stitched up my seams with thread in your favorite color, taught me how to walk and talk and smile in whatever way pleased you best. I was so happy to be your marionette, at first. So happy to be chosen.

~~What I am trying to say is~~
~~I am trying to tell you~~

ven loneliness, hollow and cold, becomes so familiar it starts to feel like a friend.